Richard Coward

CASTLES IN THE AIR

CASTLES IN THE AIR

by

RICHARD COWARD

LONDON
Richard and Erika Coward
WRITING AND PUBLISHING PARTNERSHIP
1993

First published in 1993 by
Richard and Erika Coward
Writing and Publishing Partnership
16 Sturgess Avenue
London
NW4 3TS

Photoset by BP Integraphics

Printed in Great Britain by The Bath Press, Avon
© Richard and Erika Coward 1993

British Library Cataloguing in Publication Data
A catalogue record for this book is
available from the British Library.

ISBN 0–9515019–3–3

To Erika

The young man known as Peter Kirby watched with silent relief as the last customer vanished into the cold February night. Rising to his feet, he walked to the front of the cafe and locked the door before returning to his perch beside the till. Normally he was thoroughly exhausted by closing time, yet tonight, as he gingerly tipped the contents of the till out onto the counter, he became aware that the weariness which usually engulfed him at this hour was completely absent, replaced by a sense of quiet self-satisfaction, almost of self-respect. It was a strange feeling, one to which he was not really accustomed.

There must have been coming on four hundred pounds in the till, he mused, carefully starting to count out the notes. It would be easy to remove fifty quid and stuff it into his own pocket, five lovely tenners which would make a considerable impact on his current financial impasse. Harry would never even notice they were gone.

He finished counting the notes and started on the coins. And when he had finished, he counted the whole lot again. It was only when he was absolutely sure that he had made no mistakes that he opened the large manilla envelope his boss had left him and pushed the money inside.

There was no doubt that he could have lifted fifty pounds, but he wasn't going to. It was the first time in the two years he had worked at the cafe that Harry had left him in charge of the till, and Peter did not propose to steal from the only man who had shown him any real kindness in the five long lonely years he had spent in his country's fair capital city.

He licked the envelope and sealed it. But as he did so, the pride he had felt in the trust unexpectedly placed in him by his employer faded almost as fast as it had arisen, this time replaced by an empty melancholy. Despite himself he glanced at the clock on the wall, confirming what he already knew, that midnight had long since passed and a new day had begun. A special day, or at least it should have been. His twenty-first birthday.

He tried hard to prevent himself from becoming too depressed. For this was certainly better than other birthdays he had endured. Birthdays in more children's homes than he cared to remember, where well-meaning staff had tried to make up for the real family he had never had but somehow only seemed to make things worse. And afterwards, when the children's homes proved their fundamental

1

insincerity by throwing him out at the age of sixteen, birthdays spent out rough, birthdays shivering inside a cardboard box pushed between two bins at the back end of some West End nightclub.

At the time, when he was sleeping on the streets, he'd found it faintly amusing that they'd given him a 'birthday' in February, the month when life in the open air was at its bleakest. Why couldn't they have chosen June or July, when the evenings were long and the temperatures high? Even October would have been bearable. But February?

Peter smiled wryly as he recalled that his birthday, the birthday which had prompted this uncharacteristic burst of melancholy, was no more real than his name, a bureaucratic convenience designed by some well-meaning social worker to ensure he could at least pretend to be like other people, people with names given by parents who could tell their children the precise moment at which they had been born ...

A sudden sound startled him. There was a creak on the stairs leading to the flat over the cafe. Someone was coming down, treading softly so as not to be heard. Sadly, he looked down at the manilla envelope on the counter, the envelope he had erroneously believed was a symbol of his employer's trust. For the only person living upstairs was Harry Kaye, the owner of the cafe, the same Harry Kaye who had said earlier that he wanted an early night. Yet here he came, sneaking surreptitiously down the stairs as if trying to catch Peter red-handed in the act of theft.

The door to the stairwell creaked slowly open and Harry poked his head round, wire-rimmed spectacles perched precariously on the end of his slender hooked nose.

Peter remained seated and looked sullenly at his boss's wrinkled face.

"So you don't trust me after all," he said.

"I couldn't sleep," Harry announced. Despite the best part of a lifetime in Hackney, his accent retained a pronounced Germanic lilt which betrayed his continental origins.

"Thinking of all that money walking away must be giving you nightmares," Peter muttered. "I thought it was uncharacteristic of you to leave me in charge."

Harry snorted but said nothing. He remained standing behind the door with only his head visible.

"Well. If you've come to check up on me then you're too late. I've already counted the money like you asked."

Harry's bony head turned to peer at the envelope on the counter.

"How much?" he asked gruffly.

"Four hundred and twenty-six pounds, seventy-five pence."

"Not bad," Harry grunted. "You've done well this evening."

"Correction," said Peter, beginning to feel slightly rattled by his boss's peculiar manner. "You've done well. The tips were rubbish."

"Oh well, tonight at least it doesn't matter."

Peter was beginning to tire of the conversation. It might not matter to Harry, but with the crummy basic rate he was paid it certainly mattered to him. His feet ached, he wanted to go and lie down in the tiny bedsit Harry let him use behind the kitchens, perhaps read for half an hour before dropping off to sleep.

"If it's all right with you, Mr Kaye," he said, rising to his feet, "I think I'll hit the sack."

Harry's face cracked into a grin.

"Soon, but not until we've had a chance to celebrate!"

With a flourish he pushed the door wide open and entered the room, triumphantly clutching in his hand what appeared to be an extremely expensive bottle of champagne.

"It's your birthday, isn't it? Your twenty-first. You should drink champagne on your twenty-first."

Peter stared at him in open astonishment. For although he secretly liked Harry, his boss was generally a difficult man for whom to work, a man who had no doubt worked hard in his time and now expected others to do the same.

"And that," said Harry, poking his head in the general direction of the counter, "is your birthday present."

Peter stared at the counter to see what his boss could possibly be talking about. But there was only the manilla envelope. He glanced hesitantly at Harry.

"That's right, young man," the old man said. "It's yours. The contents of the envelope is my birthday present. Make sure you spend it wisely."

Harry had started fiddling with the champagne bottle, his aged fingers trying unsuccessfully to loosen the cork. Peter remained speechless, trying hard to control the emotion he could begin to feel overwhelm him. He could handle people treating him like dirt because he didn't really expect anything else. But people were so rarely kind to him that he didn't know how to react.

Harry stopped struggling with the cork and held the bottle out to Peter.

"Didn't they even try to teach you any manners in those lousy children's homes you went to? You're supposed to say 'thank you' when somebody gives you a present."

3

"Thanks," Peter said, taking the champagne bottle in his hand. "But it's too much. It's not reasonable."

Harry shrugged. "That's what I've been telling myself all evening, so if I were you I wouldn't try to talk me into taking it back."

"Thanks, Mr Kaye," Peter said quickly. "It's very kind of you."

Harry nodded approvingly.

Peter grabbed a couple of glasses and poured out the champagne. The old man took his glass and held it aloft. "Here's to a better life!"

Peter sipped the champagne.

"It's good, Mr Kaye. I've never drunk champagne before."

Harry looked at him thoughtfully for a few moments.

"Sit down, young man," he said. "I've been wanting to talk to you for a while."

They sat down opposite each other at one of the tables. Harry took another sip of champagne.

"Are you happy here, Peter?" he asked suddenly.

The directness of the question caught him entirely off guard.

"No," Peter replied. "Should I be?"

Harry said nothing.

"Don't get me wrong, Mr Kaye. I'm grateful to you for giving me this job and a room to live in. You didn't ask for references or experience. I knew two years ago you were giving me a lucky break."

Harry shook his head.

"I knew two years ago that you weren't afraid of hard work. That was enough for me."

He was lying and Peter knew it. Two years before, when Peter was still a teenager, Harry had found him asleep one morning by the back entrance of the cafe, lying in an impromptu bed hastily assembled from cardboard boxes and old newspaper. The first Peter had known about it was when he found himself being woken up by a grumpy old man kicking him in the ribs and telling him he was trespassing. And then, before he had had a chance to wake up properly, the man had shoved a broom into his hand and told him to clear up the mess he had made. Only after three hours hard labour was he finally given breakfast. But despite it all, he knew at the time that Harry cared. Harry was the only person who had ever really cared.

Unless, a long time ago, he had had a mother who had cared for him. But he had to admit that even that seemed unlikely, because a caring mother could not have abandoned a one year old child in a hospital waiting room without so much as an explanatory note.

After that the children's homes had started. As a child it was all he had known, an endless stream of minders who would wash him and dress him and feed him but never love him. At first he had regarded it as normal, but after school started, as he gradually became more knowing, he had begun to glimpse the extent to which he had been shortchanged in life. As a teenager it had made him bitter, hurtful to those who tried to help. He had closed into a private shell, a solitary island where he couldn't be hurt because nobody could ever get close. He was never disruptive, never a bother. He had melted into the background and had been allowed to remain there.

But at sixteen the world had come to assault his lonely island. They had promised him after-care, hostel places and help with finding a job. No doubt they had meant the promises when they had made them. But it had all come to nought.

For a few months he had wandered along the familiar south coast towns of his childhood looking for work and a place to live. But he was a February child, cast adrift on his administrative birthday when seasonal unemployment in the windswept seaside resorts was at its peak. He could no more find work as a young adult than he could find love as a child. And so he had hitched a lift to London in search of better things.

But London too had been a great disappointment. The eighties' boom was still in full spate, the yuppy dreams of Fulham and Docklands and Islington still unchecked. Yet for young people like Peter Kirby, the new social security regulations were a more meaningful measure of economic welfare, and a place in cardboard city the only kind of home he was able to find. Until one day an old man called Harry had kicked him in the ribs and given him a broom.

Harry slowly refilled the champagne glasses.

"Memories?" he asked.

Peter nodded.

"When you're my age you'll have more."

"I suppose you're right. But you never talk about your past, even when there are no customers here."

Harry grunted.

"When there are no customers I am too busy thinking of what to say to the bank manager to waste my time reminiscing."

Again he was lying. Peter had seen the look on his face too often, a look of distant loss for which no thoughts of bank managers could ever be held responsible.

Peter raised his glass and took another sip.

"Why did you ask me if I was happy?"

"It's your twenty-first birthday. When I was young it was the day on which you became an adult, the day when the overture stopped and the show began. It's the time for taking stock, planning a future, making some decisions about where you're going in life."

Peter shrugged. Frankly, he was too busy working in the cafe to spend much time thinking about where he was going. Only when Sandra had been with him had he thought about his future – their future – but she had left him and that had brought nothing but pain. Since then, he had just concentrated on getting by, grateful for the roof over his head and regular hot meals.

"Well, Mr Kaye," he said at last. "What do you think I should do with my life?"

Harry studied him for a while.

"Well . . .," he muttered, "I'd get out of this dead end job for a start. You're on a hiding to nothing working for me."

This was not what Peter was expecting. The cafe had been the only real home he had ever known. Unlike Sandra, he knew when he was onto a good thing.

"What do you mean?" he said. "I like it here."

Harry looked at him with a mixture of pity and desperation.

"It's better than living on the streets, you mean," he said. "But you deserve something better. You've got a brain, you can think, you even read books. You need to get out of this rut and start doing something worthwhile."

"Are you trying to get rid of me or something?"

Harry laughed.

"There you go again, Peter. Here I am, trying to pluck up the strength to do the decent thing and give you a bit of sound fatherly advice and all you do is try to make me behave in my usual selfish way. Of course I don't want you to go. You're probably the best worker I've ever had and I'll even admit that I sometimes like your company. But I still think this is a dead end job."

Peter shrugged.

"Maybe it is. But it's no more dead end than all the other dead end jobs on offer to a bloke like me with no qualifications, is it?"

"You should have worked harder at school."

"You sound like the teachers."

"The teachers were right. You've got a brain on your head – why didn't you use it?"

"I did get a Grade A in history GCSE."

"And . . .?" Harry added.

"And nothing – well, nothing worth talking about."

"So how come you got a Grade A in history but nothing else?"

Peter was silent for a while.

6

"It was the only thing I was interested in," he said at last.

"School's not about being interested in things. It's about getting trained for adult life."

Peter smiled.

"I know that now. Then I didn't."

Harry's face turned serious.

"You know, that's what struck me when I first met you out the back. A kid on the street, sleeping rough, and by his bed, if you can call that thing you'd made a bed, an open copy of 'Tudor England' by C.B.James. It was a bit odd."

"It's a good book, a social history. Better than most of the patriotic junk written about the Tudors."

"So just how much history do you know, then?"

"Quite a bit, I suppose. History makes you realise how dreadful people's lives were in the past, how lucky we are today."

Harry looked at him askance.

"Even when you're sleeping on the streets?"

"Particularly when you're sleeping on the streets. Nowadays it's pretty rare to be sleeping rough, but in the past it was much more common. So the scraps are better these days. You'd be surprised what you can pick up outside Fortnum and Mason with a harmonica. I think it's what Tories like to call the trickle down effect."

Harry peered at Peter over his spectacles, a twinkle appearing in his eye.

"Well then, since you're so interested in history, why don't you get yourself a job which involves history? Find a job as a history teacher."

Peter looked at him wearily.

"You mean qualifications. Don't think I haven't thought about it, Mr Kaye. Get some more GCSEs, A-Levels, a degree perhaps. But it's a very long road and frankly I don't think I've the stamina for it. Not with working here in the cafe at the same time. It's one thing reading a few books on the side, quite another embarking on a full blown academic career."

Harry eyed him carefully.

"So don't bother with the qualifications."

"You're talking in riddles, Mr Kaye. Really I don't understand what you're talking about."

"I mean forget the qualifications. Go straight for the job."

Peter examined the old man with curiosity.

"You're not serious, are you?" he asked.

Harry fixed him with a penetrating gaze.

"Perfectly. You've been dealt a hard hand by your beloved

7

history. While other kids your age were being mollycoddled through their education by loving mummies and daddies, you were trying to survive in a series of half-rate children's homes or sleeping out under the open sky. If life's a game then the rules aren't fair. You should have the courage to change them."

"More riddles, Mr Kaye?"

Harry looked round furtively, as if checking to see that none of the customers were still lurking beneath the tables.

"You know Mr Keighley, that rather fat chap who comes in most Saturdays?"

Peter nodded.

"He's some sort of lecturer at Oxford University. Divorced, of course, like most of the men his age. But his ex-wife lives round the corner from here and he has access to the kids on Saturdays. Generally he pops in here for lunch before picking them up."

"So?"

"Well, you could say he's an old friend of mine. A few years ago, before the divorce, he sometimes used to slip through to the back bedroom with his research assistant."

"My room! You used to let the customers use my room to have sex?"

Harry looked embarrassed.

"Only the regulars. I reckoned it was good for business. They'd always have a good meal afterwards."

"And now he's divorced and working at Oxford?"

"Yup. Living with the same research assistant, I think. But that's not really the point. The point is I think he owes me. So I'll tell him I'd like to use his Oxford college address for some private letters I don't want sent here. Make out it's something to do with Inland Revenue. He'll tip off the man on the college gate to push anything addressed to me into his pigeonhole. Then he can bring it here on Saturday when he sees his kids. In the meantime, you can visit his college and fetch me a few sheets of blank headed notepaper."

Harry raised his glass. "And then," he said triumphantly, "it's good-bye Peter Kirby, erstwhile tramp and general dogsbody at Harry's Cafe, and hallo Peter Kirby, first class honours in history from Oxford University."

Peter looked at him in amazement.

"You are joking, aren't you?" he said.

"Well," Harry muttered. "If you mean do I think it's funny, then yes. But if you mean will I do it, then the answer's also yes. As your director of studies I can promise you a marvellous reference."

For several minutes Peter said nothing. For the first time in a long time, perhaps for the first time ever, his mind was working on overdrive, trying to spot the flaws in Harry's appealingly simple short-cut to a life of comfortable middle-class respectability.

"But I won't have a degree," he objected.

"A minor problem. But perhaps you should avoid the state sector. There're too many bureaucrats around in town halls. Go for some really third rate private school, somewhere that needs a bit of talent on the books to impress the parents but where they're not going to check too carefully."

"But what if they want to see the degree certificate?"

"Say you're just out of college, haven't been to the ceremony yet. If they get fussy, simply say you're withdrawing your application and going elsewhere because they're too slow making up their minds."

"You're serious, aren't you, Mr Kaye? You really do think it might work."

Harry snorted.

"If there's one thing I've learnt it's that people are gullible fools. They fall for anything if it's sold to them with enough panache. It's panache you need, not qualifications."

* * * * * *

It was gone three the following afternoon before Peter was able to return to his room for his mid-afternoon break. He wanted to be alone for a while, to try and make sense of the crazy ideas Harry had been throwing around over a bottle of champagne in the middle of the night.

He opened the door of his tiny bedsit and peered inside. It was a poorly-lit room even in mid-summer, the tiny north-facing window inadequate even for such a small room, but on an overcast afternoon in February it looked positively dreary. Peter flicked on the electric light and collapsed onto the sagging single bed beneath the window, gazing despondently at his surroundings.

Not that there was a great deal to look at. Besides the bed, the only furniture was a scruffy armchair, an equally scruffy chest of drawers and a small bedside table. All of these things were exactly as they had been the previous day, yet the previous day he had been almost proud of them. For a child of the streets they had represented almost unimaginable wealth, a veritable orgy of materialist control over his own life. And if Harry had come down in the night and told him what a lucky chap he was to have landed such a cushy job with a room thrown in he would have agreed with him wholeheartedly, pleased that somebody else could recognise how well he had done for himself.

But instead, Harry had advised him in no uncertain terms that his life was a shambles, that he needed to break out and build himself a better life, even if that new life was built upon a not particularly sophisticated fraud. And suddenly, depressingly, the room of which he had previously felt so proud had turned into a cramped prison cell, a physical symbol of the depths to which a young man could fall.

Without being able to help himself, he picked up the copy of the Times Educational Supplement which Harry had silently handed him first thing that morning and flicked through to the advertisement pages. Most of the adverts were for the state sector, but there was a briefer section covering jobs in independent schools. And sure enough, there they were: half a dozen adverts for history posts. They all seemed to be much the same, their text littered with phrases such as 'good graduate sought', 'keen interest in the subject expected', 'willingness to take part in extra-curricular activities an advantage'. None of them actually specified the pay, but it would no doubt be very considerably better than he was getting at the cafe.

He had just started working his way through the adverts for a second time, trying to establish which school might conceivably be a target for his attentions, when his thoughts were interrupted by a loud knocking on the front door of the cafe. Glancing at his watch, he walked through to see who could be interrupting his afternoon break.

There was an old woman at the door, her slender frame protected against the elements by a thick grey overcoat. When she caught sight of Peter, she stopped banging on the door and waited quietly while he approached.

"We're closed until five-thirty," he called impatiently, without making any attempt to open the door.

"I can read that," the old woman called, "but it's you I've come to see."

Peter suddenly became aware that the woman was looking at him far too closely. Normally he was just the waiter, a mere functionary to be addressed only when somebody wanted something. But the old woman was peering at him through the glass with an intense interest.

He unlocked the door and held it open.

"How can I help you?" he asked.

The visitor stepped gratefully into the warmth of the cafe.

"I don't know that you can help me, Peter," she said presently. "It's not why I've come."

He looked at her in surprise. She wasn't a regular, and as far as he was aware he had never set eyes on her before. Yet she knew his name and addressed him with a jarring familiarity.

"Give me a hand with my coat, will you, love," she said, struggling to divest herself of the enormous garment.

Peter lifted the coat from her frail shoulders.

"Do we know each other?" he asked cautiously.

The old woman met his gaze.

"You don't know me, but I know you. Is there somewhere we can talk? You have a flat here, don't you?"

"A room. Come through if you like."

The old woman followed silently as he led her through to his bedsit. As soon as the door was closed, Peter turned to her with an enquiring glance.

"Why do you want to see me?" he asked.

Again he became aware of the intensity with which she was looking at him.

"I've wanted to see you again for a very long time, Peter. But I swore to myself I would wait until this day and that is what I have done."

"This day?"

"Your twenty-first birthday. When I left you I vowed I would not return until you were twenty-one."

It took several moments for the words to sink in, but as they did Peter could begin to feel his legs giving way beneath him. Her words echoed around inside his brain.

"When you left me ...?" he murmured.

For a few moments the old woman continued looking at him, as if trying to confirm a decision she had taken many years before.

"I'm your grandmother," she said at last. "I was the one who left you in the waiting room of Worthing General Hospital on the 15th June 1973. I haven't set eyes on you since that day."

Peter could feel the room spinning. He sank down onto the bed, staring at the old woman as he did so. He didn't doubt for a moment that she was speaking the truth. It was a moment he had both prayed for and dreaded throughout his childhood years, a lingering dream which he felt sure was shared by all other abandoned children in the world. Yet now that it had actually happened it left him feeling cold, desolate beyond measure at the cruelty inherent in that bitter June day so long before.

"How did you know this is my birthday?" he asked suddenly.

The woman looked at him with genuine surprise.

"Of course I know your birthday. You are my grandson."

"But today is just an administrative birthday. I was told they didn't know my real birthday."

The woman looked at him sharply.

"But the letter I left. Didn't they give it to you? I left a letter, saying it should be given to you when you were sixteen, a letter in which I told you there were good reasons for my decision to abandon you, reasons which would become clear when you were twenty-one. It was in the letter that I gave the date of your birthday."

"I was given nothing."

The old woman's eyes glazed over. She leant forward and touched his arm.

"So you know nothing at all then? Absolutely nothing?"

"I was told I was abandoned in the waiting room of Worthing General Hospital on 15th June 1973. That is when my life began."

The woman who claimed to be his grandmother released his arm and leant back in her chair.

"But they must have found it," she said with a frown. "If they hadn't they wouldn't have known this was your birthday. But then they must have decided for some reason that it was best not to give it to you. Either that or they simply lost it while you were growing up."

The feeling of coldness was passing, gradually being edged aside by anger.

"Listen to me," he said, rising to his feet, "I really don't know what you're talking about. Nobody gave me any letters. You say it was you who dumped me. Well, if that's the truth then I frankly don't know how you've got the nerve to come in here after twenty years and start talking to me about letters."

Despite himself, he could feel the suppressed emotion of two decades of neglect rising to an unbearable crescendo within him. He moved to the door, intending to throw her out, but before his hand had touched the handle the old woman spoke.

"Hear me out," she said, her voice gentle yet firm.

Peter checked himself. There was something about the tone of her voice that told him he had been wrong to pass judgement so quickly. He turned to face her.

"I left you because I thought it for the best," she said quietly. "I believed that then and despite the sad life you have led since I believe it still."

Peter sat down again on the bed, his face ashen.

"When I walked away from you I hoped you would be happy, that you would find a family to adopt you and give you a happy home to replace the one they had ripped away."

Her words caught him unawares.

"They ...?" he repeated.

She nodded.

"Who are 'they'?"

The old woman lifted up her handbag and pulled out a paper bag.

"You haven't asked about your parents," she said.

"I don't have any parents. The old Jew who runs this lousy cafe is the nearest thing I've ever had to a parent. Why should I want to know about parents who were never there when I needed them?"

She peered at him, tears forming in her eyes. It was as if her careful self-control was gradually falling apart, revealing the pent-up emotion which lay beneath.

"Don't lie, Peter. Don't pretend you don't care when you do."

Her words silenced him. He sat down again on the bed and stared through the tiny window at the back yard beyond. He knew that she was right. In the homes every child had cared but none dare admit it. It was a hard habit to break.

The old woman pushed her hand into the paper bag and produced a photograph.

"That's you with your parents," she said quietly, holding it out to him.

He took the photograph and gazed at it. There was nothing special about it, just a man and a woman kneeling down in a summer garden beside a tiny toddler in a push-chair.

"Your name is not Peter Kirby," she continued. "You were born with the name William Fitzpatrick on your birth certificate, although that too was not really your name. Fitzpatrick is my maiden name, and I am your father's mother."

The old woman leant forward and looked at the photograph in his hand.

"Your mother was called Jennifer. In the brief time you shared with her she was always good to you. Your father's name was Reginald. He was also a kind man. A little impulsive perhaps, but essentially kind. With those two as parents you should have enjoyed a bright and happy childhood. But when you were one year old, only about an hour after I took that photograph, their lives were both snuffed out, smashed to bits one bright June afternoon as they drove down the suburban street where you lived. An articulated lorry lost control at a junction and crushed their car. So on the day that photograph was taken your life with them came to an end. It was 13th June 1973. Two days later I left you in the hospital."

"Who are 'they'?" Peter repeated.

His grandmother again touched his arm.

"Be patient, Peter, and I will tell you everything. But before I do, I will tell you about your father. He was my only son and he was born shortly before the war, in the early summer of 1939. He was officially registered on his birth certificate as my illegitimate son. But in the early years of his life, despite my difficult status as a single parent and despite the war, we led a prosperous life. Reginald was a bright and intelligent child, and I hoped I would be able to support him through private school and university. But when he was eight years old our lives suddenly changed. Overnight we lost everything. We had to swap our comfortable home for a municipal bedsit not much larger than this room and I had to withdraw him from his school and transfer him to a rough local primary.

"When he was fourteen he left school and started work in a local shop. He always said he wanted to leave, but I know that really he did it for me, so that I wouldn't have to pay for him any more. Over the years he worked hard, and by the time you were born he had a good post in a smart central London clothing store.

"Poor Reginald. He carried himself with dignity and never grumbled about his work, but I knew all along that he hated it. He used to spend a good deal of his working life attending to the needs of the rich clients who frequented the shop and he loathed the servile way he was treated by the customers. He always felt they were looking down at him, as if they were morally superior simply because they had so much more than he had. As the years went by I could see the frustration growing within him."

Peter remembered the look of arrogant contempt on the faces of the people he had seen outside Fortnum and Mason's when he had been playing his harmonica. Perhaps, long before, his father had seen the same faces, the same sanctimonious sense of moral superiority.

He noticed his grandmother's face. It was twisted into a strange grimace.

"Are you all right?" he asked.

"If only he'd been happy I might never have told him," she whispered.

"Told him what?"

"The story I've come here to tell you today. The story that led to your parents' deaths."

Peter looked at her sharply.

"I thought you said my parents were killed in a car accident."

"They were killed in a car. But I don't think it was an accident. I think they were killed deliberately, murdered because your father posed a threat to a family with a great deal of money. I think he must have frightened them. So they tried unsuccessfully to destroy the threat."

"If what you say is true, it sounds as though they succeeded in destroying the threat," Peter mumbled drily.

His grandmother gazed at him steadily.

"No," she said quietly. "No they didn't."

"I don't understand."

"You see, Peter, the threat lived on. With Reginald gone his son became the threat. They knew that, just as they knew that you would normally have been in that car with them. But instead you were with me, with your grandmother, and so you survived."

"And I became the threat?"

"Yes. Earlier I told you your surname was Fitzpatrick, the name you inherited from your father and before that from me. But in law that is not your rightful surname. Your rightful name is William Troughton, the 16th Earl of Southdown. And without doubt, one of the richest men in Europe."

The shock lasted only a few moments. Then he started to laugh.

"The Earl of Southdown! That bastard owns half of central London and the Home Counties, doesn't he?"

His grandmother nodded.

"Not he. You."

In his agitation Peter had stood up. Now he sat down again.

"This isn't a joke, is it? You really think I am the Earl of Southdown."

His grandmother's face was deadly serious.

"I don't think, Peter. I know. I know because when I was young I was lawfully married to the Earl of Southdown. I was his one and only lawful wife. Your father was the only child from that marriage. Reginald is now dead. You are his only son. So you are the rightful legal inheritor of the Earldom of Southdown and all the vast wealth associated with it."

"And the present Earl?"

"An imposter."

Peter's mind was racing.

"And this is what you told my father shortly before his death?"

She nodded.

"I told you before that your father was impulsive. I think he must have gone to see the family, perhaps threatened them with exposure. He never said anything to me so I'll never know. But I'm pretty sure that's why he was killed."

Peter was silent for a while.

"And yet now you've come here to tell me the same story you told my father."

His grandmother nodded.

"You have a title and property which is yours by right. When you were a child it was my duty to protect you from any careless and foolish remarks you may have made. But when your parents were killed I knew in my heart that I had no right to deny you the opportunity to claim that which is truly your own. But now I have told you. And if you wish, you may carry on with your life as if I had never come."

Peter glanced down again at the photograph in his hand. It was as if his beloved history was trying to haunt him, throwing him an extraordinary revelation from the past which held within it the power to transform his future. And yet besides the opportunity of unimaginable wealth lay a hidden threat of violence, a violence which his grandmother believed had already claimed the lives of both his parents. In the circumstances it might well be best to allow his grandmother to go no further.

"I'm listening," he said at last.

"I was born the daughter of the gamekeeper on the Southdown estate in West Sussex. I had a tranquil childhood, carefree and untroubled, and I can safely say it was one of the happiest times of my life. My father was only a servant on the estate, just as his forbears had been for generations, but the gamekeeper was a man of some seniority in the complex hierarchy of retainers surrounding the Troughtons. As such, he was a respected member of the rural community.

"As a young girl I befriended the Viscount Winston, first son of the 13th Earl. He was about my own age and we often played together in the grounds. When we were children, both my parents and his thought it harmless fun and left us alone. But later, when we became teenagers, our childhood frolics gradually turned more serious. We fell in love and stayed in love, our feelings for each other shrouded in ever greater secrecy as time went by and our parents became more concerned about our continuing friendship.

"Even my own parents were fearful. Unlike me, they knew their place. They said no good ever came of love between the classes. But it was only much later that I discovered they were right.

"The Earl's family were different to mine. They didn't care how many servant girls their son took to his bed. In those days it was regarded as a healthy sign in a young lord to excise droit du seigneur over the girls on his estate. It was common enough for recalcitrant targets of their master's affections to be threatened with their own dismissal or that of their parents if they refused to oblige. But Winston would never behave like that. He loved me. He treasured me. And although I would willingly have submitted to him he steadfastly refused. I think it was his way of proving he was sincere.

"When I was eighteen he secretly proposed and I accepted. But of course we knew there wasn't a chance of winning his parents' consent, so we waited until we were both over twenty-one and able to obtain a marriage licence without their permission. By that time I was working as a domestic maid in the house itself, and when Winston went to Italy in the summer of 1938 he was able to persuade his father to allow me to accompany him as a personal servant.

"That summer in Italy was idyllic. Freed from the need for subterfuge, Winston bought me fine clothes and introduced me as his travelling companion rather than his maid. And it was while we were in Italy that we were secretly married, at the British Consulate in Rome. It was May of 1938."

"Properly married," Peter interjected.

"Oh yes. We obtained the licence and were married by the Vice-Consul in person."

"So you have a marriage certificate."

"I am certain one exists."

Peter frowned.

"What do you mean by that?"

"I'll tell you presently. Winston believed that while his parents would never agree to our marriage they would have no choice but to accept a fait accompli. He thought that if he returned home and showed them the certificate they would simply have to accept me as his wife. But while he was away in Italy, unknown to him, they had secretly prepared the ground for him to marry a rich American heiress by the name of Alexandra. When he told them about me, they were apoplectic with anger."

"But if you were already married ... ''

"That's what Winston had thought. He had the marriage certificate and there was a copy at the Consulate in Rome. It was a simple fact that I was his legal wife."

"They could have disowned him, I suppose."

"No. He was the Earl's first son. The title was inalienable, and since the property was held in the name of the Earldom rather than any particular incumbent so was the wealth. Under the rather strange rules governing the assets of the Earldom, any adult heirs to the title could block in the courts any attempt by the incumbent Earl to dispose of the property without their consent. So you see, he really thought his parents would have no choice but to accept what he had done even if they didn't like it."

17

Peter looked at his grandmother thoughtfully for a moment.

"But he was wrong?"

The old woman opposite him nodded.

"They simply denied our marriage had happened. I was sacked and Winston was more or less instructed to marry Alexandra forthwith."

"And the certificate? You said your marriage was legal."

"As indeed it was."

"But I don't understand. Winston knew his parents wouldn't have approved of him marrying a servant girl. He must have been expecting their hostility. I don't understand why he allowed them to stand in his way."

His grandmother smiled.

"You don't understand the Troughton family and nor it seemed did he. Winston was a kind and loving man, but he proved to be the exception rather than the rule. I'm afraid his father called his bluff. He threatened Winston with my death if he didn't agree to his terms."

Peter stared at her in amazement.

"Your death ...?"

She nodded.

"Easily arranged for someone as wealthy as the Earl of Southdown, believe me. And Winston knew his father meant it. He could either marry Alexandra as a bachelor or he could marry her as a widower. The choice was his.

"So he came up with a plan. He told his father that he accepted his terms, agreeing to pretend that his marriage with me had never happened. He also agreed to marry the American. His only conditions were that I would be allowed a comfortable pension from the Southdown estate and that he would be allowed to visit me as his mistress whenever he wished.

"But Winston knew his father's health was failing. It would only be a few years until he inherited the Earldom and sole control of everything that went with it. So he hid the marriage certificate, telling his family he had destroyed it. When his father finally died, Winston had planned to produce the certificate, dissolve his second and illegal marriage with the Lady Alexandra and restore me as his rightful wife and your father as his rightful son and heir.

"But the old man lived longer than Winston had anticipated, for nine more years. Throughout that time, the old Earl and Winston kept to their bargain. Winston married again and I was given a pension. Whenever he could, he would come to see me and his child, your father, although neither he nor I told Reginald who he really was. And despite the war, despite the subterfuge, they too were happy years.

"It was the autumn of 1947 when I finally heard of the old Earl's death. For days I waited for Winston to contact me, to tell me that the years of deceit were finally over. Now that he was free, I knew he would honour the vows he had made to me that day in Rome. But he didn't come. For days I heard nothing, until by chance I came across an article in the newspaper ..."

Peter's grandmother produced from her bag an old copy of The Times. Laying it carefully on the bed, she turned to one of the inside pages.

It was a short piece under the heading 'Double Tragedy Hits Noble House': 'It was announced yesterday that the young Earl of Southdown, who succeeded his father to the title only last week, has met with a tragic accident at his ancestral home in Sussex. Mr Roger St Clair Hetherton, the family solicitor, told reporters that death was caused by a fault in a recently installed electrical system at Southdown House. The Earl's tragic demise leaves his wife, Countess Alexandra, in full control of the family estates until the new Earl, six year old Rupert Troughton, comes of age."

Peter looked up at his grandmother.

"And you don't think it was an accident?" he asked.

"It could have been, just like your parents' death could have been."

Peter accepted her remark without comment.

"What happened then?" he asked.

"The allowance I had received while Winston was alive was discontinued without explanation the following month. I wrote and begged Countess Alexandra to continue the financial assistance so that I could complete the education of the Earl's child. I received no reply to my first letter. Shortly afterwards I wrote again. I was desperate, so I intimated I might go to the press unless the payments continued. Three days later I returned home to find all my windows broken."

This time Peter knew better than to ask whether that too had been an accident.

"The Troughtons seem to have a rough streak," he said at last.

The old woman opposite nodded her head.

"It's best you know that, Peter. If you ever decide to tangle with the House of Southdown you mustn't expect them to play by the Queensbury rules. It might really be for the best if you leave them well alone."

Peter gazed at the photograph of his parents kneeling down beside him, their eyes filled with pride and happiness at the sight of their little son. It seemed they would certainly have been well advised to leave well alone.

He looked up at his grandmother.

"You didn't track me down after twenty years for me to leave them alone," he said quietly. "You want me to go after them, don't you? To get revenge for everything they've done to you."

The old woman's eyes closed and for a long time she remained silent. It was only when she opened them again and met his gaze that he could see how unfair his remark had been.

"My husband, my son and my daughter-in-law were killed by these people and you were all that was left to me. And then I had to force myself to give you away as well, cutting myself off from you absolutely so there would be no chance of them tracing you. I have already lost most of my family to the Troughtons. Do you really think I want to lose my only grandchild as well?"

"So why tell me?"

"Because it's no longer a decision for me to take. Your history belongs to you, not me. And what you do with it is your affair."

Peter lowered his head with embarrassment. It was the first day of his adult life yet he was still behaving like a child, still expecting someone else to take the decisions for him.

"Sorry," he mumbled.

She nodded a silent acknowledgement of his apology.

"And what do you think you will do?" she asked.

He remembered Harry's recent comment that he had been dealt an unfair hand in life. Up until an hour before he had always regarded the unfair hand as an impersonal act of fate, a random event which was nobody's fault. Yet now he knew that was not the case. His parents and his childhood had been stolen from him by real people, people with faces and names and families. People who should have known better.

He looked down at the fading photograph of his parents again, the life in their smiling faces so soon to be extinguished.

"I don't know," he said. "I really don't know."

* * * * * *

The man at the enquiry desk in St Catherine's House was genuinely puzzled.

"Are you sure it was May 1938, sir?"

Peter nodded.

"Certain. The ceremony was performed by the British Vice-Consul in Rome. A wife wouldn't forget her own wedding, would she?"

Suitably rebuffed, the man went through the motions of checking the records again.

"Nothing for May, sir. Plenty in April. Plenty in July again. But nothing at all between 28th April and 5th July."

Peter looked at him sharply.

"What did you say?" he asked.

"I said there weren't any marriages performed by the British Vice-Consul in Rome in May or June. Your relative just must be confused."

"How many were there in April?"

The clerk placed his finger on the terminal screen and counted.

"Fifteen."

"And July?"

"Twelve."

"Can I look myself, please?" Peter asked.

The somewhat bemused official gratefully swung the terminal around so that Peter could check for himself. And sure enough, the British Vice-Consul in Rome had been a busy man during most of the months in 1937 and 1938. Grabbing a piece of paper from his pocket, he jotted down the frequency of the marriages. It was a pretty steady flow, between ten and twenty-five a month. Except for May and June 1938.

"Why do you think there's a gap?" he asked.

The official shrugged.

"How should I know? Maybe the Vice-Consul went on holiday. Maybe he was sick."

It didn't make sense. If the normal man was unavailable, there would have been somebody else at the Consulate to take his place.

"Can you find out who the Vice-Consul was?" Peter asked.

"Oh yes," the clerk said, "that's not hard." He tapped in a few details and examined the computer screen. "Well, at the wedding on the 28th April it was a Mr John H.Frederick."

Peter scribbled down the name. A thought had occurred to him, an unpleasant theory which could easily be eliminated.

"And afterwards? Who was the Vice-Consul after the gap?"

The official tapped in the particulars.

"A different man, name of Mr Martin Gillespie. Perhaps that explains our gap. It must have been something to do with the change-over."

Peter hurriedly wrote down the replacement's name.

"Perhaps," he murmured, "but I wonder if I could ask you one more question. Did the Consulate in Rome keep records of British nationals who died in Italy during that period?"

The man looked at him with a confused expression.

"I thought we were doing marriages?"

Peter smiled grimly at him.

"We were. But now we've moved on to deaths."

The man glanced at his watch as if praying for an opportunity to escape to his coffee break.

"Overseas Consulates did keep records of British nationals who died abroad when they were drawn to their attention."

Peter nodded.

"Check June and July 1938, please. And see if you can find any record of the death from accidental causes of John H. Frederick, British Vice-Consul in Rome."

The official looked at him in consternation.

"What makes you think he died?"

Peter could feel the tension rising within him.

"Just look, will you," he said brusquely.

The official checked a reference manual and then typed some more information into the computer terminal. Seconds later, a new list appeared. After a few moments careful concentration the man's eyes rose to meet Peter's.

"You must be psychic," he mouthed. "John H. Frederick died in a swimming accident on 3rd July 1938."

Peter hurriedly copied down the details and bade the clerk farewell. He was angry with himself, angry that he had expected it to be so easy. Of course they had disposed of the Vice-Consul and arranged for the marriage records to be accidentally 'mislaid'. The particulars of the marriage would no doubt have been listed alongside all the others for those months, which explained why there was a two-month gap in the entries.

Peter shoved his way through the swing doors and out into the winter cold. Big black snow clouds were hovering menacingly overhead, but as yet the snow had not started to fall. He started trudging up towards High Holborn, intent upon catching a bus to the City. And as he walked he thought, trying to persuade himself to pull back from what was almost certainly going to be an impossible quest.

The accidental demise of John H. Frederick in pre-war Rome had finally removed any lingering doubts over the untimely deaths of his parents and his grandfather. And he was becoming increasingly sure that the final tally of 'accidental' deaths would rise considerably higher. There were the two witnesses to his grandparents' 1938 marriage, a married couple they had met by chance at the opera several nights before the wedding. His grandmother couldn't even remember their names, but he was sure it would be the same sorry story if he could find out who they were. Peter suspected the same would be true of the 1947 electrician who had installed the faulty wiring which had killed his grandfather and the careless lorry driver who had been given a six month suspended prison sentence in 1973 for the manslaughter of his parents. And for all he knew, there may have been yet others whose lives had already been sacrificed in order to protect the current owners of the Southdown inheritance. It all amounted to a pretty sobering prospect.

He arrived at the bus stop and joined the queue. It wasn't that long ago that he hadn't had the small change for a bus ticket, when the only form of transport he could afford was his own two legs. It was precisely for that reason that up until two days before he been reasonably content with his life at Harry's. But then he had briefly dreamed of becoming a history teacher, and now he was seriously contemplating an attempt at requisitioning the fortune of one of the richest men in Europe. Perhaps indeed it was time to slow the pace, to decide whether it was really worth the risk.

He decided to try and think about the situation logically, to split up the legality from the illegality. For even without the threat to his life, proving that he was rightful Earl of Southdown was not going to be easy. In the light of his recent discovery at St Catherine's House, the establishment of even a prima facie case would hinge on whether he could recover his grandfather's original copy of the marriage certificate.

His grandmother had last seen the certificate on the day of her return from Italy in the summer of 1938. Her husband had taken it with him to Southdown House, intending to use it to prove that his marriage had really taken place. But although he had not foreseen his father's threat to kill his pretty young wife, he had nevertheless had the good sense to hide the certificate when he had first broken the news to his parents. Later, when he had agreed to their terms and was instructed to produce the document, he had told his parents he had burnt it.

So the certificate was almost certainly still somewhere in Southdown House, lying hidden exactly where he had left it. Although his grandmother was not certain of its precise whereabouts, she had given him detailed descriptions of several secret places where they had hidden love letters when they were teenagers. Her husband had once told her that he was using those secret places to hide the certificate, moving it around from time to time if building or cleaning work threatened to disturb one of them. But of one thing his grandmother was sure: the certificate still existed, even if its precise whereabouts remained a mystery.

Finding the certificate would clearly be the essential first step to establishing a legal claim to the Earldom. Normally, the second, official, copy lodged at St Catherine's House would also have been required, but here Peter was pretty confident he would have the law on his side. Because of the way the records had been kept, the Southdown agents in pre-war Rome had been forced to be too crude, the weight of circumstantial evidence in his favour too high, and any court would easily be able to see that the marriage records had been deliberately suppressed.

So if he could only find the marriage certificate the legal side of establishing his grandmother's marriage and consequently his father's claim to the title would probably be fairly straightforward. But then a further problem remained, the problem of how to connect him to his parents, of proving that Peter Kirby was really William Fitzpatrick, legal heir to the deceased Earl of Southdown. In view of the vast wealth involved, there were certain to be suspicions that the whole thing was a cleverly constructed fraud.

The bus arrived and he clambered aboard, going up to the top deck so he could smoke a cigarette and calm his ragged nerves. It was fortunate that his grandmother had been on the ball so many years before, trying to plan for every possible eventuality on his behalf. Hers had been an odd kind of guardianship, watching over her only grandchild with a few strategic decisions during his infancy which had probably already saved his life and might yet secure his future.

Some time later the bus pulled to a halt in a busy City street and Peter alighted. Pulling out the notebook where he had written down the particulars his grandmother had given him, he elbowed his way through the throng of besuited office-workers and mounted the steps of a tall building with an imposing neo-classical façade.

He pushed open a heavy oak door and entered another world. The bustle of the street outside suddenly vanished, replaced by a hushed silence in which even his footsteps were stilled by the deep-piled burgundy carpet. As he entered, a doorman wearing an overly ornate red uniform rose from behind a desk and approached the scruffily dressed visitor with a suspicious eye.

"Deliveries are round the back in Percy Street," he said imperiously.

Peter looked at him, annoyance at the man's assumptions temporarily overcoming his nerves.

"Do I look as if I'm delivering something, mate?" he said gruffly.

The man checked himself.

"I'm sorry," he said. "You've come to see ..."

"Fricknell, Percival and Smythe. This is the right place, isn't it?"

"Oh yes, sir," the man replied. "Which partner did you wish to see?"

Peter glanced uncertainly at his notebook.

"Well ...," he said. "One of those three, I suppose."

The man in uniform gave up. He returned to his desk and spoke briefly into his intercom. Moments later, a door opened in a corridor leading off from the main hallway and a man of about forty in a pinstriped suit appeared.

"Roger Thompson," he announced, approaching Peter with a smile and holding out his hand. "Can I help you, sir?"

Peter glanced at the notebook.

"I'm looking for a Mr Fricknell, a Mr Percival or a Mr Smythe. Do they work here?"

The man smiled.

"I believe Messrs Fricknell and Smythe died before the last war," he said. "Mr Percival retired sometime in the 1960s. But perhaps I can be of some assistance."

Peter looked at him suspiciously.

"I'm William Fitzpatrick," he blurted out. "I believe a sealed packet was left with you in 1973. I've come to see whether it's still here.

Mr Thompson smiled faintly.

"We might have lost our three original partners, Mr Fitzpatrick, but we never lose our papers. Do please come through to my office."

He led Peter into an imposing office and pressed a buzzer on his desk. Moments later, a neat young secretary appeared.

"Check the registry for some papers relating to a Mr William Fitzpatrick which were deposited in 1973, please, Miss Walton."

The secretary vanished softly, leaving an awkward silence in her wake.

"To what do the papers refer, if I may be so bold as to enquire?" asked the lawyer.

Peter shrugged.

"Well, to me, I suppose. I just wanted to check exactly what you had."

The man nodded and allowed the silence to continue unchecked. Ten minutes later the secretary returned carrying a brown paper envelope. Roger Thompson patiently took the package from her and lifted out the contents. There appeared to be a single sheet of paper inside, some kind of office memorandum. As he read the note, his eyebrows raised perceptibly. Finally, his eyes rose to meet Peter's.

"And you are Mr William Fitzpatrick?" he asked.

Peter nodded.

The lawyer carefully re-read the sheet of paper. Then he took a deep breath.

"I am instructed to check your identity by inspecting your back," he mumbled.

For a moment Peter stared at the man. Then he burst out laughing. His grandmother had told him that they would know who he was at the solicitors. At the time, he hadn't thought to enquire how.

"Some thing's never change, eh," he said, rising to his feet.

The lawyer flinched.

"Sorry?"

"I've a birthmark. It's on my back."

He pulled up his shirt and turned his back towards the lawyer.

"Thank you, sir," the flustered Mr Thompson replied. "Your birthmark is exactly as it was described by the lady who deposited the package with us in 1973. I believe we must assume you are indeed who you say you are. But I am also instructed that I am only to give you one of the two packages under seal unless you are in the presence of an officer of the court."

Peter nodded quietly. It was just as his grandmother had said, two identical packages deposited with the same firm of solicitors, both sealed in June 1973. One was for his personal use in preparing his case, the other to be used to establish his identity at a subsequent court hearing.

The solicitor handed him one of the packages. Peter already knew what it contained. Twenty years before, his grandmother had been consumed with grief at the loss of her only son and the impending loss of her only grandchild. But despite the grief, or perhaps because of it, she had found it within herself to plan for Peter's future with almost military thoroughness. Each package contained certified copies of Peter's birth certificate, his father's birth and marriage certificates, his grandmother's birth certificate and a sworn testimonial of her extraordinary story. But besides these papers, the packages also contained photographs of his birthmark, fingerprints taken in the presence of a solicitor and tiny samples of his hair and skin.

Peter eyed the lawyer suspiciously, wondering whether he could be trusted.

The lawyer must have read his mind.

"If you require some confidential advice from my firm, Mr Fitzpatrick, please do not hesitate to ask. I see from the enclosed memorandum that a fairly substantial amount has already been paid on account of our fees. It has been accumulating interest ever since."

It was another little detail his grandmother had forgotten to mention.

"Can you explain how to claim a title?"

"What sort of title?"

"A noble title. A peerage."

The lawyer shrugged.

"In principle it is relatively straightforward, particularly if handled through a firm of solicitors such as ourselves with some experience in these matters. An application form is completed and submitted to the Home Office. The Home Secretary passes the application to the Attorney-General who examines the case to see whether a prima facie case exists. If it does, then the matter is referred to the Committee of Privileges of the House of Lords for a full judicial hearing. After that, if the case is successful, the Crown will issue the letters patent."

Peter looked at him in surprise.

"You say you have experience of these things. Is it common, then?"

Roger Thompson shrugged.

"Not common. But cases do occur from time to time. A title becomes dormant and then somebody pops up and claims it. Usually it's some obscure tenth cousin from the farther reaches of the New World."

Peter hesitated. He wanted the information, but he didn't want to give too much away. Not until he was ready.

"Do people ever challenge the holders of titles?" he asked.

Mr Thompson looked at him with a frown.

"I've never heard of such a case. A title is only granted in the first place if a pretty watertight claim is established."

"But would such a challenge be technically possible? In theory?"

Mr Thompson thought for a moment.

"I can see no reason why not," he answered quietly. "If a first rate prima facie case could be established, I can think of no legal reason why the Committee of Privileges would not examine the circumstances to see whether the title should be restored to its proper owner. No reason whatsoever."

* * * * * *

He stood before the tall mirror in the changing room and stared with incredulity at the complete stranger standing before him. Gone was the scruffy and faded open-neck shirt, the tatty pair of green corduroy trousers which had served him faithfully from morning till night for nearly ten months, the tarnished pair of trainers he had picked up in the local Oxfam shop for little more than the price of a burger. And in their place were a clean white shirt, a brightly patterned tie and, most striking of all, a smartly pressed suit of the very latest fashion.

His raised his hand slowly towards his ear. Harry had warned him it would have to go, but at the time he had refused to accept it. Yet now, looking at himself in his new outfit, he could see for himself that there was a certain inevitability about its removal. For while a real Oxford graduate might possibly have been able to carry it off, flaunting it as a symbol of rugged individualism, Peter could sense that for him the gesture would be a dangerous and foolish provocation of a fate which he badly needed on his side.

He solemnly removed the tiny earring and cupped it lovingly in his hand. For he had worn it every day since the age of fourteen, and over the years had come to think of it as a faithful friend, a kind of domestic pet which would slavishly follow him around wherever he went. Whenever he had felt lonely or afraid, as he had often done during the long colourless years of his youth, he had often turned to his earring for comfort, fingering it nervously while he wrestled with whatever difficult issue confronted him at the time. With a sigh, he tucked it carefully into his breast pocket. One day, perhaps, he would feel able to wear it again.

The earring safely gone, he examined himself carefully in the mirror for clues as to his former self. His hair had already been cut, reduced to the kind of regulation crop he had often observed on the heads of aspiring yuppies as they marched up and down the streets of central London in search of a high-flying career. His nails too had been transformed under Harry's strict instruction, manicured and cleaned in a way they had never been before.

There remained the small matter of his accent. It could certainly not be described as posh, but for once perhaps chance had been on his side, blessing him with a nondescript south coast drool which gave little away about his social origins provided that he avoided at all times the temptation to swear.

Finally satisfied with his clothing and general appearance, he started to examine his face, searching his features for some tell-tale sign that would give the game away. For Harry had warned him to avoid the kind of hang-dog look which often spoiled his youthful good looks, told him to try and feel as well as appear bright and alert and cheerful. It was easier said than done, but as Peter gazed at himself in the mirror he began to see how much the new clothes helped. It was as if the muscles of his face somehow mirrored the smartness of the clothes, refusing to be outdone in the sense of outward confidence they exuded.

A quiet smile slowly spread across Peter's face. Soon, very soon perhaps, he would be ready to begin his long journey into the unknown.

* * * * * *

Miss Trumpington-Fetherby rose to her feet as he entered the room and approached him with a bright smile.

"Welcome, Peter," she said cheerfully, extending her hand. "Welcome to Raley-le-Street!"

Peter grasped her extended hand firmly in the manner Harry had instructed him.

"Thank you, Miss Trumpington-Fetherby."

The headmistress of Raley-le-Street School for Girls was a lady in late middle age, her rather stiff appearance and prim clothing contradicted by her warm and friendly manner. She steered him towards two large armchairs neatly arranged beside a bay window overlooking the school playing fields.

"Sherry?" she asked as soon as he was seated. "I know you Oxford fellows always like a glass of sherry before your supper."

"Please."

She poured out two glasses and settled down in the second armchair.

"Is your flat all right?" she asked with a concerned tone. "Not too small I trust?"

The flat came with the job, a smart and well-appointed apartment over the old stables. It was accommodation of a standard and spaciousness to which Peter had until recently not dared believe he could ever aspire, yet the headmistress seemed seriously concerned that he might find it cramped.

"It's fine, thank you."

The headmistress looked immensely relieved. She leaned conspiringly towards him.

"Unless we are with the girls," she whispered, "you must call me Penelope. As a boarding school we are a tight-knit community here, a family you might say. Excessive formality is rather inappropriate in such circumstances, don't you agree?"

"Oh yes, Miss Trumping ... I quite agree."

She took a sip of her sherry and looked dreamily through the window.

"I expect you're missing Oxford dreadfully, Peter. I know I still do even after all these years."

Peter winced. Already at the interview he'd been more than a little shaken to discover that the headmistress of Raley-le-Street had not only been to Oxford herself but seemed to know the college he had supposedly attended rather well.

"Yes," he replied, vainly hoping the conversation would turn to other things.

"I expect a fit young man like you was seriously into eights?" she asked expectantly.

Peter looked at her in consternation, not having the faintest idea what she was talking about.

"Actually I wasn't that keen on eights," he mumbled.

She looked disappointed.

"Oh but you should have been. When I was up I had a dear friend called Frank at your college. In those days everyone was into eights."

Peter searched for something to say but nothing came.

"So what sports did you like?" she asked.

Again Peter flinched. Harry had advised him to put down sports as an interest on the application form, on the grounds that it would make him look more wholesome. It might perhaps have been a foolish thing to do.

"Oh ...," he said, "you know, all the usual ones. Rugby, rowing that sort of thing."

Miss Trumpington-Fetherby looked at him with a puzzled expression.

"I thought you said you weren't keen on eights," she said.

The penny dropped. Inwardly he kicked himself for not realising sooner.

"Well, at first I was. Later I was more interested in rugby."

He could see her visibly relaxing.

"Rugby," she said with a smile. "Frank would have approved of that too, but I'm afraid you won't have much opportunity to play rugby here. Our girls seem to prefer netball and lacrosse."

The smile lasted only a few seconds and then her face grew serious.

"You know, Peter," she confided, "we really are terribly pleased to have you on board. Terribly pleased."

"The pleasure is all mine."

She stretched back in her chair and examined him carefully.

"You remind me more than a little of Frank," she said wistfully. "I know he would have fitted in well at Raley. And I'm sure you will as well."

Peter smiled grimly to himself. From the outset, Penelope Trumpington-Fetherby had appeared to be transfixed not only by the fact that he had a first class honours degree from Oxford but also by his college connections. Yet only now did he begin to realise that it was also because he reminded her of a young man called Frank, a long lost sweetheart of her youth.

There was a knock at the door. Miss Trumpington-Fetherby looked up.

"Ah, that'll be Frances Beattie, our Deputy Head. I asked her to pop in and join us before dinner." She turned to face the door. "Do come in, Frances."

The door swung open and another primly dressed lady in her late fifties appeared. But in sharp contrast with the headmistress's warm and welcoming manner, the newcomer's face displayed an innate hostility to his presence.

"How nice to meet you again," Miss Beattie said, her words formal and hollow.

"The pleasure is mine," Peter replied.

Miss Trumpington-Fetherby poured another glass of sherry and eyed the Deputy Head silently.

"I should warn you that Frances doesn't quite approve of your appointment, do you, Frances?" she said, handing her the sherry.

Miss Beattie looked at Miss Trumpington-Fetherby with scarcely-disguised contempt.

"I have nothing against Mr Kirby personally," she observed.

At the interview, Peter had learned that the Deputy Head, having spent almost her entire adult life at Raley, had recently been denied the long coveted headship when Miss Trumpington-Fetherby, an outsider from another more academic school, had been appointed. From this inauspicious start, relations between the two women had been deteriorating ever since.

"Until your arrival Raley had an all-female staff room. Frances is worried your presence will unsettle the girls."

Peter remained silent, unwilling to be drawn into a dispute which could serve him no useful purpose.

"I am merely concerned with the smooth running of the school," Miss Beattie interjected. "The older girls are at an impressionable age. I fear they might find Mr Kirby a distraction, that's all."

"Is it just because I'm a man that you're worried, or because I'm so young," Peter interjected, feeling he had to say something.

For the first time, Miss Beattie smiled.

"You are a good-looking young man, not many years older than some of our senior girls. It would be surprising if they did not find you a distraction, would it not?"

Miss Trumpington-Fetherby rose imperiously to her feet and glowered down at her deputy.

"I am sure Peter is fully aware of his professional responsibilities," she said sharply. "And now I think we should make our way to the dining hall. The girls will be waiting for us."

They walked in frosty silence through the wood-panelled corridors towards the dining hall. Raley-le-Street occupied an old stately home deep in the heart of rural Gloucestershire and still retained a sense of aristocratic grandeur inherited from a previous era. The walls of the corridors along which they passed were adorned with paintings of long dead headmistresses, their stern faces a reminder to any girls foolish enough to glance up at them that their childish pranks were being overlooked from beyond the grave.

Finally Miss Trumpington-Fetherby pushed open one of a pair of ornate double doors and they entered the dining hall, a spacious gallery in which tapestries were interspersed with windows along one wall and high gilt-edged mirrors along the other. The gallery was jammed full of long wooden tables at which several hundred girls were sitting arranged in order of age, their bright red uniforms reminiscent of a military parade. Nearest to the door through which they had passed were the girls from the preparatory department, tiny little things no more than seven or eight years old. They then grew progressively larger until at the far end, just beneath the raised podium on which the staff were sitting, the sixth form were assembled, advertising their exalted status by their much coveted right to wear their own clothes rather than the official school uniform.

As they entered the hall a hush rapidly descended, followed almost instantaneously by a deafening scraping of chairs as the girls and the staff simultaneously rose to their feet. Only when silence had once more returned did Miss Trumpington-Fetherby begin to walk down the central aisle towards the high table on the podium, flanked on either side by her two companions.

Peter noticed it the second he entered the hall. For although the headmistress was in the centre of their little triumvirate as it swept imperiously down the aisle, he knew that all eyes were focussed on him. In the silence he could feel them staring at him, dissecting him, analysing him, silently preparing themselves to discuss his every feature and every mannerism as soon as the opportunity permitted. Deliberately he avoided the eyes, concentrating on reaching the raised platform ahead.

They reached the podium and he took his place at the dining table beside the headmistress's place, standing behind his chair along with the other members of staff. Miss Trumpington-Fetherby glanced around the hall and then inclined her head to indicate that everyone besides herself should sit.

"Good evening, girls," she announced as soon as the chairs stopped scraping and silence was restored.

"Good evening, Miss Trumpington-Fetherby," came the ritualised response. Only when the echo had finally faded away did the headmistress begin to address the sea of faces before her.

"I am sure we are all pleased to be able to welcome a new member of staff this evening." She stopped and indicated Peter with a gracious wave of her hand. "Mr Kirby has just completed his B.A. in history at Oxford University with first class honours. I am sure you will all be as pleased as I that he has chosen to come and teach at Raley. And I am also sure that you will welcome him into our little community with open arms."

Peter winced. It was almost imperceptible, but he was sure he could sense a ripple of repressed amusement at the headmistress's words. But Miss Trumpington-Fetherby continued unperturbed.

"It is my belief that Mr Kirby's magnificent academic achievements at both school and university will act as a beacon to you all, glittering prizes towards which your labours here should be aimed. It is my hope that as many of you as possible will benefit from coming into contact with him."

This time the ripple of repressed amusement was unmistakeable. Out of the corner of his eye, Peter became aware of Frances Beattie. She was sitting with her head hunched forward, as if waiting in silent resignation for her dire warnings about his presence to come true.

Miss Trumpington-Fetherby made several more routine announcements before at last sitting down. She, at least, seemed not to have noticed the effect her words had had upon the girls.

Peter turned to her with a smile.

"What sort of homes do most of these girls come from?" he asked with feigned innocence.

Miss Trumpington-Fetherby leant conspiringly towards him.

"Frankly," she whispered, "most of them are what I like to call rural squirearchy, not at all like the London intelligentsia at my last school. Put rather crudely, that means their parents have plenty of money but couldn't get them into any more academically exciting establishments. When I came here last year, Raley's exam results were not exactly top of the league. But it's something I plan to change."

"Rural squirearchy," Peter said. "Does that mean you have a lot of girls from noble families here?"

Miss Trumpington-Fetherby smiled.

"One or two," she whispered. "They're terribly good for the school's reputation, you know. One of our little flock is even the daughter of an Earl."

Peter looked out at the sea of faces before him.

"Oh yes," he said with interest.

Miss Trumpington-Fetherby understood his meaning.

"Over there," she said. "The surly-looking one in the Upper Fifth sitting just beneath the window. That's the Lady Julia, youngest daughter of the Earl of Southdown."

* * * * * *

The bright April sunshine was streaming in through the window as he awoke. Compared to his old bedsit at Harry's, his bedroom was spacious indeed, converted from an old storeroom above the stables and decorated with a tasteful floral-design wallpaper which would never have been selected if the person responsible had realised it would be occupied by a man. But despite the rather feminine feel of the room, or perhaps because of it, Peter felt comfortable in his new lodgings, more comfortable than he had ever felt before.

He glanced apprehensively at the alarm clock beside his bed and saw to his relief that he did not have to get up for nearly half-an-hour. Time enough to doze a while, to think again about exactly how he would handle the Lady Julia when he met her in their first lesson together immediately after morning assembly.

The idea of getting a job at Raley-le-Street in order to gain access to Southdown House had occurred to him shortly after his visit to the firm of solicitors in the City. When he had told his grandmother that he intended to try and reclaim his inheritance, she had handed him a small file of press cuttings concerning the Troughton family and the Southdown estate. Most of the material had been relatively uninteresting, conveying a rather stereotypic impression of a settled aristocratic family placidly enjoying the fruits of their vast unearned wealth in a variety of innocent rural pursuits.

From the press cuttings, it appeared the current Earl was particularly keen on shooting, periodically carrying off a prize in some competition or other. He seemed to have a special interest in wildlife conservation in Africa, having provoked some considerable controversy in the press for financing a huge private game reserve in Zimbabwe for his own personal use. But besides his hunting activities, the Earl himself did not appear to have any real interests. His wife, who in her day had been a noted socialite, had died of cancer in the early 1980s. Since then the Earl had appeared at fewer society functions, preferring the quiet rural pursuits of Southdown House to the hurly-burly of his Belgravia home.

Besides the Earl, the only other Troughtons living at Southdown House were the Dowager Countess Alexandra and the Earl's two children. The Countess Alexandra, the current Earl's mother and official "wife" of Peter's grandfather, was now in her mid-seventies. In her youth she too had preferred the excitement of Belgravia to the sedate ways of the rural estate, but in recent years there was increasingly little reference to her in the social columns of the newspapers. Occasionally she would open a country fête or award the prizes at a county vegetable contest, but the rich American heiress who had successfully captured the House of Southdown in her youth appeared to have retired into relative obscurity during the twilight of her life.

The same obscurity did not however surround the Earl's only son, the Viscount James. Although only twenty years old, he had already begun to make a name for himself in motor racing. He was by all accounts highly proficient as a mechanic as well as a racing driver, and had already won a number of important international events. On the sports pages, he was reported as being a spirited young man capable of extraordinary flashes of genius on the racetrack, and his image as a dashing young man with plenty of money had earned him considerable attention from the ladies.

It was only as he had read through the press cuttings handed to him by his grandmother that Peter had begun to realise how difficult it would be to gain access to Southdown House in order to search for the vital missing copy of his grandmother's marriage certificate. The House itself was never open to the public, and in view of the priceless collections of art treasures and antiquities in the Earl's possession, it was no doubt protected by extremely sophisticated security and surveillance equipment. A break-in was therefore out of the question. He could have made a casual visit on some pretext or other, but although he would probably have gained access to the building he would have neither the time nor the privacy on such a visit to find the hiding places described to him by his grandmother. He therefore knew he had to find a better way, a way of gaining access to the House so that he could search without interruption.

If the school had had a less unusual name he would probably never have noticed it. There, tucked away in the corner of an otherwise uninteresting report about the inhabitants of Southdown House, was a one-line mention of the fact that Lady Julia, second child of the Earl of Southdown, was a boarder at Raley-le-Street School for Girls in Gloucestershire. He had realised the possible significance of the words as soon as he had read them, for Raley- le-Street had been one of the independent schools he had seen advertising in the Times Educational Supplement earlier that week. A school with a vacancy for a history teacher.

And so it had all fitted neatly together. Harry's original plan about becoming a history teacher in a third rate public school had coincided conveniently with his need to gain access to Southdown House. So without telling Harry the real purpose of his actions, he had applied for the post and won it against some pretty stiff competition from experienced teachers, largely thanks to the wholehearted support of Miss Trumpington-Fetherby. But if everything had gone smoothly in Stage One of his plan, Stage Two looked like being a far more difficult nut to crack. For now he was safely ensconced within the school as a member of the academic staff, he faced the far more difficult task of persuading the sixteen year old Lady Julia to arrange an invitation to stay in her father's home.

It was already April, with only the first half of the summer term to go before the GCSE examinations began. After the examinations were over anything might happen: Julia might transfer to a different school for her A-Levels or she might decide not to continue her education at all. And if she left, then all chance of using her to gain access to Southdown House would promptly vanish. He had to act fast.

Peter realised that two approaches presented themselves. One was to persuade Julia and her parents that she required urgent tutoring in history during the May half-term holiday immediately preceding the summer examinations. If it worked, this first approach appeared to pose little risk. But as Peter lay in bed and listened to the sound of the birds singing outside his window, he knew that first approach also carried little chance of success. Julia would probably neither wish nor require extra tuition in history. And even if she did need additional coaching, she would probably seek it from a teacher she knew already or from someone outside the school. Even if he approached her with a direct offer of help, she would almost certainly refuse his overtures.

But although this first approach seemed to carry little possibility of success, Peter tried hard to convince himself that it did. For the alternative strategy he had devised was not only far more difficult, but was also considerably more dangerous.

He could read them like a book. Twenty-three young faces who were far more interested in him than in his well-rehearsed recitation of the events leading up to the Munich crisis of 1938. Twenty-three reluctant conscripts in a single-sex institution who could gaze upon his body and transform him into the man of their dreams. Twenty-three impressionable girls with whom he sensed he could make some progress if only he were to make a determined attempt to win their hearts.

And then there was the twenty-fourth girl. The twenty-fourth girl in the Upper Fifth history class. The girl in the back row who looked upon him with such deep and unnerving contempt. The Lady Julia.

A bright-faced girl called Claire-Marie raised her hand and Peter stopped speaking.

"Could you excuse me, please?" she asked politely.

"Why?"

"I have to go to the loo," she replied nervously.

Peter flinched. He had been warned only the previous day by Miss Beattie against girls trying to escape to the toilets during his lessons. She had told him to expect it as a routine challenge to his authority as a new teacher.

"Can't it wait?" he replied. "It's only a quarter of an hour to the end of the lesson."

Claire-Marie looked at him, her baleful eyes pleading for understanding. And as she did so, she seemed to wriggle uncomfortably in her seat.

"Sorry," she said apologetically, "but it really is urgent."

Still Peter hesitated. Miss Beattie had warned him about this. It was standard fare, served up regularly to new teachers. He should be firm, toe the line.

"I can't let you go," he said. "You know that."

Claire-Marie looked away sulkily, still fidgeting. The other girls turned silently to face Peter.

"As I was saying," he continued, "the powers opposed to German expansionism in the summer of 1938 were in something of a fix. Hitler was always careful to phrase his demands in language which appeared perfectly reasonable to foreign public opinion, and there could be no denying that the German-speaking minority in the Sudetenland wished to be incorporated into the Third Reich. It was this very reasonableness that ... Yes, Claire-Marie?"

Again she had raised her hand, a look of genuine concern on her face.

"Please, sir," she said quietly but insistently. "I've really got to go now."

You could hear a pin drop as the rest of the class watched the silent struggle. Miss Beattie had warned him they would look genuine in their appeals. She had expressly instructed him to resist at all costs or face a progressive and potentially destructive undermining of his authority.

"No!" he repeated firmly.

He could feel the tension in class dissipating, a test successfully overcome. He wasn't sure, but he wondered if he could detect a suppressed hint of a smile even in Claire-Marie's anguished face. He was just about to continue with his account of the Munich crisis when he was interrupted by a softly spoken voice from the back of the room.

"Are you influenced in your actions by the history you're teaching us, sir?"

He froze. It was the first time Julia had spoken to him. She was sitting in her place at the back of the room and staring at him with a penetrating gaze. And unlike the contributions during his lesson from the other girls in the group there was no attempt at flirtation in her words. Just a sharp straight intellectual challenge.

He tried unsuccessfully to meet her gaze.

"In what way?" he asked.

"In your superficially callous treatment of Claire-Marie?"

Peter relaxed, allowing himself to sit casually on the teacher's desk.

"You said 'superficially', not me."

He had hoped she would smile at his riposte, allowing the incident to close. But her face remained set.

"Do you really believe Claire-Marie is like Hitler, Mr Kirby?" she said.

"What on earth are you talking about?"

"Just now Claire-Marie asked you if she could go to the toilet. A perfectly reasonable request, I would have thought, just like Hitler's claim to defend the democratic rights of the German minority in Czechoslovakia in 1938. But you refused. It suggests you considered her to have a wider purpose, rather like Hitler did."

"And what do you think I should have done?" he asked, disoriented by her unexpected challenge.

Julia thought for a moment.

"I think you should have considered her case on its merits rather than according to some arbitrary preconceived formula dictated to you in a teachers' training college."

The eyes of the rest of the class were bouncing back and forth across the room, rather as if they were watching a tennis match.

"And what do you suppose the merits of this case are?" Peter asked.

For the first time Julia allowed herself to smile. But it wasn't a cheeky smile, far less an aggressive smile. Just a quiet self-satisfied smile of total triumph.

"You don't know us yet, do you, Mr Kirby? You don't know anything about Claire-Marie or any of the other girls in this school. She might suddenly have got her period, or she might have a bladder problem which nobody has mentioned to you. So I think you should give her the benefit of the doubt until you know better, don't you?"

Peter glanced nervously at Claire-Marie. She certainly did look uncomfortable now, although whether it was because of her physical circumstances or because she was the subject of his discourse with Julia he could not tell.

In his mind he could see Miss Beattie telling him to resist, above all to maintain a firm line with the girls and not weaken. But before his eyes he could see the Lady Julia, his first cousin and adversary, and he knew already that the Troughtons had won the first round of the battle that was to come.

"You can go this once, Claire-Marie," he said quietly, "provided that you don't make a habit of it."

* * * * * *

It was late afternoon. Peter walked alone through the formal gardens surrounding the school and looked with scarcely concealed impatience at the cherry trees lining the path. For the blossom of April had long since given way to the leaves of May but still he had made no progress in his concerted attempt to find a way of penetrating the protective wall which surrounded Lady Julia. Yet the half-term holidays were only two weeks away, and soon it would be too late to secure the invitation to Southdown House he so desperately sought.

He had long since given up any idea that he could persuade her to invite him simply to help her with her studies. For one thing, Julia didn't need any help with her studies and knew it. Her written work was as sharp as her barbed verbal ripostes in class, and there was no doubt in Peter's mind that she would do well in the summer examination.

So for several weeks now he had been trying to summon up the courage to make a serious attempt to win his first cousin's heart, but somehow the opportunity had never presented itself. Since their first lesson together she had been perfectly civil to him, both in class and on the numerous occasions when they had spoken individually, but always he had sensed that she would push him firmly away if he were to make any determined approach.

Ironically enough, the task of pursuing Julia was made more difficult by the fact that Peter found himself more than a little attracted to his sharp-witted first cousin. Like him, she appeared to be a closed and private person, hiding her true feelings behind a veneer of courteous formality. But he sensed that despite the differences in their backgrounds those true feelings if uncovered would be remarkably similar to his own: an overwhelming sense of isolation and loneliness.

Julia was a girl apart from her peers, respected by them for her intellect and her general demeanour, but also a little feared for her aloofness. It was as if she were somehow above her classmates, not just in her inherited aristocratic status but also in herself, an idol and a champion perhaps, but never a friend.

He spotted her the moment she turned the corner. She too was walking alone, returning late from the redundant stately home in which the lessons were held to her dormitory in the coachhouse adjoining the stables. He could feel himself tensing, knowing the second he saw her that it was probably his best chance, perhaps the only chance remaining to him before the holidays. For normally he spoke with her in school, when others were either present or likely to interrupt at any moment. But today they were the only two people in the garden together, their paths soon to cross as he knew their destinies had crossed many years before they had even been born.

As she approached him she smiled. Ever since her victory in their first encounter together she had smiled at him. But it was a formal smile, a smile which gave nothing away.

"Good afternoon, Mr Kirby," she said.

"Hallo," Peter replied. "You're late today."

"A netball practice," she explained.

He nodded.

"I prefer rugby," he said.

Again she smiled politely, beginning to walk on.

"I wonder if you have time for a quick word?" he said hurriedly.

She stopped and nodded.

"I've been wanting to talk to you for some time," he continued quickly.

Again the formal smile.

"Oh yes."

"You're very good at history. I was wondering if you were planning to continue with it at A-Level next year."

Her face fell.

"That rather depends on my father," she said.

"Does it?"

"He wants me to take science."

"What's it got to do with him?"

Again she smiled.

"My father's a strong-minded man."

"So?"

"He who pays the piper calls the tune, I suppose."

"But Julia, what do you want to do?"

"I want to do history, of course. You knew that already, didn't you?"

"But there must be a way of persuading him. Shall we talk about it?"

She nodded. Peter motioned her towards a wooden bench some way away from the path and they walked towards it in silence. It was a perfect place to talk: public and therefore not dangerous, but also a place where they would not be overheard. When they were seated Peter turned to face her.

"So what's your dad got against history, Julia?" he asked.

She shrugged.

"He says there's no point in dragging up the past. Science is more useful because it's about making the future work."

Peter smiled wryly to himself. He could understand better than Julia the Earl's reluctance to drag up the past.

"It's a point of view," he commented.

Julia turned to face him.

"My father doesn't recognise the legitimacy of 'points of view'," she said. "In his eyes, things are either right or else they're wrong. There's no middle ground."

"But you're sixteen now. You've got to make up your own mind. You can't keep passing the buck to him or you'll go on blaming him for screwing up your life for evermore."

He realised what he had done the moment the word slipped past his lips. It was a reversion to the carefully concealed language of the street urchin, the rough tough vocabulary of the dispossessed which he had successfully hidden from everyone at Raley-le-Street since the moment of his arrival.

Although she said nothing he could see Julia's reaction. Somewhere, deep down inside her, he knew she had stored the information away.

"Sorry?" he mumbled.

"What for?" she asked.

41

"The language I used."

She smiled sarcastically.

"Oh, don't worry about that. My father swears all the time."

For the first time since knowing her he could feel some emotion in her words. He hesitated.

"Your father's an Earl, isn't he?"

She nodded but said nothing.

"I imagine that means he's used to people doing what he says."

She looked up at him sadly and smiled.

"He's certainly used to me doing what he says, if that's what you mean."

They sat in silence for a few moments.

"Does he respect qualifications?" Peter asked suddenly.

"My father? Of course he does. He's got money and status, but somehow he never managed to get his act together when it came to exams. It's something neither his money nor his status could buy him. That's why he wants me to do well at school. I think maybe it explains why he won't leave me alone to make up my own mind."

"I've got some pretty good qualifications," Peter said brightly. "Do you think it's possible I might be able to persuade him to change his mind about you doing history. You know, tell him how good your chances would be of getting into Oxford or Cambridge, that sort of thing."

Julia looked at him in surprise.

"You'd talk to him?"

"Of course. It's my job."

"Do you really think it might do some good?"

"It might. I couldn't do it in half-an-hour, of course. I'd need to wear him down with a concerted campaign of flattery about your academic prospects if you choose the right discipline."

A cloud suddenly passed over her face and she looked at him suspiciously.

"Why do you care so much?" she asked.

"It's my job to care. You're the best history student in the Upper Fifth. I want to have you in my A-Level class next year."

"None of the other teachers here would put themselves out like that."

Peter shrugged.

"That's their business. Call it the idealism of a young teacher if you like, but I don't want to see you messing up a promising future because nobody can be bothered to give you a helping hand at a crucial stage."

42

The explanation seemed to convince her and her face momentarily cleared, but then another disturbing thought seemed to occur to her.

"But when could you see him?"

Peter was silent for a while. It was an outrageous suggestion, one which might well bring instant and outright rejection. When he spoke, he tried to make the words sound as casual as possible.

"The holidays, I suppose. If you can arrange it."

She looked at him with astonishment.

"Half-term?" she mouthed.

"I'm free. I'm sure your dad's got a big house. Get me invited."

"To stay, you mean?"

"Do you think he'd have me if you asked him, if you told him I wanted to come and discuss your future with him."

She laughed.

"You don't know my dad. He'd probably tell me you can discuss my future with him on the telephone. Especially if he knows you're History."

"Think of a better pretext, then."

She hesitated, and he could immediately see in her face that he was making progress. Already she was conspiring with him, trying to find a way to ingratiate him into her father's home.

For several minutes they sat in silence together. Then she turned and looked thoughtfully at him.

"You don't shoot, do you?" she asked.

"Shoot? Shoot what?"

Again she laughed.

"Well, in my father's case, just about anything that moves. He's absolutely manic about hunting. If I said how much you'd helped me this term with my work and how keen you were on shooting, then if I egged him on he just might ask you down to the estate by way of saying thank you."

Peter could feel his heart sinking. The only sport he'd ever played in the children's homes and at school was football, the one pastime in which the upper classes seemed to have absolutely no interest.

"I love shooting," he said brightly. "You might say I was a leading light in the Oxford hunting scene. I regularly went on safari in Africa during the vacs."

Julia's eyes lit up.

"Big game!" she exclaimed. "That'll clinch it. My dad gets even more excited about killing elephants than about killing pheasant."

"So you think you might be able to arrange me an invitation?"

"I'll ring him tonight, Mr Kirby, see what he says."

43

"I think you're stark raving bonkers. That's what I think."

Harry prowled up and down the dingy living room of his flat above the cafe and tried unsuccessfully to contain his consternation at the story Peter had just recounted.

"It's you who said I should change the rules because life hadn't been fair to me," Peter mumbled, his words a futile attempt to pacify the old man.

Harry stopped pacing in front of the armchair in which Peter was sitting and glowered down at him.

"Correction. I advised you to move up in life, young man. Not down into a six foot hole in the ground."

"It's my title and it's my money. They shouldn't have nicked it."

Harry grunted.

"'My title and my money'," he mimicked. "What makes you think it's yours? Did you work for it?"

Peter shrugged.

"It's still mine."

Harry was still standing motionless but had now resorted to taking deep breaths. The only other time Peter had seen him deliberately taking deep breaths was just after a visit from Customs and Excise.

"For the sake of argument I'll accept the money's yours," he said as soon as he had recovered himself. "I'll even accept that you might be able to win your claim in a court of law if you could find that damned marriage certificate. But don't you see they'll never let you get as far as a court. As soon as you raise your silly little head above the parapet, they'll simply chop it off."

"I'll be all right," Peter said, trying to sound more convinced than he felt.

Suddenly Harry's face froze rigid.

"I can still hear my father saying those very words only days before the Nazis came to pick him up," he said eventually.

His remark reduced Peter to temporary silence. He knew Harry was right, he knew that from the moment he arrived at Southdown House the following weekend the danger to his life would start increasing exponentially.

Harry sat down opposite Peter and scratched his balding head.

"Why did you come and tell me all this now, Peter? You didn't breathe a word of it before, when I was helping you get the job."

Peter looked down at his feet.

"I don't know. I suppose it didn't seem so real then. But now that

I'm actually going to Southdown House it does. So I wanted to tell you."

"You enjoy seeing an old man suffer! Some sport."

"And also I wondered if you knew anything about hunting?"

Harry's naturally protruding eyes seemed to protrude even more.

"Hunting! Why do you want to know about hunting, for goodness sake?"

"I told them I was something of an expert. Actually that's partly why the Earl is asking me down. From what Julia says I think he likes to gossip about big game hunting."

Harry rolled his eyes upwards.

"May your God protect you," he breathed.

"Does that mean you don't know anything?" Peter asked sadly.

"Of course I don't. You think just because I'm so old I know everything. When would I have had a chance to learn about hunting?"

Peter shrugged.

"Never mind," he said. "I'll think of something."

"Within five minutes of arriving he'll ask you what your favourite gun is," Harry said. "What are you going to say then?"

"A Colt 45?" Peter replied with a pretence at a smile.

Harry also pretended to smile.

"Do yourself a favour, Peter. Phone them up, tell them you're sick. Forget the whole bloody thing before it's too late."

Peter's face grew serious.

"I'm not going to do that, Mr Kaye."

"But why?" Harry pleaded. "It's crazy. You'll just get yourself killed, that's all."

"When you were my age, what would you have done if you had had a chance to get even with Hitler?"

Harry snarled.

"I'd have done the same as most Jews. You know that."

"But what about the dangers? What if there'd been a good chance of getting yourself killed in the process?"

"No difference."

"Well, that just about sums up how I feel about the people at Southdown House. They didn't just nick my property, did they? They also killed my parents and destroyed my childhood. And now I reckon they owe me. Isn't that a good enough reason for me to take the risks I'm taking?"

This time it was Harry who hung his head.

"I suppose it is," he murmured.

Peter smiled.

"Thanks, Mr Kaye," he said quietly.

Harry looked up at him with a look of wry resignation.

"If you like," he said, "you can call me Harry."

* * * * * *

The tiny rural railway station of Chumley Halt looked like a throwback to a previous era, an era when time moved at a slower pace. The freshly painted lettering of the signs, the faded green of the ornate iron pillars, the pastel shades on the posters advertising day trips to London and the south coast towns: all conspired to fend off the relentless passage of the years, reminding the increasingly rare travellers who used the station that the great age of rail was not quite over.

As Peter alighted from the train there was only one other person on the platform, an old gentleman in a crumpled railway uniform bending low over a neat flower bed. But despite the fact that he was only yards away from the train he appeared to take no notice of either its arrival or its departure, as if resentful of this modern intrusion into a world more suited to steam.

Peter picked up his suitcase and started walking down the platform towards the station buildings, expecting to find the driver Julia had told him would be waiting to escort him to Southdown House. But before he had reached the exit he was stopped by a sharp tap on the shoulder.

"You must be Peter Kirby," came an ancient voice, its intonation dull and lifeless.

He turned and saw that the words came from the old man in the crumpled uniform.

"Yes," Peter said. "How did you know?"

The old man shrugged and indicated the deserted platform.

"Nobody else here, is there?"

Peter glanced through the small station building to the deserted car park beyond.

"I'm expecting to be met."

The station-master shrugged.

"I'm afraid you'll have to wait. They telephoned to say all the cars were out."

The old man turned away, content to have delivered his message as instructed.

Peter glanced again at the empty car park.

"Did they say how long?" he called after the man, but he continued to walk away, oblivious of all except his beloved flowerbeds.

Peter ambled through the deserted station lobby into the empty car
park beyond and sat down on his suitcase. The early afternoon sun
was beating down overhead, throwing up a good deal of reflected heat
from the concrete car park. Even in the protective shade of the station
building, the temperature was becoming oppressive.

He glanced at his watch, wondering whether he himself should
telephone for a taxi, but before he could make up his mind he became
aware of a bright yellow bicycle sweeping towards him across the
empty car park.

The bicycle skidded to a halt beside him and Julia dismounted,
allowing the discarded cycle to fall to the ground. Instead of her
school uniform, she was wearing a worn stripy blouse and a pair of
jeans several sizes too large for her. Her generally tatty appearance
was reinforced by the gaping hole in the jeans just above her right
knee.

"Hallo, Mr Kirby," she said brightly. "I only just heard about the
cars, so I came down as quickly as I could."

He smiled.

"Thanks, I was just beginning to wonder if I should call a taxi
myself."

She smiled maliciously.

"What an excellent idea!" she said. "That'll show 'em."

He looked at her askance.

"It's deliberate, you know," she added. "They've got plenty of cars,
they just want to make you wait a bit."

She said it so naturally that it caught him off-guard.

"Why?" he mumbled.

"To make a point, of course."

"What sort of point?"

"To show you you're not important."

"I know I'm not important. But I still don't understand why it's so
important to rub my nose in it."

Julia laughed.

"That's Daddy," she said. "You'll soon see."

She picked up her bicycle from where she had left it lying on the
ground and lent it against the station wall. When she returned she sat
down beside him on his suitcase.

"I thought you told me I was welcome here," Peter said suspiciously.

"Oh don't worry," she said with a grin. "When you do finally arrive
he'll be charm itself. It's just their way of making sure you know your
place, that's all."

Peter looked at her.

"There's something else, isn't there? Something you've not told me yet."

She met his gaze.

"Well . . ."

"You're hiding something, Julia. Don't you think you ought to tell me what it is before we arrive?"

She thought for a moment before replying.

"O.K.," she said. "Since you ask, I'll tell you what really happened. When I told Daddy about you, he told me you could go and get stuffed."

He looked at her with amazement.

"Yup," she continued. "When I suggested he might like to invite you down in view of how helpful you'd been to me last term and how interested you were in hunting and all that, he just said it was your job to be helpful to me. He warned me you were probably nothing more than a young man on the make, trying to make a pass at a vulnerable young girl likely to inherit a fortune."

"So what happened?"

A sheepish look came over her face.

"I'm afraid I got rather angry. I didn't see that he had a right to speak about you like that, as if you were simply using me in order to get your hands on part of his precious millions."

Peter winced.

"Maybe he's got a point," he said hurriedly. "I suppose I wouldn't be the first."

She shrugged.

"Perhaps not. But I'm perfectly capable of looking after myself."

Peter remembered their conversation together in the school grounds.

"It's hard to believe you're the same girl who won't do history A-Level because her Daddy says so."

She was sitting beside him, nervously picking her fingernails.

"You don't understand Daddy yet," she said. "On some things – things he considers to be unimportant – I can make him change his mind simply by threatening to sulk. He loathes it when I sulk. But on anything he considers to be important, woe betide anyone who crosses him, including me."

"So my visit is unimportant, but your academic future isn't, is that it?"

Julia nodded.

"I'm afraid that just about sums it up."

Peter watched her carefully out of the corner of his eye. If what she was saying was true, then it didn't augur well for his chances of being able to influence the Earl's thinking about her choice of A-Level subjects. Julia must have been aware of that fact. Yet she had still persisted in forcing through his visit in spite of her father's opposition. It made one wonder.

Despite himself, he found his eye wandering downwards towards the seductive slit in her jeans just above the knee. Ever since he had met her, he had tried to ignore the fact that he was increasingly coming to like his first cousin, not only for her sharp manner but also for her youthful good looks. Yet he had identified her prior to his arrival at the school as a necessary tool in gaining access to her father's house. It was and continued to be an act of calculated manipulation.

"I tore it myself," she said, seeing him looking at her knee.

"Did you? Why?"

When he had been sleeping rough, he had known plenty of people with torn clothing. But never before had he met someone who had deliberately ripped their own things.

"It's fashionable. All the girls wear them like this. Usually the tear is on the right knee."

"A mark of affluence?"

She looked puzzled.

"You're all from well-to-do homes at Raley-le-Street," he continued. "Is that why you tear your jeans and try to look poor?"

Again she shrugged.

"I've never really thought about it," she said, "but I suppose you might be right. Do you think I shouldn't have?"

"I suppose it's up to you. You can wear your clothes how you like."

She eyed him suspiciously.

"You're not a socialist, are you, Mr Kirby?"

He shook his head violently. She had mistaken his remark for a statement of abstract political dissent from a member of the educated middle classes rather than a simple reflection on life's oddities from one who had never had any money of his own. It was a lucky escape.

"No," he said. "Are you?"

She grinned.

"When I'm eighteen, I might vote Labour, if that's what you mean."

He raised his eyebrows.

"Hardly in your own interests, surely?"

If she understood she pretended not to.

"Why not?"

"Because you're from a rich home."

Julia smiled.

"You think it's just an adolescent phase. In a few years time I'll become like all the other reactionary bastards in my family."

"So would you really renounce your inheritance?"

She fell silent, a strained look on her face.

"What inheritance?" she said at last. "What makes you think I'm going to get an inheritance?"

Suddenly Peter remembered his grandmother's words. The property was as inalienable as the title, owned by the Earldom rather than the Earl. It was why their mutual grandfather had not feared disinheritance when he had returned from Italy with his serving girl wife.

"What do you mean?" he asked innocently.

"My father's wealth is all held in the name of the Earldom. You might say he holds it on trust for future generations. I don't understand all the legal ins and outs, but when the Earldom was established centuries ago the property of the Earl was somehow linked with the title. When a new Earl is created, he has to agree to dispose of any personal money he might hold by either giving it away or granting it to the Earldom. Only then can he come into the Earldom."

"And your father did that?"

"Yes. He had no real choice if he wanted to inherit."

"But he must control the money, surely. I mean, if he wants to he can buy things or give money away."

"Until last week he had absolute control. But now he doesn't any longer."

"Why not?"

Julia scowled, and Peter suddenly sensed an anger in her far deeper than anything he had felt when she spoke about her father.

"Last week my brother James celebrated his twenty-first birthday. Now he must countersign every expenditure my father makes."

Peter slowly nodded his head. It was a legal system cleverly designed many centuries before to maintain the family fortune intact, preventing a weak or spendthrift Earl from recklessly dissipating the family fortune. Generally speaking at least two adult generations in the direct line would be alive at once, each carefully watching over the actions of the other.

"And you don't think your brother will agree to your father giving you any part of his fortune?"

Julia turned to face him, her face white with suppressed emotion.

"Frankly," she said, "my brother would rather see me dead."

The ensuing silence did not last long. A vintage Rolls-Royce swept majestically into the car park and approached them, its young driver smartly dressed in a pale green livery which looked more suited to a footman than a chauffeur. As soon as the car drew to a halt the driver stepped smartly out and stood to attention.

"His lordship sends his apologies for the unavoidable delay," he said politely, his remark addressed to Julia rather than to her guest.

"Pressing engagements elsewhere, eh, Roberts?" Julia commented drily, making little attempt to hide the sarcasm in her voice.

"Indeed, my lady," the driver replied with an embarrassed look. "Shall I load the gentleman's luggage?"

"And my bike, Roberts. I'll be coming too."

As the chauffeur started to stow the luggage away, Julia clambered up into the rear seat.

"I forgot to mention," she said, seeing Peter eyeing the car, "Daddy likes vintage cars almost as much as hunting. He says he has one of the finest collections of inter-war Rolls-Royces anywhere in the world."

Peter's excitement at the prospect of a ride in such an unusual vehicle temporarily elbowed aside his discomfort at the thought of his impending meeting with the Earl. He climbed up beside Julia and looked admiringly at the controls of the car.

"It's impressive," he said.

"You think so," she replied. "Personally I think they're disgustingly uncomfortable."

Her remark reduced Peter to silence. He remembered her as she had first arrived at the station, a scruffy girl on a bright yellow bicycle, and could not help but find himself wishing that the car had not come to pick them up. For while they were alone in the station car park she had seemed so relaxed, certainly more natural than her carefully controlled manner when at school. But the car's arrival and the aristocratic authority with which she had instructed the driver in his duties had forcefully reminded him of the gulf between their two worlds, a gulf which even a designer rip in a trouser leg could not serve to bridge.

They drove in silence through winding country lanes between fields full of unripe corn for what seemed like many miles. Villages were nonexistent, the few farmhouses which could be seen set far back from the twisting road, almost hidden from view behind fences and high bushes. Geographically the West Sussex countryside through which they were passing was close to the south coast bustle of his childhood and the packed London streets of his adult life, but in every other respect it was far removed, a remoter world, a quiet haven suited to those who found the frenzy of modern life too much to bear.

His thoughts returned to the car in which he was sitting and with a shock he realised that for the first time he had entered into disputed territory. For the car, like everything else belonging to the Earldom, was rightfully his, a tiny portion of the vast domain over which he was proposing to claim possession.

They turned a corner and started to drive along beside a high brick wall. Julia jerked her thumb towards it.

"My home," she observed.

"Behind the wall?" Peter asked.

"Behind the wall, the dog runs, the trip wires, the electronic sensors, the armed guards. You name it, Daddy's got it. He's obsessed with security."

"Did you say armed guards? I thought they were illegal in this country."

She laughed.

"I think they're called gamekeepers for official purposes, but they amount to the same thing."

Peter stared morosely at the brick wall. Several of the hiding places described by his grandmother lay in the grounds rather than in the house, one of them actually on the inside of the wall itself. Armed guards would not make his life any easier.

The car swept on until it reached an ornate iron gate set between two brick gatehouses. The driver pulled the car to a halt and produced from the dashboard a small electronic device rather like a television remote control unit. Swiftly punching in a series of numbers, he waited patiently as the gate automatically swung open before entering the drive.

For a long time the car continued its stately passage along a single track road beyond the gate. After a while the open fields gave way to high flowering rhododendrons, their dense foliage interspersed with trees which must have already been tall when Peter's great-grandfather had worked as senior gamekeeper on the estate before the war.

They turned a corner and the car braked sharply, pulling over onto the grass verge beside the single track drive. Approaching them from the opposite direction was a dark limousine, its sleek lines accentuated by the darkened glass in the windows. As the car passed them Julia breathed a sigh of relief.

"At least he's gone," she muttered.

"Who?"

"Axel Hablinski, my father's chief business advisor."

"I take it you don't like him?"

52

"No I don't. He's like a snake. When he smiles, he makes my spine chill."

Suddenly the rambling chaos of the rhododendron bushes vanished and they were driving across a carefully manicured formal garden. A myriad different flowering plants had been laced and interlaced by some early philosopher-gardener into an ornate and intricate pattern, as if to convince a lingering sceptic in the Age of Enlightenment of Man's capacity to subdue nature. And beyond and within the formal garden, surrounded on all sides by all its splendour and beauty, lay the gemstone at the heart of the Troughton empire, the vast elegant edifice of Southdown House itself.

Peter gasped. The bright afternoon sun was glinting off the clean classical lines of what he had hitherto understood to be his ancestral home. But as he gazed upon the magnificent structure before him, he realised that this building was no home at all, but rather a symbol of a family's ruthless determination to control all around it, to subjugate nature itself if nature dared resist. And as he stared in silence at the building which should have been beautiful but was instead menacing, he could feel a dark sense of forboding rising up within him. For the architects of this awesome building, the people so desperate to impose their will upon their surroundings whatever the consequences, were none other than his own flesh and blood. And if all his painful experience of life told him he should dislike the enormity of their arrogance, he sensed that deep down it was as much a part of him as it had been of all the other generations who had once owned this place.

"Are you all right?"

Julia's words cut across his thoughts like a knife. He glanced at her and saw the look of concern on her face.

"You look as if you've come over feeling ill," she said.

He shook himself.

"No," he said. "I was just admiring your home."

His explanation seemed to satisfy her and she lapsed temporarily into silence. But seconds later she leant forward and tapped the driver smartly on the shoulder.

"Stop the car, Roberts," she commanded, even though they were still some way away from the house.

The car pulled up and she jumped out.

"Over there," she said to Peter, pointing to a solitary figure walking a dog. "It's Daddy. We'll go and meet him."

She turned to the driver.

"Take Mr Kirby's luggage up to his room and unpack it, will you, Roberts."

Peter had already climbed down from the car before he remembered.

"Stop!" he yelled after the disappearing Rolls-Royce. Julia looked on as Roberts applied the brakes.

"Just put my suitcase in my room, Roberts. Don't unpack it."

Roberts inclined his head slightly, almost as if reassured by the tone of authority in Peter's voice.

"As you wish, sir," he said.

"Why wouldn't you let Roberts unpack?" Julia asked after the car had driven on.

Peter turned.

"Oh, nothing," he murmured. "Just a quirk of mine. I don't like other people going through my things."

She shrugged and started to walk towards the distant figure of her father. Peter followed nervously several paces behind. He hadn't yet arrived, but already he had nearly made a fatal mistake. For if Roberts had unpacked his clothes, he would surely have discovered the detailed plans of the house and estate lying amongst his underclothes at the bottom of the case.

Julia's father had spotted them and was waiting silently beside a small rectangular pond. He was an upright angular man in late middle age, the austere lines on his face set into a stern expression which gave little away about his feelings. But as they approached he seemed to wince, as if wrenching his mind away from some weighty topic on which he had been concentrating.

"Hallo, Daddy," Julia called as they approached, bending down to stroke the dog. "I want you to meet Mr Kirby. He's just arrived."

The reigning Earl of Southdown smiled gracefully and extended his hand.

"A pleasure to meet you, young man," he offered, no trace of falsehood in his voice. "We have heard a great deal about you from Julia."

Peter shook the Earl's outstretched hand, wondering whether Earls like Kings were accustomed to speaking to lesser mortals in the first person plural.

"It was very kind of you to invite me to stay for a few days."

The Earl's face cracked into a thin smile and he looked at his daughter.

"Julia suggested it. We were glad to agree."

It was obvious that despite his polite words the Earl's mind was still firmly elsewhere. Julia stopped playing with the dog and straightened herself up.

"Did the old serpent upset you again, Daddy?" she asked pointedly.

For a second her father looked down at her angrily before recovering his composure.

"Why don't you take Mr Kirby on a tour of the house and grounds?" he remarked frostily. He turned to Peter. "Julia will be pleased to show you round, Mr Kirby. I am sure we will meet again at dinner."

Without further ado he turned on his heel and strode briskly away, his dog running along faithfully by his side.

Julia looked after him and scowled.

"He's in a pretty stinking mood," she muttered.

"Who's the old serpent?" Peter asked.

"Hablinski. The man in the car which drove past us as we arrived. He's far older than Daddy, and when Daddy was little Hablinski virtually ran the estate for my grandmother. I think Daddy used to think of him as some sort of father-figure. But recently his visits always seem to bring an ill-wind."

She had sat down by the edge of the pond, absent-mindedly running her finger back and forth in the water.

Suddenly she looked up at him, her eyes probing, uncertain.

"Why did you come here?" she asked.

The words caught him unawares.

"I told you why. To try and persuade your father to let you study history next year."

Slowly she shook her head.

"No," she murmured. "I don't believe that. There's another reason, one you've not told me."

He hesitated, entirely unprepared for her challenge. Earlier, at the station, she had seemed to be so relaxed. And even the subsequent encounter with her father had not seemed to completely dispel her good humour. Until her wholly unexpected question he had assumed she had taken everything at face value.

Reluctantly he met her gaze.

"Why did you ask me, Julia?" he asked.

She looked away, down into the water.

"I don't know," she said, her eyes averted. "All along I knew Daddy wouldn't take a blind bit of notice of you."

Peter could feel his mind spinning. Suddenly he knew full well why she had invited him. It was because despite all the odds he had succeeded in doing what he had set out to do even before he had met her. He had succeeded in awakening her interest in him. Yet despite his carefully laid plans everything was rapidly going wrong. Julia had not turned out to be the inanimate Trojan Horse he had foolishly imagined her to be. She was real flesh and blood, and the irony of it was that despite himself he was beginning to share the feelings he now saw that she felt for him. If he told her now that he enjoyed her company and wanted to see more of her he would be speaking nothing but the truth. They were only five years apart in age, close enough perhaps for something lasting and worthwhile to develop between them. Yet he knew that he could never tell her of his true feelings. For she had already served the purpose he had so cynically proscribed, already gained him access to her father's house. And as he watched her gazing into the pond, he tried hard not to think about the grievous hurt he would surely cause her when she finally discovered the real reason behind his feigned concern for her welfare.

She looked up at him, her lonely eyes full of sorrow.

"You don't have to tell me why you came," she said softly. "For me, it's simply enough that you did."

* * * * * *

There was a knock on the door. Peter quickly straightened his tie in front of the mirror.

"Come in!" he called.

The door opened and Julia appeared. The old clothes had disappeared, to be replaced by an elegant green evening dress. It made her look older, more knowing.

"Hi," she said brightly. "If you're ready, I thought I'd show you round the house before dinner."

"Thanks," he said, following her out into the deserted corridor.

They walked in silence through several hundred yards of broad wood-panelled passageway until Julia pushed open a large door. Before him, stretching away for what seemed like an eternity, was a vast white gallery. The evening sun was streaming through tall windows placed at regular intervals along one side, its pale light gently illuminating the intricate plasterwork adorning the walls. Under their feet gleamed a multi-coloured marble floor, while overhead a thousand angels seemed to be peering down at them from a vast expanse of blue that was the ceiling.

Julia looked at it admiringly.

"What do you think?" she asked.

Peter gazed in wonder at the gallery. Other than the odd Queen Anne chair dotted about there was little furniture, little to draw the eye away from the sheer size and majesty of the room before their eyes.

"It's beautiful," he said. "More than beautiful."

He followed her as she walked slowly towards the centre of the gallery. Then, suddenly, she lay down on the floor.

"Come on," she said, "you can't really appreciate it standing up. You have to lie down to understand this room."

Gingerly he lowered himself down onto the cold marble floor beside her and looked upwards. From all around, the tiny angels seemed to be flying towards them, as if intent upon protecting them from unseen dangers.

"I see what you mean," Peter said, glancing around at the gallery from his unusual position.

Julia gazed up at the ceiling.

"I used to come and lie here for hours when I was little," she said. "I would look up at those angels and dream about what the future would hold in store for me."

Peter allowed his eye to roam around the room, savouring the sensation of space. But then, with a shock, his eye came to rest on a painting hanging above the fireplace. It was a portrait of a young man in tweeds standing beside a fine dark horse.

Julia had noticed him looking. Suddenly she jumped to her feet, staring down at him with excitement.

"Bloody hell," she exclaimed.

Peter rose swiftly to his feet.

"Who is it?" he asked.

Julia glanced at the painting again.

"The 14th Earl. My grandfather. But it could just as well be a painting of you. You're the splitting image of him."

"That's what I noticed," Peter added, seeing little point in denying a resemblance that was so uncannily close.

"You're not a Troughton, are you?" Julia asked.

Peter shook his head and forced himself to laugh.

"I'm afraid not," he said.

Julia glanced again at the painting, but before she could pass any further comment the door at the far end of the gallery swung open and a tall young man entered.

He strode towards them.

"Hallo, little sister," he said. "I thought I might find you in here."

Julia looked at him with a sour expression.

"What do you want?" she said.

James arrived at her side and turned to face Peter.

"I wanted to meet your ... your friend."

The insinuation was deliberate.

"Hallo," Peter said, deliberately ignoring the provocation. "I was just admiring the gallery. It's very beautiful."

James looked around disparagingly.

"I suppose we'll have to keep it like this while the old man's alive," he said, "but then I think I'll rip all this crap out and turn it into a disco or something." He glanced pointedly at Julia. "I can't stand all those sanctimonious angels up there."

Julia was standing with her head lowered, taking her brother's deliberate jibes without comment.

"You're a teacher, aren't you?" James continued, turning to face Peter again.

"Yes. Julia's history teacher."

"Never could stand all that history junk myself," he continued. "Can't see what you people see in it."

Peter couldn't help but smile.

"You'd be surprised," he replied.

James jerked his head towards Julia.

"She likes history," he said.

"I know she does. And what's more she good at it. She should carry on with it."

James smiled.

"Quite frankly, I don't give a toss what my dear little sister does as long as she goes and does it somewhere else. But I must dash now, I'm meeting someone before dinner."

He swung on his heels and strode swiftly out of the room.

"Charming," Peter muttered, turning to face Julia. But she was no longer beside him. She had walked over to one of the windows overlooking the garden and was standing with her back to him.

He approached her slowly and she turned to face him. In her eyes he could see how hurt she had been by the deliberate humiliation. And suddenly Peter knew he wanted to embrace her, to give her the comfort she so obviously needed. But he knew that if he touched her he would end up kissing her. And that, he knew, could only make things worse.

"I'm sorry," she said.

"Why are you sorry?"

"I really didn't think he'd carry on like that in front of you. Normally he makes at least some kind of effort to control himself in public."

Peter glanced at the door through which her brother had just left.

"Why does he treat you like that?" he asked.

For a while she said nothing, gazing out over the beauty of the formal garden outside. When she did finally speak, her voice was calm and gentle, showing no trace of anger.

"I think James has hated me ever since I was a little girl. Even as a kid he was a nasty brat, bullying and fighting at every opportunity."

"But why does he hate you so much, that's what I don't see?"

"Oh, that's easy," she said. "He hates me because I don't approve of him. All that theatre just now was simply his way of trying to get a reaction out of me. But I won't oblige, and that just makes him even madder."

* * * * * *

The enormous dining room was only intimate by comparison with the white gallery, filled as it was by a heavy oak dining table which could easily have accommodated forty people. Yet on this occasion, besides Peter, only five people were present.

At one end of the table sat the Earl himself. His walk in the garden did not seem to have greatly revived his spirits, and after a few opening pleasantries he had remained silent, his back upright, mechanically consuming his meal. His two children sat to either side of him, although the sheer size of the table meant that they were sitting a considerable distance away. Peter was seated next to Julia, opposite a good-looking young man by the name of Roderick Willoughby who had been introduced as one of James's motor racing friends.

Presiding over the entire company at the far end of the table was the tall figure of the Dowager Countess Alexandra. Although apparently a woman of few words, she had spent the entire meal examining Peter with a hawk-like eye, as if intrigued by his face.

The meal itself was excellent, an exotic dish prepared from partridge which the Earl himself had shot that morning, but the lack of conversation coupled with the Dowager Countess's unwavering stare gave little opportunity for Peter to enjoy his food.

It was only when the dessert had been served that the Countess finally allowed herself to make public a thought which had clearly been troubling her throughout the meal.

"You remind me of someone, Mr Kirby," she said, her British upper class drool still tinged by the American accent of her youth.

Peter remembered the portrait of his grandfather in the white gallery.

"I agree," said Julia. "He's the splitting image of grandfather, don't you think?"

The Countess nodded slowly.

"A remarkable likeness," Peter added swiftly. "I must be the same racial type."

The Countess nodded again, and as she did so, Peter tried to imagine how she had appeared as a young woman, as she must have looked at the time of her husband's premature death in 1947. But in the worn and ancient features of her face it was difficult to summon up any very clear image.

"You say you are a teacher," she said, and Peter was not very clear whether her remark was a question or a statement.

"Yes. Julia's history teacher at Raley-le-Street."

"And how long have you been working there?"

"Not very long at all, your ladyship. Since the Easter holidays. I only finished at Oxford last summer."

"That's interesting," the Countess added, lapsing into silence again as she turned her attention back to the dessert before her.

Peter eyed her nervously out the corner of his eye, but her mask-like face gave no clue as to her thoughts.

Suddenly, for the first time during the entire meal, Roderick opened his mouth to speak.

"Jolly nice weather today, chaps, don't you think?"

At this even the Countess looked up.

"I beg your pardon," she said drily.

"The weather. Simply super weather."

Although it was not yet dark outside, the heavy damask curtains had already been pulled shut, the rather gloomy artificial lighting in the room adding to an already sombre atmosphere. Peter glanced down the table to see how James would react to his friend's unexpected words, but he was sitting quite still with a thin superior smile on his lips, casting his eye slowly round the table to see how the rest of the company would respond.

"Rather too hot if anything," Peter remarked casually, grateful for any topic of conversation which would turn the Countess's mind away from his physical similarity with her erstwhile husband.

The Countess put down the fork she was holding in her hand and turned to Roderick.

"Are you also a racing driver, Mr Willougby, like James?"

Roderick smiled.

"Oh yes. But not as good as your grandson. He's tops. He really is."

"So I hear," the Countess added, exchanging a knowing glance with James which suggested they were quite intimate.

"Actually, grandma, Roddy's come down to see what he thinks about my latest ideas for the estate."

At these words the Earl stopped eating and looked up sharply at his son.

"Ideas?" he said. "What ideas?"

James turned to his father.

"Well, there's so much space here, father. I thought it might be a good idea to put some of it to good use. Roddy's something of a specialist on the design side, so I thought I'd seek his advice before talking to you about it."

"And what exactly did you have in mind?" the Earl enquired.

"A Formula One racecourse. Somewhere to practice in my own back garden, you might say. Roddy thinks we can build a cracker here, don't you Roddy?"

"Absolutely, old chum. The contours are perfect. Everywhere else will look like yesterday's news when Southdown's on the map."

The Earl looked at his son askance.

"And whatever makes you think I will agree to the estate being vandalised in such a way, James? You know that a racetrack would do irreparable damage to the rural environment."

James grinned.

"You're just worried about the hunting, aren't you, father?"

The Earl pursed his lips.

"Amongst other things," he replied. "But to rip up a beautiful estate like this which has been lovingly built up over so many generations would be an act of criminal folly. It's a ridiculous notion."

"Some people would object to your grandiose schemes for turning Zimbabwe into a private gamepark, too, wouldn't they father?"

Peter stared at James. He had only just turned twenty-one, but he was certainly not slow in exploiting his new-found power of veto within the Earldom to secure his own ends. The Earl of Southdown didn't reply. Instead, without a word, he quietly pushed his chair back and rose to his feet. With a polite inclination of his head to everyone except his son, he walked slowly out of the room.

The ensuing silence was broken by Julia.

"You bastard," she muttered under her breath.

James turned to Roderick, who by now was fidgeting uncomfortably in his seat.

"I must apologise for my little sister," he said. He flicked a pointed glance at Peter. "Frankly, I suspect she picks up her bad language at school."

61

Roderick said nothing, clearly not wishing to join in a family dispute of which he appeared to have no knowledge.

Julia rose quietly to her feet.

"If you'll excuse us, grandma," she said, "I'd promised to show Mr Kirby the library before we turn in."

The Countess gracefully inclined her head and Julia left the room. Peter rose silently to his feet, and after bowing politely to the Countess, followed her outside.

She was already half way up the main staircase when he caught up with her. She was still fuming, yet she said nothing until they had reached the library, a spacious room surrounded by row upon row of ancient leather-bound volumes. She slouched down behind a desk and started flicking nervously through one of the books which had been left open.

"Your father's got problems, hasn't he?" Peter remarked.

She threw a glance at him.

"I've known all along this would happen. But Daddy never faced up to it. He let James get away with blue murder when he was a child. Now he's got the legal powers as well there'll be no stopping him."

"Not quite what the architects of this dual control idea had in mind, perhaps?"

She shrugged.

"I don't know. Maybe it is, maybe it isn't. How can you plan for somebody like James?"

"Is he crazy?" Peter asked hesitantly.

Julia smiled.

"I know what you're thinking," she said. "If father could establish that James was off his rocker, then he might be able to get the courts to agree to suspending his power of veto."

Peter nodded.

"I thought of that ages ago," Julia continued. "I even asked father once, but it was a big mistake. Although James infuriates him, he can't seem to find it within himself to take a firm stand."

"Maybe the thought of a Formula One racecourse in his back garden will help him change his mind?"

"Perhaps. But even if it did, I don't know that you'd ever get a doctor to certify him. You've seen him at home, the real James. But when he wants to, he can be charm itself. Most outsiders think I'm the prickly one in the family, not him."

It seemed to be a good time to change the subject.

"There's something I've been meaning to ask you, Julia?"

She looked up at him.

"The first time I taught you, when you challenged me about Claire-Marie's moral right to go to the toilet in my lesson. Did she really want to go or was it a try-on?"

The cloud passed from Julia's face.

"A try-on of course. Claire-Marie always comes that line with new teachers. She's pretty good, isn't she? The plaintive look, the deceptive wriggle of the bottom. You'd have to be as hard as old nails to resist her, don't you think?"

Peter smiled.

"I was certainly fooled. But I'd been warned to expect no mercy from a class if I failed that particular test."

Again Julia smiled.

"That would normally have been the case. But you're special, you see. You're so good-looking. Surely you know that most of the girls at school fancy you like crazy. These days they talk of little else."

Despite himself, Peter flinched at her choice of words.

"They?" he murmured.

Her face grew serious. Rising to her feet, she walked silently over to the window. It was nearly dark outside, and she stood with her back to him, gazing out over the twilight world beyond.

"I don't understand you," she said in a voice so faint it was barely audible.

He rose and walked towards her.

"Why not?" he asked.

"You obviously want me," she murmured. "I'd have to be a fool not to see that. It upsets you even to contemplate that I did not lie in bed at night and dream of what it would be like to be held in your arms. Yet even though you must know I'm here for the asking you make no move towards me."

Peter looked away. Ever since he had arrived at Southdown House he had feared he was falling hopelessly in love with his enigmatic first cousin. But there was no way he could admit his love to her.

"It's getting late," he said quietly, "and I think I ought to go to bed."

* * * * * *

From somewhere outside in the corridor, the sonorous chime of an ancient grandfather clock rang out eleven times. Peter took a deep breath and rose from the fourposter bed on which he had been re-clining. Lifting his suitcase up onto the bed, he carefully pulled out the detailed map of Southdown House and tucked it into the inside pocket of his jacket before stepping out into the deserted corridor.

Julia's tour had been a great help to him, enabling him to visualise much more clearly the layout of the House detailed in his grand-mother's plans. Aware that he could encounter one of the family or a member of the domestic staff at any moment, he sauntered along with a deliberately casual air, stopping every now or then to admire a vase or a painting. If anyone met him and seemed curious about his movements, he would freely volunteer the information that he was going to the library to borrow a book to read in bed. With his known interest in history, it seemed a solid enough cover story.

He had originally planned to start hunting for the papers in the middle of the night, when everyone was fast asleep, but on reflection had changed his mind. For although the chance of discovery in the late evening was far higher than in the early hours, so also was the ease with which he could explain his movements.

Some way ahead of him, one of the wooden panels in the corridor suddenly swung open and a young man dressed as a servant appeared, carrying on his arm a silver tray with a glass of milk on it. The man glanced towards him and Peter could see that it was Roberts, the driver who had brought them up earlier from the station.

"Good evening, sir," said Roberts, politely inclining his head.

"I'm going to the library to borrow a book," Peter explained.

"Indeed, sir," Roberts commented, and Peter could just detect a slight rise in one of his eyebrows. "Can I help you with directions, sir?"

Peter shook his head.

"No, Roberts, it's all right. Down to the end and turn right, if I'm not mistaken."

"That is correct, sir," the young man replied. "Will that be all, sir?"

Peter nodded and Roberts walked silently on towards the wing of the house where the family's bedrooms were located. Without looking back, Peter walked on swiftly towards his destination.

Moments later he was once again inside the library. He glanced quickly at the bay window at the far end, remembering the words Julia had muttered, but then quickly started searching along the shelves. Just maybe, if he was really lucky, he would find it straightaway, and then he would be able to make his excuses and leave the next day.

In her instructions, his grandmother had listed separately the three secret hiding places which she had used in her youth. Two of them were outside, one in a stable block, another behind a loose brick in the estate's perimeter wall. Only one of them was actually in the house itself, inside an edition of the Parliamentary Gazette dating from 1757.

He scanned rapidly and systematically along the shelves and soon spotted the tall volume high up towards the ceiling. Quietly collecting an old wooden library stairs from the other side of the room, he gingerly climbed up and started pulling it from its resting place.

The book was not yet fully in his hand when the door began to creak slowly open. Quickly pushing the book back into its place, he started climbing back down the steps.

"Hallo!"

Julia stood by the open door. The elegant green evening dress had gone, replaced by a long pink dressing gown.

"What are you doing there?" she said. "I thought you went to bed."

Peter gratefully reached the floor and stood holding the steps.

"Couldn't sleep, Julia," he said.

"Couldn't you?"

"No."

"So you came to have another look at the library."

He nodded.

She glanced at the steps.

"It's funny how the one you want is always on the top shelf," she said. "It must be somebody's law."

Peter smiled and picked up the steps, carefully carrying them back to where he had found them. She watched him.

"Peter?" she asked, and he noticed that for the first time she had addressed him by his first name.

"Yes."

"Haven't you forgotten something?"

He looked at her with a confused expression.

"Your book," she said with a faint smile. "You were going up to fetch a book when I came in."

"Was I?"

"Isn't that why you got the stairs?"

Peter glanced back at the shelf.

"Oh yes," he said, "how silly of me."

He put the steps back where they had been when she entered. Then he climbed up and grabbed a volume of the Parliamentary Gazette a little way along the shelf from the copy he had started pulling out before, carrying the heavy book carefully back down and laying it on the desk.

"There," he said triumphantly, carefully returning the steps to their original resting place on the far side of the room.

Julia was eyeing him suspiciously.

"Happy now?" she asked.

Peter opened the book and pretended to examine the boring compendium in the manner of a true scholar. Julia looked over his shoulder.

"What's so interesting about that one?" she said.

"Absolutely fascinating material," Peter replied. "You'd be surprised what you can find in the Parliamentary Gazette."

"Are you looking for something in particular?"

Peter cursed himself for not taking a note of the year to which the volume referred.

"Oh no," he said. "Just browsing."

There was a deep leather armchair several feet away from the desk. She curled herself up in it.

"Mind if I watch you?" she asked.

Peter pretended to look up from his studies.

"Of course not," he said. "Be my guest."

For about a quarter of an hour they remained in silence. Peter sat at the desk and tried hard to concentrate on the book before him in order that he could make some knowing remark about its contents. Out of the corner of his eye he could just see Julia, curled up in the armchair, watching him with a strangely inscrutable look.

He abandoned the book and looked up at her.

"Why did you come back, Julia? It's late."

She smiled.

"The library's another of my haunts, I'm afraid. I only like the white gallery during the day, when the sun's streaming in through the windows. After dark it's better here."

She smiled softly again. Peter allowed his eye to fall back onto the book.

"Oh well," he said after a what seemed like a decent interval, "I think I'll call it a night."

She remained in the chair. Awkwardly, he glanced at the wooden steps.

"Yes," Julia said from the armchair, seeing what was in his mind, "it would have been easier if you had left them there in the first place."

He nodded and fetched the offending piece of furniture, aware that this would be the fourth time he had carried it across the room since she had entered. He positioned it carefully and turned to fetch the book. But there was no need, because Julia had risen silently from the armchair and was standing just beside him, clutching the old volume in her hand.

"It's all right," she said, "I'll do it."

Peter stood to one side as she started to climb the steps. Glancing apprehensively at the 1757 volume, he noticed he had not pushed it back quite far enough when he had heard her enter. Its spine was several inches further forward than its neighbours.

She reached the top of the stairs and placed the volume he had been examining back in its correct place. Then, noticing the other volume was too far forward, she reached her hand out towards it and started to push it back. But then she glanced down at him.

"Peter," she said innocently, "were you looking at this one too?"

She was looking straight at the 1757 volume.

"No," he said quickly. "Why do you ask?"

"It looks as if you've left some papers lying inside it."

Peter flinched.

"Nothing to do with me," he said hurriedly.

To his relief, she seemed to accept his denial and climbed down the steps again. He hurriedly picked them up and carried them back to the far side of the room. But when he turned he noticed to his horror that Julia was still staring up at the top shelf.

"Peter," she said, "bring the steps back, will you, please."

"Why?"

"That book up there, the one I just pushed back in, it had a lot of old papers stuffed between the pages. I'm curious to see what they are."

"Oh, I shouldn't think they're anything much."

"Maybe not," she said, her imagination clearly fired, "but I still want to have a look at them. Sometimes you find handwritten stuff in old books, really interesting old stuff. Get the steps, will you."

"They're heavy."

She stared at him in disbelief.

"All right," she muttered, "I'll get them."

Peter watched her in consternation as she dragged the heavy stairs across the carpet.

"Please don't look!" he said abruptly.

She lowered the steps to the ground and faced him.

"Why not?" she said. "Why don't you want me to look?"

He should have made up some lie, some explanation of his concern which would protect her. But her bright clear eyes held his gaze, and he knew that his secret was lost.

She looked away from him and continued carrying the steps across the room. When they were in position she climbed to the top and reached her hand out towards the book. But then, before she had touched it, she hesitated and turned to face him once more.

"There's something important in here, isn't there? Something you were looking for when I came in, something you didn't want me to see."

His face ashen, he sank down into the armchair in which she had so recently been sitting.

"Yes," he said, looking down into his lap. "I think there quite possibly is."

She glanced back at the book. He was sure she was going to take it off the shelf, but then she seemed to change her mind. She pushed it neatly back into position and climbed back down.

"You were right about the stairs," she said. "They are heavy. Would you mind very much carrying them back for me before you go to bed?"

His downcast eyes rose to meet hers.

"You're not going to look?" he asked.

Quietly she shook her head.

"No," she said. "Whatever it is, it's not my business."

She turned towards the door and started to walk away. And as she did so, Peter knew for certain something that he had suspected for a long time. He knew that he wanted her to know.

"Julia!" he called. "Please stay."

She turned again and faced him.

Without a word, he clambered up the stairs and fetched the heavy volume from the shelf, laying it on the desk. Then he opened it up and carefully removed the ageing papers lying within.

Julia had approached him silently and was looking over his shoulder.

"What are they?" she asked.

Most of the papers hidden in the book were love letters from his grandmother. The paper on which they were written was going yellow with age, but Peter could clearly recognise his grandmother's angular script. There were also a number of photographs: some of his grandmother alone as a young woman, some of her together with his grandfather, the late Earl, and some of a young boy who Peter guessed was his father as a child. But he took little notice of the letters or the photographs, and instead picked up an old brown envelope. Opening the flap, he carefully withdrew the fading marriage certificate.

"Here," he said, handing it to Julia.

She took it in her hand and studied it carefully for a while.

"I don't understand," she said at last.

Peter pointed to her grandfather's name.

"Look. Don't you recognise the name?"

She stared at it in bewilderment.

"My grandfather," she murmured.

He took the certificate back.

"Your grandfather," he said, "and mine. The likeness you noticed before was no coincidence."

"But ..."

Peter watched her helplessly as she wrestled with the information he had thrown at her. But then, without a word, she sat down at the desk and picked up one of the letters, reading it through swiftly and fluently. When she had finished she picked up another and read it, and then another, until finally she had read them all.

"Oh my God," she whispered, staring at the old photographs. She picked up one of his father as a young child and looked at Peter.

"Your father?" she asked uncertainly.

He nodded.

"But then your father should be the Earl?" she whispered.

"No, Julia. My father is dead. He died a very long time ago."

She stared at him wide-eyed.

"You?" she mouthed.

He nodded silently.

"I didn't realise it until a few months ago, on my twenty-first birthday. Then, out of the blue, I was visited by a grandmother I'd never known ..."

The story took a long time in the telling. Julia sat quietly at the desk, her head resting on her hands, looking down intently at the photographs before her. Each time he told her of a fresh act of violence committed by her forbears against his she seemed to flinch, but she said nothing, waiting passively for him to finish his account. Only when he had finally stopped did she look up at him.

"But if you're right and they find out what you're doing, they might try to hurt you too."

He nodded glumly.

"I suppose the choice is yours," he said quietly.

"If I tell them?"

Again he nodded.

She thought.

"Peter ..." she began, but before she had finished her sentence her voice faded away.

"Yes?" he asked.

She looked at him sadly, but her eyes showed no bitterness.

"You used me, didn't you? You simply used me to gain access to my father's home so you could search for these papers?"

Once again he nodded. There was little point in denying it.

"At first I used you," he admitted.

"What do you mean 'at first'?"

He glanced towards the door.

"Just now you were going to leave, weren't you? I don't know why, but you were. Despite catching me red-handed, you were going to leave. So why do you think I asked you to come back?"

There was a kind of forlorn desperate hope in her eyes.

"You see, Julia," he continued, "even the best laid plans go astray. How could I predict that I would fall hopelessly in love with my adversary's daughter?"

He looked at the ageing certificate in his hand and suddenly wondered what it was all for. He had sensed at the time that Harry was right, that the Southdown inheritance would bring him nothing but misery. They were wise words spoken by a wise old man, and if he had had any sense at all he would have listened. But he hadn't listened. He had allowed the impetuosity of youth to overcome the wise counsel of experience, and had allowed himself to chase after an impossible dream.

Suddenly his mind was made up. He pushed the certificate across the desk towards Julia. Reaching his hand deep into his pocket, he pulled out a small cigarette lighter and placed it on the desk.

She looked at him but said nothing.

"This might make the choice easier," he said quietly.

Her hand hovered over the certificate but she seemed afraid to touch it. Then she looked up.

"Why?"

"Because I love you." He jerked his thumb at the certificate lying on the desk. "Because I've decided you're more important to me than all this."

She rose to her feet and walked silently round the desk until she was standing just in front of him, her eyes looking up tenderly into his. And at the sight of the love in her eyes he forgot the certificate, he forgot the wrongs her family had inflicted on his, he forgot everything in his past life that had led him into this bizarre situation, and all he knew was that he had found the girl with whom he would share his life for ever.

He was sure the moment their lips touched that he was the first man she had ever kissed. There was an uncertainty about her, a hesitancy which only inexperience could explain. But as he held her body close to his, he could also feel within her a sense of almost desperate urgency, a desire which surprised him by its sheer intensity, almost as if the discovery of the certificate had made her fear for them both.

She pulled her lips away from his and walked towards the door. Turning the key firmly in the lock, she turned towards him, her face a strange mixture between love and anxiety.

"This is for real, isn't it, Peter?"

He nodded.

"And for ever?" she asked.

Again he nodded.

She was still standing on the far side of the room from him, beside the door. Yet now, without a word, she drew apart the cord on her dressing gown and let it to fall limply from her shoulders. Wearing nothing but a flimsy white nightdress, she walked slowly towards him, allowing him once again to engulf her in his arms.

"I've never met anyone like you before," she said softly. "I knew immediately I met you that you were going to be special to me."

Peter smiled.

"I suppose I am a bit odd. The only Earl in England who's slept rough on the streets of London."

"You'll be a better Earl for it," she said.

Her remark caught him by surprise.

"Surely you don't want me to pursue my claim?"

By way of answer she picked up the marriage certificate from the desk and pushed it into his pocket.

"Yes," she said, "I think so. Despite what I've said about Daddy, I do love him in a funny sort of way, but you could see at dinner that he's finished. My brother is the new powerbroker in this family, backed up by that snake Hablinski and my grandmother. Daddy doesn't stand a chance against the three of them together. And anyway, you'll make a far better Earl than my brother could ever be."

Peter smiled. He lifted her up in his arms and sat down in the large leather armchair, relishing the curve of her body as she curled up on his lap.

"And you, Julia? Would you be my Countess?"

She laughed.

"Perhaps," she replied. "If you meant what you said about this being for ever then I suppose I would be, wouldn't I?" Her pretty face grew serious. "But that's not why I'm saying it. I really do think you'd be a better Earl, even if you leave me for someone else."

"Julia," he asked, "do you think we stand a chance against them. Once they find out what's going on there's no knowing what they'll do. Your forebears have a pretty ferocious track-record."

She frowned.

71

"I suppose with the marriage certificate you'll have the law on your side," she said uncertainly.

"I wasn't thinking of the law," he muttered.

She looked up at him thoughtfully.

"I don't think Daddy will do anything illegal," she said slowly. "Despite his love of killing animals he's not a violent man. But I couldn't be sure about James, particularly if he thinks his back is against the wall." She eyed him carefully for a moment. "But you must have thought about all this before you came here."

He nodded.

"I did. But that was before I met you. Until then, I thought I knew what I wanted. I thought I wanted to undo the injustice that had been inflicted on my family by yours. Perhaps I felt bitter about the way they had stolen my childhood. And to be perfectly honest, when you've been as poor as I have the thought of all that money does have a certain appeal. But now I've met you I'm not sure that matters any more. You've become more important to me than everything else in the world."

She said nothing for a long time. Then she rose to her feet, quickly scooping the papers from the desk and handing them to Peter. He folded them up and stuffed them into his pocket.

"Take me away with you, Peter," she said, standing before him. "Now. Tonight. I don't think I can stand it here any longer. And when we've found somewhere quiet to think, then we can decide what to do next."

"But where could we go?"

"I don't care. Anywhere."

Peter looked at her innocent face and tried to imagine her living the life he had once led.

"You come from a sheltered background, Julia. I'm not sure you realise just how rough life can be. And anyway, you've got exams to do in a few weeks. It doesn't make any sense to throw all that away now."

"I don't care about that. I want to be with you. Forever."

"I want to be with you, too. But I've got a better idea. You'll be back at school next week. We can be together there. You can do your exams and we can plan our future together at the same time. How does that sound?"

She thought for a minute.

"I suppose I have to admit it sounds fairly sensible," she said.

She pulled him to his feet and held him close to her.

"Make love to me," she whispered. "Right now. Right here in this room."

Her words surprised him and he gazed at her uncertainly for several moments. In his mind, he suddenly remembered his grandmother as she had sat beside him in his room at Harry's the first time they had met. Once before, when she had been very young, Peter's grandfather had proved his sincerity by refusing for years to make love to her.

"Are you sure you want to?" he asked hesitantly.

She said nothing, but by way of answer quietly lifted the nightdress from her shoulders and threw it onto the armchair behind him, allowing him to gaze upon her naked body.

"You're beautiful," Peter murmured, slowly removing his own clothes without taking his eyes off her for a second. Yet still he made no move to touch her. For a long time they stood in silence, savouring the sight of each other's nakedness, each thinking their own thoughts. But then at last their eyes met and he enfolded her gently in his arms.

Lowering her naked body gently to the floor beside the desk, he knelt down and began to caress her, relishing the feel of her firm smooth body beneath his fingertips. For a long time she lay passive, gazing up at him with love in her eyes, patiently allowing his fingers to explore her, but then, slowly at first and then with growing intensity, she began to writhe with pleasure at his touch, caressing him too with her hands.

"I love you," she said at last, pulling him on top of her, but no sooner had she uttered the words than there was a loud crash from the direction of the bookshelves beyond the desk. Peter looked up rapidly, just in time to see the tall figure of James appear over the desk, staring down at their interlocked bodies with a strangely anguished grimace on his face. And beside him stood Roberts, his placid expression giving little away about his thoughts.

Peter rose swiftly to his feet. Julia stood up, quickly grabbing the nightdress from the chair to hide her nakedness.

"You sanctimonious little slut," James snarled at her. "I thought I might find something interesting going on in here."

Julia pulled the rest of her clothes on and turned to face her brother. She was angry, but overlaying the anger, far more intense than the anger, was an overwhelming sense of fear.

"How did you get in?" she whispered.

James grinned.

"You always consider yourself so much better than everyone else, don't you, Julia? Far too high and mighty to take much interest in the largely unused network of servants' corridors which criss-cross this entire building." He stalked across the room and pulled one of bookcases away from the wall, revealing a hidden corridor beyond.

73

Peter had taken the opportunity of this exchange to pull on his clothing. Now he stepped forward purposely between James and his sister.

"What's Julia's private life got to do with you, anyway?" he asked angrily.

But James took no notice of him. He walked rapidly to the main door of the library and pulled the key out of the lock. As he did so, Julia seemed to wince.

"Come on, James," she said in a soothing voice. "Don't be silly, now."

James raised an eyebrow in the direction of Roberts. Peter turned, but before he could react Roberts had stepped swiftly across the room and caught his arm with a vice-like grip. He tried to pull free, but the harder he pulled the tighter the grip.

"Go on, little sister," James continued. "Get down on your knees and beg me for mercy. You know how I love to see you beg."

"Stop this!" Peter cried out, himself now more frightened than angry by the crazed expression in her brother's eyes.

"Please James," Julia pleaded, her eyes fixed on her brother's hardened face. "Please don't hurt me."

"Beg!"

Julia lowered herself passively to her knees in front of him.

"Please don't hurt me," she whispered.

James took a menacing step towards her, but then he seemed to check himself. He turned to face Roberts.

"Get that scum out of this house immediately," he ordered, jerking a thumb in Peter's direction.

Roberts nodded silently and started pushing his captive firmly towards the secret door in the bookshelf. As he passed her Julia was looking up at him, a sense of desperation filling her frightened face.

"Come back for me, Peter," she said urgently, but before he could reply Roberts had pushed him roughly out of the room and pulled the door shut behind them.

* * * * * *

Peter weaved and dodged along the crowded City streets towards the offices of Fricknell, Percival and Smythe. But he didn't see the people he was passing, in fact he was hardly aware of their existence. In his mind he could only see Julia's frightened face as she knelt before her elder brother, begging for mercy for a crime she had not committed. He smiled grimly, for James Troughton had made a foolish mistake by menacing his sister in that way, because he had unwittingly helped his adversary to make up his mind. For before James had smashed his way so brutally into their happiness, when Julia and he had been locked in each other's arms, he had already come to a private decision to abandon his quest to win the Earldom.

Julia's warm caresses, and the touching simplicity with which she had asked him to make love to her, had made him recognise that she was all he needed to find true happiness. And understanding that simple fact had suddenly rendered the Southdown inheritance completely irrelevant. Better in the circumstances to escape quietly, to elope to some remote sanctuary where they could love each other and be free.

He clutched the briefcase containing the marriage certificate tightly in his hand. James had changed everything. James had made him realise that it was not just wrongs against himself that had to be put right, but also wrongs against the girl he was now utterly convinced would be his future wife. For it was slowly becoming apparent to him that Julia had suffered far more at the hands of her brother than he had at first realised. He remembered the fear in her eyes as he had approached her, a fear which ran so deep it had caused an otherwise self-confident girl to kneel on the floor and beg for mercy.

But the young Viscount's bizarre conduct had made him realise something more. He had initially supposed that James was indifferent to his sister's fate and that he would therefore allow her to disappear quietly if she so wished. He had even supposed that James would actually welcome the fact. But now he saw that that was not the case, for he had revealed by his behaviour that far from being indifferent to his sister he was in reality obsessed with her, seeking to dominate and control her for purposes on which Peter did not care to speculate. And with such a man there would be no secret elopement, no quiet future for two ordinary people in a quiet suburban semi-detached house. For James and James's vast power would be able to track them down to the ends of the earth, smashing into their happiness wherever they were, just as he had so recently smashed into their happiness in the library at Southdown House.

Arriving at the imposing door of the solicitor's office, he pushed the door open and entered the plush foyer. The flunky in the red uniform who had previously referred him to the tradesmen's entrance glanced in silent surprise at his suit and rose politely to his feet.

"Roger Thompson, please," Peter asked, deliberately looking at the man's uniform rather than his face.

The flunky lowered his head politely and spoke briefly into an intercom. Seconds later the solicitor appeared, looking the same in every respect as he had done on Peter's previous visit.

"Ah, Mr Fitzpatrick," he said, shaking Peter by the hand, "do please come through."

Peter silently followed him through into his office and sat down, placing the briefcase carefully beside him on the floor. Roger Thompson sat down on the opposite side of the desk and smiled his friendliest professional smile.

"Can I be of service again?" he asked.

Peter nodded, lifting the briefcase onto his lap and removing the brown envelope containing the marriage certificate.

"I hope so," he began. "I wish to begin proceedings to claim a peerage."

Roger Thompson raised an eyebrow.

"I recall our previous conversation. Does the peerage in question already have an occupant?"

"It does. If I briefly summarize the situation, can you tell me whether, if I can establish the truth of what I am saying, I will be able to claim the title successfully?"

"I think I will be able to give you a general indication."

"My father was the legitimate first-born child of a previous rightful holder of the title. My father is dead. I am his only child by a legitimate marriage. Does that make me the rightful current holder of the peerage?"

The solicitor eyed him cautiously.

"You state the situation very succinctly, Mr Fitzpatrick. The answer is equally succinct. It is yes. But who then is the current holder?"

"My grandfather concealed his marriage to my grandmother and married again without having first obtained a divorce. The present incumbent is the child of that second illegal marriage."

Roger Thompson leant back in his chair and thought for a while.

"I see," he said. "Once again the situation, although certainly unusual, is straightforward. The present holder would be illegitimate if what you say is true, and therefore unable to inherit any noble title in this country. If the facts could be clearly established as you state them, then I believe the Committee of Privileges of the House of Lords would uphold your right to the title."

Peter nodded.

"Is this the kind of case you could handle?" he asked.

Roger Thompson smiled broadly at the thought of such an interesting and potentially profitable account.

"Certainly," he replied. "We are an experienced firm in such matters. I feel sure we would be able to represent you adequately."

"Good," he said. "Well in that case you're hired."

Roger Thompson inclined his head to one side by way of thanks.

"And now," he said, "I wonder if you could outline the precise particulars of the title you wish to contest."

Peter could feel himself relaxing in the warm office. He had expected the solicitor to raise all manner of tedious technicalities which would hamper his claim. But instead he had implied that as far as the courts were concerned it would all go through relatively smoothly.

"I believe," Peter said, "that I am in fact the rightful holder of the Earldom of Southdown."

* * * * * *

Harry lifted the lid on the teapot and began to pour in the boiling water.

"Tell me again," he said.

Peter shifted uncomfortably in his seat and tried to remember the exact sequence of events.

"He was sitting there at the desk, as cool as a cucumber. And up to the point when I told him I believed I was the Earl of Southdown he seemed quite happy to represent me. But the moment I named the title he suddenly flinched, almost as if I'd given him an electric shock. Then he asked me to excuse him for a few moments while he attended to something in the outer office. A few minutes later he returned and told me he had consulted with his partners and they had together reached the conclusion that they would not be able to represent me. I asked him why not, but all he did was shake his head and mutter something about conflict of interest. After that he glanced at his watch, told me he had another appointment and held the door open for me to leave."

Harry stopped making the tea and peered at him impatiently over his spectacles.

"I got all that the first time," he said. "It's the bit after which worries me."

"Well," Peter continued. "He'd told me before that they did a great deal of work for titled families, so I just assumed I'd been unlucky and that his firm was already representing the Troughtons. But before I left, I asked him if he could recommend another firm of solicitors who could represent me, assuming he'd at least know who his competitors were. But he denied point blank knowing the names of any other solicitors in that field and suggested I try the yellow pages. And then he virtually pushed me out of his office and closed the door."

Harry sat down opposite and leant forward on his knees. He fixed Peter with a questioning stare.

"Would you say he was frightened?" he asked.

"Yes," Peter replied, remembering the man's face. "One minute he was so calm, so professional. Yet the next moment he was chucking me out of his office. I haven't liked to admit it even to myself, but I suppose he did look frightened."

Harry rose to his feet and started pacing up and down.

"You haven't been anywhere else, have you?" he asked suddenly.

Peter shook his head.

"No," he said. "I was worried. I came straight here."

Harry stopped pacing up and down and gazed out into the street.

"But why should he be frightened?" he muttered. "Why should the solicitor be frightened?"

Peter looked at Harry's slender back silhouetted against the window.

"Why not?" he asked.

"Because all the violence against your family took place a very long time ago and it was all thoroughly covered up at the time. So it can't really explain why the solicitor reacted as he did."

Peter sank back into his chair with a glum expression.

"So you think there's something else? Something we don't know about yet?"

Harry nodded.

"I'm afraid so," he muttered.

He suddenly turned to face Peter.

"Do you think the girl's all right?" he asked.

"I don't know. As soon as I arrived at the house I knew there was no love lost between her and her brother. But when he interrupted us in the library and started taunting her, I felt I was witnessing something that had taken place before, some kind of sick ritual."

Harry shivered.

"You've tried telephoning of course."

"Repeatedly. But I'm always told she's unavailable. I suppose it's what you'd expect in the circumstances."

Harry had started pacing again, ploughing backwards and forwards across the room with a deep furrow running across his forehead.

"But you're sure her brother didn't overhear you talking about the certificate?" he asked.

"Not certain, but I don't think it's very likely. If he had they wouldn't have let me go."

"So it was her he was angry with, not you. You're sure of that?"

"Positive."

Harry looked relieved. But then suddenly Peter remembered the Dowager Countess Alexandra's penetrating stare at the dinner table.

"I'm not so sure about his grandmother, though."

Harry stopped in his tracks.

"What do you mean?" he said.

"Unfortunately I'm the splitting image of my grandfather as a young man. The old Countess noticed the likeness, that's all."

Harry fell silent. He quietly poured the tea and handed a cup to Peter. Only when he had added two spoonfuls of sugar to his own and unnecessarily stirred it for several minutes did he finally speak.

"I don't like to say so, but I think you've got to hide," he said solemnly.

Peter frowned.

"Because she saw a certain similarity with my grandfather?"

Harry nodded.

"There's quite a bit of circumstantial evidence to suggest that she knew about what happened all those years ago. But if she did know, she'd also know that there may be a young man alive of about your age who could cause her and her family a lot of trouble. It wouldn't take much for her to make a few enquiries about you, would it? And if they do that they'll find out from the school where you supposedly went to university, and then they'll know you lied. And after that it wouldn't take them long to trace you back here through me ... "

Harry's voice suddenly trailed off.

"Have you warned your grandmother?" he asked.

"No. Not yet. I was planning to see her tomorrow."

Harry shook his head.

"No," he said with a frown. "Don't wait that long. Go now. Go tonight."

* * * * * *

It was a hot midsummer night. Peter glanced around apprehensively as he walked along the drab concrete walkway connecting two low-rise blocks of council flats in the heart of Brixton. He had deliberately changed out of his smart public school suit into the tatty clothes he used to wear when he worked at Harry's, but the sight of a dozen West Indian youths lolling about some thirty yards ahead was nevertheless distinctly disquieting. The group had been talking in an animated way, but now, ominously, they had fallen silent and were eying him carefully as he approached.

Peter sauntered casually towards them. They continued to stare in silence as he passed, but no sooner was he a few feet beyond them than a voice called out.

"Hey, man, I don't recognise you. You're not from round here, are you?"

He stopped and turned.

"No," he said. "I'm a visitor."

The man who had addressed him was a tall Rastafarian in his late teens.

"Ain't you scared of us, man?" the Rastafarian called menacingly.

Peter smiled, pretending to a confidence he certainly did not possess.

"No. Should I be?"

As a man the entire gang of youths collapsed into helpless mirth.

"You're crazy, man!" said the tall one.

"Should I be scared of you, then?"

His remark only made them laugh louder.

"Of course, man! We could be after your money, man!"

Again Peter smiled.

"Well in that case you've got the wrong guy, because I ain't got none."

The young man grinned, revealing at the heart of the blackest of black faces a perfectly formed set of shining white teeth.

"So what's new, man! Nobody's got no money round here."

"I'm looking for my grandmother," Peter announced. "Mrs Fitzpatrick. She lives in one of the big blocks."

The young man's grin broadened.

"You're old Mrs Fitzpatrick's grandson? Well, why didn't you say so, man? Come on, I'll take you to her."

The gang swept him along into the heart of the council estate. From deep within one of the tower blocks, the heavy throb of reggae was spilling out into the warm night air. The corridors, alleyways and stairwells were virtually deserted, but despite it Peter could sense the extreme density of human beings surrounding him in the myriad tiny flats.

The man who had spoken earlier jabbed him sharply in the ribs.

"You're a pretty bad grandson, man. I didn't even know she had a family."

"You know her, then?" Peter asked.

"Yeah, she's all right."

They arrived at a large tower block. None of the lifts were working so they all started climbing the stairs. The stairwell was dingy, half the bulbs having failed in its already inadequate lighting system, and the whole place reeked of urine.

They turned a corner and passed a swarthy man coming down the stairs. The gang took no notice of him, but as he disappeared from view Peter suddenly swung around and stared after him in horror.

"Come on!" he yelled, starting to leap up the stairs three at a time. As he yelled he could hear the footsteps of the man they had just passed start running downwards. The man's flight confirmed what he had already feared. He had seen him before, pruning a hedge at Southdown House. He stopped and turned to the young blacks, who were standing watching him.

"Get that man!" Peter screamed. "And one of you get me to my grandmother."

The leader of the gang shook himself rapidly out of his reverie, thrilled at the prospect of some excitement. In an incomprehensible dialect, he barked out some orders at the others and they charged off down the stairwell after the disappearing footsteps. Then he turned and chased up the stairs after Peter.

"It's five more flights, man," he panted. "What's going on?"

But Peter didn't answer, concentrating on getting up the stairs as quickly as possible. He suspected he was too late, that the swarthy gardener from Southdown House had already finished his business with his grandmother. But still he hoped, hoped despite all the evidence to the contrary, hoped that he had misinterpreted what had happened.

But then they turned another corner and all hope instantly died. Ahead of them, the smashed door of the flat was sufficient evidence that they were indeed too late. Peter stepped cautiously into the tiny living room, nervous lest the silent assassin had left an accomplice behind, but inside were nothing but the scattered remains of his grandmother's few possessions. The murderer had done his work well, carefully disguising his visit as one of the violent sadistic robberies so common in the crowded urban world of the inner suburbs. Even the armchairs he had ripped to pieces with a knife.

"O Lord Jesus, man!" his companion called from another room.

He followed the young black through to the kitchen. He was standing motionless in the centre of the room, looking down at the twisted remains of what had once been Peter's grandmother. She was lying face-down on the floor, blood still flowing freely from the multiple knife wounds in her back.

81

Peter stared down at her, angry at his own impotence. The violence against her person had been gratuitous, like the slashed armchairs in the living room a way of fooling the police, but although Peter fully understood its purpose it still appalled and sickened him. He knelt down beside her, not caring that her blood flowed freely onto his trousers, and turned her over to face him.

He flinched. Her lifeless eyes were still open, but there was no fear in them. Instead they seemed to be smirking, as if she were silently laughing at her assailant for choosing the wrong victim, taunting the people responsible for her death that the threat was still there, still hanging over them, and that her death changed nothing.

He remembered her as she had been during the brief time their lives had crossed. To this day he had not been certain why she had sought him out, handed him so decisively the poisoned chalice which had directly caused her own untimely death. But he did know that she had been harshly abused by fate.

He had told her that he was going to Southdown House. She must have realised that sooner or later the Troughtons would realise that they were once again under threat. But despite the danger she had made no attempt to hide, waiting at home for fate's last cruel joke. At the time, while she had been patiently preparing for him the plans of Southdown House, he had asked her if she was herself afraid, but she had laughed and told him that if the Troughtons had wanted her dead they could have killed her long ago. At the time he had accepted her quietly-spoken confidence in her own irrelevance at face value, just as he had accepted the general notion that he should try to win for himself the vast Southdown inheritance which was his birthright. Yet now, looking down at her lifeless corpse, he realised that she had long before reconciled herself to death. Too old and weak to hide, she had made no attempt to conceal herself from the wrath of the Troughtons, waiting patiently in her tiny council flat for the assassin's knife to tear and rip her flesh apart. And as the knife had sunk into her aged body, she would have known for certain that her lost grandchild had found within himself the will to try and avenge the multiple injustices of her own sad life.

Peter laid the body back down on the floor and looked up. His companion was leaning anxiously out of the window, and Peter suddenly became aware of the sound of police sirens far below.

"What's going on?" he called.

"Riot squad," the young black replied, pulling his head back from the window. "We've got to clear off!"

"Why?"

The young black was already by the door.

"You're crazy, man! Who d'you think's going to get the blame for this?"

Peter glanced down at his blood-stained clothes and suddenly realised that the man was right. Picking himself up, he chased after him as he bolted out of the flat and charged down the stairs. Several flights below, the young black stopped at a door and rang the bell five times. From a few flights below, they could hear the police running up the stairwell in strength.

The door opened and a middle-aged black woman appeared. With a worried frown, she swiftly pulled them both through the door and closed it firmly behind them.

"What's going on, Leroy?" she asked anxiously.

"Mrs Fitzpatrick's been all cut up, Mum," he replied, walking hurriedly through to his bedroom and returning moments later with some clean clothes.

"Here," he said to Peter, thrusting him the clothes. "The bathroom's through that door. Shove the old things in the tub. You can sling them away later."

As Peter went silently into the bathroom, Leroy put his arm around his mother's shoulders and steered her into the living room, explaining as he went exactly what had happened in a largely incomprehensible West Indian dialect.

There was a long ring on the doorbell. Peter froze.

"Who is it?" Leroy's mother called through the door.

"Police!" came a gruff man's voice.

There was the sound of the door opening.

"Yes."

"Have you seen anything tonight, missus?"

"No."

"Heard anything?"

"A faint crash from upstairs a while back. Nothing else."

"Is Leroy here?"

His mother hesitated. Then Leroy's voice.

"I'm here."

"You heard anything, Leroy?"

"Me. Not a sound."

"Not even the crash?"

"I'm watching the football, man! Arsenal's three-one up and you expect me to listen for noises."

"Have you got any friends here with you, Leroy?"

"Only Mum. She's a friend."

"O.K. Leroy. But what happened upstairs is serious. Understand. If you hear anything about it you make sure you give me a ring. O.K?"

"O.K. officer."

The door closed and Peter could hear the policeman ringing at the flat next door. Moments later Leroy pushed open the door of the bathroom and came in, sitting down on the toilet. He eyed Peter suspiciously.

"So what's with you, man?" he asked. "Are you in some sort of trouble?"

Peter finished pulling on Leroy's clothes. In the bath beside him he could see his own clothes, still soaked in his grandmother's blood.

"You might say that."

"Are you hiding from the pigs?"

"No, from some other people. A rich family. It was them who paid for my gran to be killed.

"Some rich dudes paid a hit man to kill Mrs Fitzpatrick? Are you serious?"

Peter nodded.

"And now they want me," he added glumly.

Leroy grunted.

"In that case you're right, man. You are in a lot of trouble."

There was a long silence. Leroy sat with an expressionless face on the toilet seat. Compared to his usual effervescent manner, he seemed unusually subdued.

"You got anywhere to stay?" he said at last.

Peter shook his head.

"Nowhere safe. Nowhere they won't be able to find me."

Leroy rose to his feet and looked down at him.

"I liked your gran," he said. "If you like, you can stay here for a few days."

* * * * * *

The sun was beating down overhead, turning Hyde Park into an arid desert. Peter sat disconsolately on the grass in the shade of a horse chestnut tree and ticked off yet another firm of solicitors from his list. So far he'd been to seven, all firms which claimed to be capable of handling this kind of work, and the story had been the same at each one. Lots of interest in his case at first, but the interest rapidly faded when they discovered that he was proposing a full frontal assault on the Earldom of Southdown.

He lay back on the grass and finally allowed his thoughts to drift away from solicitors and onto Julia. Several days had now elapsed since he had last seen her at Southdown House, and as yet he had had no chance to speak with her again. Yet despite his own travails it seemed more than likely that no lasting harm would have come to her. Even though the Troughtons must have established that he was the missing threat to their fortune, there was no real reason to suppose that they would seek to hurt her on his account. Whatever the sordid reality of her relationship with her brother, she was still his flesh and blood. But despite everything, the thought of her languishing in Southdown House still worried him, and he knew he would be relieved when she returned to boarding school at the end of the holidays.

He looked up at the dense mass of foliage in the tall horse chestnut tree above his head. Seen from below, the leaves seemed to form a complex tangle, a tangle which reminded him only too clearly of the increasingly complex mess in which he now found himself. His grandmother's death had confirmed beyond doubt that he himself was now in mortal danger, and he could clearly not return to the comfortable job which Harry had arranged for him at the school. The cat was firmly out of the bag, and there was now no way it could be put back in again.

But his recent experiences with the solicitors had opened up a new and entirely unexpected obstacle. It seemed that he did indeed have the law on his side, but without any legal representation he didn't have the faintest idea how to proceed with his challenge. And even if he could somehow find out how to act without a solicitor, there seemed little he could do, since he could hardly turn up in open court while there were an unspecified number of Southdown hit-men out searching for him.

So it was altogether a rather depressing situation, worse if anything than when he had been out on the streets in his late teens. For then at least he had been an obscure nobody, not even worth robbing because he didn't have anything to steal. But now he was a fugitive, destined to keep running until some hired killer caught up with him in a back alley and finished his flight for ever.

He tried hard to look on the bright side. Leroy at least had been a lucky break, giving him a place to sleep where he was pretty certain he could not be traced. Leroy considered himself to be a kind of latter-day Robin Hood. He was by his own admission a thief, the gang of which he was the undisputed master having discovered they could intimidate wealthy passers-by into parting with their possessions by their mere presence. But he coupled his criminal activities with a remarkably robust moral code, eschewing physical violence and insisting that the proceeds of any thefts were well-distributed throughout his tight-knit community. As a result, and despite his extreme youth, he seemed to be a widely-respected figure, regarded as a kind of unofficial welfare officer who could be approached for help when the meager munificence of the regular variety failed.

Peter glanced up at the bright sun overhead. At last it was sinking lower in the sky, its gradual slide towards the horizon promising relief from the heat which he had latterly been finding so oppressive. Perhaps, when evening came, he would find it easier to work out a way of extricating himself from his current impasse.

A dark-suited man was walking along a nearby path with a newspaper tucked under his arm. Peter watched him idly as he walked, but then he suddenly had an idea. He jumped up and walked quickly out of the park, pleased with himself that he had not had to wait until darkness fell before having the bright idea which he so badly needed.

Twenty minutes later he was back beneath the broad leaves of the horse chestnut, this time equipped with a large selection of daily newspapers. Laying them carefully down on the grass, he picked up the first and started to read.

* * * * * *

It was a crowded Central London pub, full of thirsty office workers seeking a pint after work. The early birds had found seats, but most of the drinkers stood around in little clusters, the men with their regulation ties pulled loose, the women in the skimpiest dresses their employers would tolerate, and as they sat and stood, they filled the bar with the agitated emotion of endless office gossip.

Peter pushed his way through to the bar. Eventually a hard-pressed barman looked at him expectantly.

"I'm looking for a Gertrude Farrington," Peter said. "Somebody said I might find her here."

The barman grinned.

"Somebody was right. She's sitting over by the one-arm bandit."

Peter ordered himself a pint of bitter and elbowed his way through the throng in the direction the barman had indicated. An overweight woman in late middle age was sitting alone at a small table beside the dreadful machine, silently clutching a near-empty pint of lager with a vacant expression on her face.

Peter approached.

"Mrs Farrington?"

The woman put her lager down on the table and looked up at him with bloodshot eyes.

"It's Miss," she observed.

"Do you mind if I join you for a bit, Miss Farrington?"

He could see she was making an effort to concentrate through the alcoholic haze.

"Be my guest," she mumbled.

Peter glanced around to see if he could see a vacant chair but there were none. Yet Miss Farrington made no attempt to rise. Instead, she had slumped back in her chair and started sipping her lager again, almost as if she had forgotten he was there. Peter stared down at her, trying to reconcile the biting satire in the article about corruption in the procurement wing of the Ministry of Defence he had recently read with the human wreck before him. But there seemed to be no obvious connection between the two.

"I want your help," he said, squatting down beside her.

She looked at him through clouded eyes. Then she swigged the last dregs of her lager and held out the glass to him.

"Good," she said. "In that case you can get me another pint."

Peter took the glass and went to the bar to fetch the drink. And as he went, he tried to decide whether he had perhaps made a mistake in choosing to approach this particular journalist.

The barman he had spoken with before appeared.

"Does Miss Farrington always drink like that?" he asked.

The barman smiled.

"Like a fish. But usually it's double whiskies. Maybe it's the hot weather."

Peter nodded thoughtfully.

"A pint of lager," he said, "and a double whisky as well."

Moments later he elbowed his way back towards her table, clutching the two drinks and a vacant chair he had found at another table. He sat down beside her and carefully placed both drinks in front of her, tracking her eyes carefully as he did so.

For a few moments she didn't react, but then she suddenly became aware of the two drinks and flicked a taut intelligent glance towards him. Peter relaxed. The glance was enough. She had passed the test.

"I brought you the whisky for later, when it gets cooler."

Her lips cracked into a faint smile.

"Thanks," she said. "It was kind of you to take so much interest in me. Can I ask why?"

"You're a journalist."

"So are half the other people in this pub. But you didn't buy them their favourite drinks."

"I think you might be a good journalist. I read the piece you did about the Ministry of Defence."

"You want to speak to me about that?"

"No. About me. I'm in trouble. I need help from a journalist. A good journalist. I thought you might do."

She eyed him curiously.

"What kind of trouble?" she asked.

Peter glanced around at the crowded pub.

"I can't tell you here. Is there somewhere we can talk privately?"

Gertrude Farrington leant towards him across the table, pushing her face so close to his that he could smell the alcohol on her breath.

"Give me a clue what it's about," she said, "and I'll think about it."

She was clearly not going to shift her generous form from its comfortable perch until he had told her something interesting. He leant right up to her ear.

"I might look like just any little shit," he whispered, "but I have good legal grounds to believe that I am really the Earl of Southdown. The present incumbent is an impostor who landed the title through of a sordid saga of violence stretching back to the 1930s."

The journalist leant back in her chair and picked up her lager. Without taking her eyes off him for a moment, she downed the entire pint in one go. Then she picked up the whisky and downed that too. Only when she had finished both drinks did she start to heave herself to her feet.

"You have honest eyes," she said when she had finally achieved vertical. "I'll listen to your story."

The pub was near one of the small square parks which adorn the busy commercial centre of London. She led him to a wooden bench where they could not be overhead.

"And now, your lordship," she said as soon as they were seated, "please could you be so kind as to tell me what is the basis for your extraordinary belief."

Peter looked at her with curiosity. Gone was the pathetic listless drunk he had first seen in the pub, and in its place was a woman with keenly intelligent eyes, probing eyes which would search out the truth from far more than words alone.

She sat in silence as he told his story in every detail, deliberately meeting her gaze. But as he spoke she neither nodded nor frowned, giving nothing away about her reaction. Only when he had finally finished did she speak.

"Your story makes sense," she said thoughtfully.

"You believe me then?"

She smiled.

"Oh yes," she murmured, more to herself than to him. "I believe you all right."

Her words surprised him. She saw his surprise.

"Did you think I wouldn't believe you?" she asked.

"I thought you'd be more sceptical, that's all."

The journalist frowned.

"Why do you think you cannot find legal representation with firms of solicitors who claim to specialise in precisely this kind of work?" she asked.

Peter remembered Harry's surprise at the same point.

"I don't know. Despite the evidence in my favour they seem frightened to take me on."

"And why do you think that is?" she asked.

"I don't know. I'm frightened. Maybe they're frightened for the same reasons. The Troughtons aren't very nice, are they?"

She nodded.

"I've been after those evil bastards for years. Just maybe, armed with what you've got, I'll finally be able to nail them."

Peter stared at her in amazement.

"What's it got to do with you?" he said. "I thought this was personal, between me and them."

She shook her head savagely.

"Personal? There's nothing remotely personal about the activities of Gamma Holdings."

"Gamma Holdings?"

She looked at him askance, but then her face softened.

"Bloody hell," she said. "You don't know anything about all this. You're just an ordinary chap who's just stumbled across it by accident, aren't you?"

"Who are Gamma Holdings?" he repeated.

As if instinctively, she glanced around the park to make sure that nobody was eavesdropping.

"It's a pretty open secret among the people who matter, but nobody's ever managed to get an angle on it which could successfully stop them. But of course it has to be an open secret, otherwise it wouldn't work."

"What wouldn't work?" Peter asked in desperation.

She checked herself.

"Sorry. I forgot you didn't know anything. I'll try to explain it rather more coherently."

She paused, as if collecting her wits.

"You're aware of course that the Earldom of Southdown is one of the largest private repositories of wealth in Europe?"

He nodded.

"Well, Gamma Holdings is the name of the holding company which manages the Troughton fortune."

Peter looked at her with a perplexed expression.

"What's a holding company?" he asked.

"A company that doesn't actually produce anything itself. It just holds shares in other companies which do. It's a widely used device in the world of big business. Anyway, Gamma Holdings lies at the heart of a vast conglomerate multinational business empire. Property, mining, agriculture, manufacturing, service industries. You name it, Gamma's got a slice of it. And its tentacles seem to stretch wider with every year that passes."

A thought occurred to her and she glanced at Peter.

"You didn't by any chance meet a man called Axel Hablinski while you were at Southdown House, did you?"

Peter remembered the limousine with the darkened glass which had passed them on the drive. He hadn't thought to mention him during his earlier account.

"The old serpent," he said.

"You what?"

" 'The old serpent'. That's what Julia calls him. I didn't actually meet him, but she spoke of him as if he was some sort of old family retainer. He used to help run the show when her dad was little."

Gertrude smiled.

"Very quaint," she said, "but not very accurate I fear. Axel Hablinski is the brain behind Gamma Holdings, the man who over the last fifty years has transformed a moribund Earldom living off the rents of its London real estate into one of the world's largest private companies."

Peter shrugged.

"Surely there's nothing wrong with that."

"No indeed, nothing at all. Officially Gamma Holdings will go down in history as one of capitalism's more exciting success stories."

"But ..."

She smiled cynically.

"But it's all a fraud. Just like you now tell me the Earl himself is a fraud. Although nobody dares say it publicly, the success of Gamma is largely a direct by-product of the Mafia methods Hablinski imported from the United States before the war."

Peter remembered his grandmother's bleeding body, last in a long line of murders. But before he had always assumed it was personal, not part of some wider web of violence.

"Hablinski is descended from a Polish family which emigrated to the States at the end of the last century. During prohibition they emerged as major players in the East Coast organised crime scene. But by the end of the thirties things were starting to fall apart. The US Justice Department were beginning to close in and the foundations of the Hablinski empire were beginning to crumble."

As she spoke it all suddenly started to slot into place.

"Alexandra?" he whispered.

Gertrude nodded.

"Exactly. She was one of the clan. Marrying into an ancient and wealthy English noble house simultaneously provided a respectable cover for their activities and a suitable receptacle for the threatened Hablinski fortune."

"So Alexandra is also a Hablinski."

"Yes, they're some sort of cousins. I can't really remember the exact relationship. But that's not important. What is important are the brilliant methods Axel Hablinski used to develop his family's fortune. He'd learnt a great deal from his family's setbacks in America. In those days as much as today, organised crime concentrated its energies in areas of illegal economic activity. Things such as drugs, prostitution and gambling. Hablinski's genius was to completely avoid these things and concentrate instead on the normal economic life of the nation, skilfully integrating the Mafia methods of his youth with the activities of an otherwise respectable multinational business.

"Gamma Holdings operates basically like this. The subsidiaries are perfectly normal businesses run by perfectly normal businessmen. These businessmen report to the Gamma board, chaired by Hablinski. Normally Gamma doesn't intervene, but occasionally, when a seemingly insuperable problem crops up, they turn to their special operations wing. That's when the rough stuff starts."

Peter looked at her with a puzzled expression.

"I'm not sure I understand," he said.

"I'll give you a hypothetical example," Gertrude explained. "Suppose one of the Gamma subsidiaries wanted to purchase another company. It would offer the shareholders a reasonable sum of money in payment. But if the board of the company refused to recommend acceptance, if that emerged as an obstacle, then Gamma Holdings might authorise the special operations wing to step in and give them a nudge."

"A nudge? You mean kill them, don't you?"

Gertrude smiled.

"I suppose that's been done from time to time, although I've never actually heard of any well-substantiated cases. Most of the time a rumour of a special operations interest in the case would suffice. That's the real beauty of Hablinski's system. The sordid actuality of real violence is rarely if ever required. Where Gamma's concerned, the fear of terror is quite enough."

* * * * * *

"Have you got a phone here?" he shouted, trying to make himself heard over the deafening noise of the boogie-blaster perched precariously on Leroy's lap.

Leroy glanced across the tiny bedroom at him and turned down the volume.

"You what, man?"

"A phone. I was asking if you had a telephone. I need to make a call."

Leroy's face cracked into a smile, revealing once again his two gleaming rows of white teeth.

"We got a phone, man, but it's been disconnected for months. There's a pay phone in the entrance hall, but I wouldn't go down there right now."

"Why not?"

"Are you deaf, man? Load of pigs turned up again a few minutes back."

Peter looked at Leroy askance, uncertain how he could have heard anything over the music.

"Are you sure? I didn't hear anything."

"Pigs you don't hear. Pigs you smell. They've come to make an arrest. Pick up some poor dude they can nail with your grandmother's death."

Peter rose swiftly to his feet and walked to the window. Sure enough, far below in the bleak concrete car park, he could see a sleek police van. Two officers were anxiously pacing up and down beside it.

Leroy switched off the music and sauntered over to stand by his side, peering down at the scene below.

"Why the hell are they arresting someone from here?" Peter asked. "The guy running down the stairs killed her. You know that."

Leroy shrugged.

"Don't ask me. Pigs don't turn up here like that unless they're out for blood. Black blood."

No sooner had he spoken than a group of about twelve or thirteen policemen emerged from the tower block, hustling a thin young black in handcuffs towards the van.

"That makes sense," Leroy muttered. "They've taken Frankie."

Peter watched as the police officers bundled Frankie into the van. Moments later, the van drove off at speed. It was only when it had disappeared from view that Peter turned to face his companion.

"It might make sense to you, Leroy. But none of this makes any sense to me."

Leroy smiled grimly.

"You're pretty naive, ain't you, man? This place is what's known in the papers as a 'problem estate'. The poor old pigs is always being accused of treating it as a no-go area. And now a sweet little old granny with a white skin has been brutally murdered right in the heart of the estate and they need to prove they can cope. So they've picked up Frankie, because everybody knows Frankie is mean and bad and nasty and because the pigs have wanted to nail him for ages. The journalists is happy, the politicians is happy, most of the people living on the estate is happy. And of course the pigs is really happy, because they've solved a difficult and embarrassing crime."

Peter stared down at the concrete car park below. A small group of residents had appeared from nowhere and appeared to be discussing in animated tones the recent excitement.

"But Frankie didn't do it," Peter said quietly.

Leroy shrugged.

"Frankie's got a history of random violence. You can bet they'll nail him good and proper."

"Not if we tell them who really did it."

Leroy's face froze.

"You're a crazy dude, man. If we go to the pigs, it won't be Frankie who cops it. It'll be you and me."

"Why?"

"Why didn't we tell them in the first place, then? The night she was killed we was hiding our arse in here. Why are our fingerprints all over her flat? Why are traces of her blood all over my bathroom floor? I'll admit the pigs don't want me quite as bad as they want Frankie, but they'd willingly settle for second best."

Peter could feel his mind spinning. But there was more, much more.

Leroy seemed to read his mind.

"Yes, man, you're right. You may be a white man, but if you go to

93

the pigs you'll be in even more danger than me. Your grandmother's killers will be back for you, won't they? And my guess is they want your blood even more than they wanted hers."

Peter walked slowly away from the window and slumped down on Leroy's bed. After a while Leroy sat down beside him.

"You really don't need to have Frankie on your conscience, man," he said softly, "because although he didn't do this one, I can think of at least three that he did do. So you can think of it as natural justice."

Peter looked at him.

"You seem to think about justice quite a lot, don't you, Leroy?"

Leroy shrugged.

"Maybe I do. There's not much of it around, is there?"

"But your gang? Don't you worry at all about what you get up to with them?"

Leroy looked offended.

"We've never laid a finger on anyone."

"But you'll admit you nick things."

"I admit people with money sometimes share their cash around. But all we do is talk, man!"

Peter sat up on the bed.

"You can't seriously expect me to believe that, Leroy."

"Is it my fault they're frightened of us? The only reason people is frightened is because they've got so much more than we have, because somewhere deep down inside they know they've got no right."

"You frightened me when I met you the other night, all lolling about together like that on the walkway."

"There's no crime in lolling about. All we did was talk. And because you didn't have nothing to share you soon realised we was O.K. It's only the guilty ones with the wallets stuffed full of ill-gotten cash who sweat blood when we talk."

Peter rose slowly to his feet.

"Where did you say that phone was?" he asked.

Leroy grinned.

"Not convinced, eh. It's right down at the bottom of the stairwell."

Peter slipped quietly out of the door of Leroy's flat. In the corridor, a large sign announced that the lift was still out of order, so he started tramping steadily down the stairs. The excitement of Frankie's arrest had temporarily distracted him, but now his thoughts had returned to Julia. It was gone eight o'clock, and she should by now have returned to Raley-le-Street.

The telephone was still working, and he nervously dialled the school's number.

"Raley-le-Street High School for Girls," came the secretary's crisp answer.

"May I speak to Miss Trumpington-Fetherby, please? It's Peter Kirby here."

Moments later the headmistress's voice, and to his relief the voice sounded normal, not the voice of a headmistress who had just been told by an angry parent that one of her staff had seduced one the pupils in her charge.

"Why, Peter. Where are you? We were expecting you this afternoon."

"I'm afraid I've been taken unwell. I won't be back for a few days."

There was a pause.

"Unwell? Oh dear. Nothing too serious I hope."

"No. Just a summer flu."

"By the way, somebody was up at the school this morning asking for you."

He tensed.

"Who?"

"A well-spoken young man. He said he was a friend of yours from Oxford. He was just passing through and thought he'd look you up."

"Penelope," Peter began, deliberately addressing her by her first name, "I wonder if you could arrange for me to speak to Julia Troughton. I have to tell her something important about her first history exam next week. Something she asked me about when I went to see her father last week."

There was a pause.

"Didn't you know, then?" came the headmistress's voice.

"Know what?"

"She's not here. Her family phoned to say that she had been taken seriously ill and wouldn't be able to return to school for a while."

It was as if she had turned a knife in his stomach. But when he spoke, his voice remained perfectly controlled.

"Ill? She wasn't ill when I last saw her. What did they say was the matter with her?"

"Hepatitis. Apparently she'll have to be out of circulation for quite a while, certainly until the end of term."

"Who was it who telephoned?" Peter asked.

"Her brother, I think. That handsome chap who's always on television squirting champagne around racecourses. A very personable young man."

"Thanks," Peter said quietly. "I'll be back with you just as soon as I can."

With a grim expression he put down the phone and began walking back up the stairs. But then he stopped and turned. Returning to the telephone, he quietly picked up the handset and dialled Harry's number.

"Harry Nathaniel Kaye speaking," came the gruff answer.

Peter flinched, for in all the many months he had worked for Harry he had never before heard him use his middle name when answering the telephone.

"Harry. It's Peter, Harry. Are you all right?"

There was a silence.

"Where are you, Peter?"

Only a few days before Harry had specifically told him that he should on no account reveal his whereabouts.

"I thought you told me not to tell you. Don't you remember? I was phoning to check you were all right."

There was another pause.

"I have to see you urgently. Can you come round here, to the restaurant?"

Again the voice sounded normal enough, but the words were wrong. Harry never ever graced his establishment with the title 'restaurant'. He was trying to tell him something, trying to tell him that he could not speak freely, but before he could think of what to say a different voice came on the line.

"Are you Peter Kirby?" the voice said in a broad West Country accent.

"Yes. What's going on?"

"Did you know your granny's dead?"

"What do you mean my grandmother's dead? I don't have a grandmother."

The voice laughed.

"You're right about that," it said. Peter remained silent.

"But your professor chum with the fertile imagination is still very much alive," the voice continued. "And you've got precisely one hour to come here with that little piece of paper you stole if you want him to stay that way."

There was a click and the line went dead.

Peter stared in horror at the telephone. He thought of calling the police, but he knew it wouldn't do any good. Even if they believed him they would probably go crashing in and bring forward the moment of Harry's execution. He turned and sat on the bottom stair, looking morosely around him at the crumbling graffiti-covered paint on the walls. There wasn't much time to think: from Brixton to

Hackney would take a good half an hour, even if he was lucky enough to find a cab.

With a sickening sensation he realised that he had finally run out of ideas. He couldn't simply let them kill Harry, poor innocent old Harry Kaye who had been just about the only person in the world who had ever shown him any true kindness. For although the Troughton inheritance might have been worth risking his own life and perhaps even that of his grandmother, he knew with a sickening moral certainty that it was not worth Harry's, and that if he simply let Harry die he would never be able to face himself again.

Feeling in his pocket to check that he still had the certificate, he rose slowly to his feet.

He was already half-way across the concrete car park when he heard the sound of running footsteps coming up behind him.

Leroy fell in beside him.

"What's up, man. I thought you was just going to the telephone."

Peter's pace didn't slow.

"Don't worry, Leroy. I'm not going to the cops."

"Is it the bad dudes, then?"

Peter nodded.

"So they got you?"

"They got my friend, mate. And if I'm not at Harry's Cafe in Hackney in precisely one hour then his life ain't worth very much."

Leroy fell silent.

"If you go they'll kill you too, man!"

Peter shrugged.

"Maybe. But it's the piece of paper in my pocket they really want, not me."

Leroy reached out and caught his arm, forcing Peter to stop.

"You're a pretty cool dude for a white man," he said when he had met his gaze. And then he turned and walked smartly away.

* * * * * *

It was growing dark by the time he reached the front door of the cafe. There was nobody inside, and a hurriedly handwritten sign on the door in Harry's shaky script declared that the cafe was temporarily closed. His hand hovered hesitantly over the bell beside the door, but before he could ring there was the sound of a window being opened on the first floor. He looked up and saw Harry's taut face looking down.

"Run for it, you crazy idiot!" he called out urgently, but no sooner had he uttered the words than he was pulled roughly away.

97

Seconds ticked by and nothing happened. But then there was a sharp sound on the ground beside him. He looked down, and saw that a key had been thrown through the open window above. Picking it up, he unlocked the door to the cafe and went inside.

The inside of the cafe was eerily deserted, the usual animated chatter of the customers silenced. Glancing nervously around, he walked slowly past the familiar tables and chairs until he came to the bottom of the stairs which led up to Harry's flat.

"Are you alone?"

It was the West Country voice he had heard on the phone.

"Yes."

"And have you brought what I want?"

"Yes."

"Come upstairs with your hands held high. Hold the paper I want in your right hand. If you try anything stupid I'll blast your head off."

He began to climb the stairs as instructed. When he was half way up a masked figure appeared at the top of the stairwell pointing a shotgun at his chest. And despite the mask, there was now no longer any doubt that it was the same man he had seen running down the stairs in the tower block, the one who had killed his grandmother.

As Peter reached the top of the stairs the masked man snatched the marriage certificate from his hand before roughly shoving him through to the tiny living room of Harry's flat. Harry himself was sitting uncomfortably in his armchair, his hands tied behind his back, sticking plaster over his mouth.

Peter could feel his heart pounding. He dared not look back at the door, half certain that the killer was now going to kill them both. For several seconds he waited, but no shot rang out. Finally he turned to face his assailant.

The man was carefully checking the details on the certificate, as if trying to judge its authenticity.

"It's the real one: the only one," Peter said, trying to sound as calm as he could.

The masked man nodded silently.

"I think it is," he said at last.

"And are you going to kill us now?"

The man slowly raised his gun.

"Not the old man. I have no reason to harm the old man."

To Peter's surprise, there was a kind of cold professionalism about the hired killer. Previously, when he had seen the wanton violence inflicted on his grandmother, he had assumed the killer had enjoyed the killing, that he was nothing more than a bloodthirsty maniac. But the manner of the violence in the tiny council flat had been as calculated as his own death was now. There was no joy in it, merely a determination to fulfil to the letter an employer's instructions.

"If you kill me the story will be all over the newspapers tomorrow. Of that you may be sure."

The gun was still pointing at him.

"I have left instructions," he continued. "An insurance policy, you might say."

Still the gun was pointing at him, but it had not yet fired. It was just a hunch, but Peter was pretty sure the man was not competent to handle this kind of situation.

"What are you talking about?"

"You have the certificate. I cannot make a legal claim on the title without it. Yet I can make a lot of noise if I wish, even beyond the grave. I am simply offering my silence in exchange for my life. To me that seems like a fair deal. Don't you think you ought to at least check with your boss before you unleash events that can no longer be controlled?"

The gun seemed to waiver.

"There's a phone over there. Why don't you check?"

The masked man slowly edged round to the phone and picked it up. After exchanging a few hurried words in what sounded like a Slavic language he replaced the handset.

"I am to tell you this," he said quietly. "You have trodden on some very powerful toes and made some very important people unhappy. If you are now silent, you will be left alone, just as your father and your grandmother were left alone for as long as they remained silent. But if you ever breathe a word about this to anyone ever again you will be killed, along with anyone else who may be dear to you."

From within his pocket the man produced a length of thin wire. Minutes later, he and Harry were both tightly bound together and tethered to a heavy oak table, their mouths covered in sticking plaster. The man edged towards the door and silently disappeared.

As soon as he had gone, Peter started to wriggle his hands, trying the loosen the wire, but the more he wriggled the more deeply the thin wire dug into his flesh, achieving little but excruciating pain. Eventually he lay back exhausted, trying hard to fend off the overwhelming feeling of impotence and depression which was starting to engulf his whole being.

He gradually became aware of a commotion in the street outside. There was a lot of rowdy swearing and cursing, and then, several moments later, the sound of many footsteps clambering up the stairs towards them.

The living room door crashed wide open and Leroy appeared. At the sight of Harry and Peter lying tightly bound together on the ground, his face broke into an enormous grin.

"Having a spot of bother, man!" he exclaimed, bundling into the room closely followed by seven or eight of his youthful gang.

Pulling a penknife from his pocket he quickly cut the wire and pulled the sticking plaster from their mouths.

"Leroy!" Peter exclaimed. "What the hell are you doing here?"

"Followed you on the train, man. But never mind that. What do you want us to do with the lump of meat downstairs?"

"The what?"

"The dude who was causing you trouble. Some of the lads are sitting on him downstairs in the cafe."

They all trooped silently down the stairs. Behind the bar, three particularly heavy members of Leroy's gang were sitting astride Peter's assailant, leaving only his head visible. Leroy peered down at him and spat straight into his eyes.

"That's for Mrs Fitzpatrick," he growled, before turning away and allowing Peter to pass.

"Where's the certificate?" Peter asked, his voice cold and controlled.

"In my pocket," the man replied. Professional or not, the fear in his voice was unmistakable.

One of the young men sitting astride him pulled the piece of paper out and handed it to Peter.

Peter suddenly remembered his grandmother's mutilated body as she lay on the floor of her council flat. And as he did so, a strange sensation came over him, a cold sensation, a sensation he had never before felt. Without a word, he picked up a knife and held it at the man's throat. But no sooner had he done so than he became aware of Harry's restraining hand on his shoulder.

"Don't!" the old man whispered.

Peter turned.

"He's not worth it," Harry persisted with a firm shake of his head.

The moment of rage passed. But the knife remained in his hand. He knelt down beside the prostrate killer.

"Who were you speaking to on the phone?"

The man said nothing. Peter pushed the knife up hard against his Adam's apple.

"I said who?"

Silence.

He flicked a glance in Leroy's direction.

"Do you want Leroy here to help you talk? Leroy enjoys playing games."

Leroy leered down at him, his eyes flashing menacingly. The look of terror on the man's face magnified several times.

"Hablinski. I take my orders directly from Hablinski. It was Hablinski I was talking to."

"And it was Hablinski who ordered my grandmother's death?"

"Yes."

"And mine?"

"Yes."

"Where is Julia?"

"Julia?"

"Yes. The Earl's daughter. Where is she now?"

"I don't know. I know nothing of her."

"Is she really ill?"

"I said I know nothing."

Peter gave up. It was clear that the man was terrified of being handed over to Leroy. There seemed little doubt he was telling the truth.

He rose slowly to his feet and turned to Leroy.

"I need this creep alive for a while. He might be useful. Can you think of anywhere we can hide him?"

Leroy thought for a moment.

"I know a place," he said. "He won't like it much, but it'll certainly keep him quiet."

* * * * * *

Harry and Leroy were both snoring soundly beside him in the tiny bedroom, but try as he might Peter could not himself find rest. For the drama of the evening had given way to the silence of the night, and with it the terrible vision he had glimpsed earlier had returned. He could see in his mind's eye the awesome edifice of Southdown House, and deep within the house he could hear a faint voice calling to him. An anguished voice. A terrified voice. The voice of the Lady Julia.

He remembered her as she had been in his arms that night in the library, the sheer strength of the emotion which had engulfed them both as they had allowed themselves to accept the truth of their love. He had trusted her, and she had trusted him, and with that trust the barriers with which they had both surrounded themselves for as long as they could remember had suddenly come tumbling down.

101

But her trust in him had been horribly misplaced, for now he was becoming increasingly certain that Julia was being held against her wishes as some kind of obscene pawn in a developing power-struggle. Axel Hablinski himself had hinted as much, for he had specifically warned that it would not just be Peter who would be hunted down if he pursued his claim, but also those who were dear to him.

He slipped silently out of bed and walked through to the living room. Without turning on the lights, he pulled aside the curtains and gazed out across the Thames towards the soaring office blocks of the City of London. Somewhere in that vast mass of glass and concrete Hablinski was sitting and scheming, prepared to go to any lengths to prevent his vast European empire from collapsing in the same way as his family's American empire had done over fifty years before.

The sombre outlines of the City skyscrapers did little to lighten his mood. There was an awesome power about the Southdown fortune which almost defied belief, as its tentacles extended into every branch of human society, enveloping and enfolding everything into which it came into contact. Everyone who mattered seemed to know without really knowing why that its wishes were not to be challenged; only he, an insignificant waiter in an East End cafe, had been naive enough to dare and raise a challenge.

At first he had supposed it was nothing more than a personal struggle to right the wrongs which had been inflicted on him and his family over the generations. The sordid reality of his own early life, the years spent trying to find a role in a society which had always ignored his plight, all had conspired to encourage him to make a determined grab for better things.

But now, as he gazed across the river at the pinnacles of European financial power, he was beginning to glimpse the depths of his own naivity, the extent to which he had been as bad as all the rest. For Harry had been right to say that it wasn't his money. It wasn't his money any more than it was Hablinski's money or the Earl's money. Perhaps, for all the vast power and status it conferred on those who controlled it, it was really nobody's money, and it would be better if the whole sick edifice of property and power and greed would simply drop into a big hole in the ground and disappear.

In his mind's eye he remembered the days he had played the harmonica outside Fortnum and Mason, the contempt which he had seen on the faces of the people passing him by. Ever since his grandmother had told him about the fortune he might one day possess, he had been haunted by a recurrent nightmare, a nightmare which was becoming stronger with every day that passed. It was that the roles would one day be reversed, that he would be the fat cat with the chauffeur-driven limousine, and that as he walked towards the car he would catch sight of some poor lad like he had once been and look upon him with the same look of contempt.

But however much he was secretly growing to fear the fortune he might one day inherit, he knew full well he could no longer simply walk away. For he was gradually coming to realise that wider issues were at stake than simply his own life. Despite himself, he had become pivotal in a wider struggle, a struggle which was no longer personal, a struggle against tyranny and evil in which he was emerging as the crucial player.

Although he knew it seemed like rather a pompous conception for one so very young, he realised that he was gradually coming to think of himself as a kind of resistance leader. Perhaps that was why he got on so well with Leroy, because Leroy also thought of himself in a wider, almost political, context. And just as Leroy seemed to reflect about the moral dilemmas which he faced in his tough existence in the ghetto of London life, so he now found himself reflecting on his own role.

It was about time there was a clean-up. It wasn't just his own family who had been victimised and bullied and hurt by greedy people without scruple. It was going on all the time, certainly in Hablinski's sordid commercial empire and perhaps in others as well. Under the cover of the sanctimonious social superiority of an ancient noble house, ordinary people, little people, were being manipulated and abused and exploited. And he, perhaps, could stop it.

He smiled to himself at the arrogance of his own thoughts. For in his own way he was displaying exactly the same arrogance as his noble forbears had displayed throughout the generations. It was a kind of noblesse oblige, a willingness to stand over and above his fellows and state unequivocally that he knew what was for the best. It was hardly a democratic notion; after all, he wasn't seeking democratic nomination for the role of official protector of human decency.

But as he gazed around him at the London which so clearly summarised everything that was wrong with a society built on a crumbling foundation of unbridled human greed, he knew he now faced the terrible dilemma which had so often faced resistance leaders in the past. For he had made a terrible mistake for one with a mission in life, a mistake that he now knew could cost him very dear.

He had made the mistake of falling in love.

The alcoholic stupor was gone, replaced by a keenness of intellect which almost frightened him by its virility.

Gertrude Farrington swigged down the glass of lemonade she had been sipping when he arrived and elbowed her way out of the pub, clutching in her hand an enormous briefcase. As soon as they were outside she took Peter firmly by the arm and steered him towards the park where they had spoken a few days earlier.

"Sleep well?" she said, as soon as they were out of earshot of the other drinkers in the pub.

"Not really," Peter replied, "but it doesn't matter."

Despite her enquiry Miss Farrington did not seem in the least bit interested in his recent attack of insomnia.

"I've made a lot of progress," she said. "In a few days time we should be ready to launch the whole story."

Peter flinched.

"I can see you're surprised," she said, "but Gertrude Farrington is a fast mover when she comes off the bottle. Last time we met I was pissed."

"Listen carefully," she said, not waiting for him to reply. "I've lined up a solicitor with some guts, a retired friend of mine who has his own personal reasons for disliking people like Axel Hablinski. As soon as the finishing touches of the media campaign are in place, which will still take a couple of days, he will formally file the application on your behalf."

"What media campaign?" Peter asked.

She laughed.

"I am a journalist. Media campaigns are my speciality. I thought that's why you came to me."

"And you've arranged one?"

She nodded.

"Sorry," she said. "I forgot how inexperienced you are. I'll try and explain it a bit more slowly."

She steered him towards a park bench and sat down.

"Your story is what is known in media circles as a scoop," she began. "That is to say, I can have my name plastered all over the media as being the clever little shit who found everything out. But this story, as I'm sure you've already surmised, is not an easy one to break. It requires careful handling."

Peter smiled.

"You can say that again," he said cynically. "One squeak and we're dead."

She puffed herself up like some giant bull-frog and looked him straight in the eye.

"Listen sonny, do you know where I learned my trade," she said.

He shook his head.

"Lebanon. So don't treat me like some naive little sports reporter on a local paper."

Suitably rebuffed, he fell silent.

"You must understand that the media aspect is crucial to protecting both your life and mine. With sufficient media exposure of the threats against us, it will be very difficult for them to deal with us. Media coverage also brings a good measure of official protection as the politicians run for cover. So at first we go into hiding, only emerging when the full glare of publicity is firmly upon us."

Peter watched her apprehensively.

"Will the story be covered?"

She frowned.

"A good point," she said. "Even where the newspapers aren't already directly owned by the Southdown empire, which a lot of them are, the editors will be scared witless about legal action and worse. But you need only one weak link in the chain, because once the story has firmly broken the rest of the pack has to provide some kind of coverage, even if it isn't very sympathetic coverage."

"And you think you've found a weak link?"

She nodded.

"I think so. A national paper which is currently being threatened with take-over by a Gamma subsidiary. In the circumstances I'm pretty sure the editor will think this story is worth running on his front page despite all the risks involved. And that'll force the rest of the rat-pack to follow suit. Before you know it, you're going to be the biggest news item to hit this country for years. It'll force Hablinski and company onto the defensive, make them rely upon their legal guns rather than the explosive variety."

She stopped and looked at him.

"You're already in hiding, aren't you?"

Peter nodded.

"I'll have to join you," she said. "We have to be able to communicate with each other hourly, as well as with the outside world."

Peter thought of Leroy's tiny bedroom. Now that Harry had joined them, it was already becoming rather overcrowded.

"It's in the middle of a council estate," he explained.

She frowned.

"Hopeless," she said, "but don't you worry, leave the practical arrangements to me. We'll visit the solicitor and sort out the paperwork this week, then on Thursday evening we'll make ourselves scarce. Friday afternoon the solicitor will file the formal application. My friendly editor will get his scoop on Saturday morning, leaving the Sundays to pick up the story in depth. By Monday the story will have an unstoppable momentum behind it and the politicians will have no choice but to wade in."

She sat back and heaved a huge sigh of relief, clearly pleased with herself that the journalist scoop of a lifetime was all but in the bag.

Peter looked at her with a forlorn expression.

"There's only one little snag," he lied.

She glanced at him with a worried frown.

"What's that?"

He looked her straight in the eye.

"I'm afraid I've lost the marriage certificate."

* * * * * *

September had been warm and bright, a long Indian summer which had stretched on for day after glorious cloudless day. But now the leaves on the trees had turned from the green of summer to the varied russet hues of autumn, and the weather had finally begun to turn. A biting wind had been sweeping in from the English channel for several days, driving the last remaining tourists away from the beach and back to their cosy home fires.

Harry sat slumped in the driver's seat of the little ice cream van which was now their home, forlornly watching an elderly couple walking along the promenade without so much as flicking a glance in their direction. When they had gone he turned to Peter.

"Let's go," he said. "There's no point in hanging about here any more."

Without a word, Peter started putting away the various tools of their new professional trade: the wafer cones, the milk chocolate flakes and the all the other paraphernalia which cluttered the interior of the ancient ice cream van.

He glanced at Harry's crumpled form in the passenger seat and felt, as he usually felt when he looked at Harry, an almost unbearable wave of guilt sweeping across him. For if Leroy's unrequested assistance some four months previously had recovered the marriage certificate on which his future hinged, it had certainly done little to improve the quality of Harry's life. For a few weeks they had both slept in Leroy's flat but then, with their money running out, they had finally been forced to make some more durable decisions.

There was quite clearly no way that Harry could return to his cafe, not even for an hour or two. For the second time in his long life he had been forced to become a refugee, running from a fate he understood all too well.

Yet Harry had shown no bitterness towards him, neither during those difficult early days in Leroy's tiny flat nor during the weeks and months which followed. And if he resented the way in which the security of his old age had been ripped away from him, he had not allowed it to show. Indeed, in adversity he appeared to have found a renewed vigour, as if the plight of his young friend had given him a meaning and a richness to his life which had hitherto been missing.

It had in fact been Harry's plan to lay low and await developments. For Peter, with all the impetuosity of youth, had come up with all sorts of crazy plans to break into Southdown House and rescue Julia from her captors. It was of course an absurd notion, and Harry had persuaded him that his best chance of seeing Julia again was to do precisely nothing and wait until she resurfaced again.

But if the idea of lying low had been Harry's plan, the ice cream van had been Peter's, inspired no doubt by his childhood memories of life on the south coast beaches. In the heat of summer, it offered the chance to earn a decent enough income without vast initial outlay. And more importantly, it enabled them to keep constantly on the move, avoiding the prying eyes of interfering officials whose sole aim in life seemed to be to insert people into the kind of computer listings which would enable Hablinski to trace them.

So by day they had plied their new trade, constantly moving with the shifting crowds of summer holiday-makers, and by night they had found haven wherever they could, sleeping on makeshift mattresses in the back of the van. It was rough, and it was uncomfortable, but they had both known that they were at least safe, that they were unlikely to be shot in the back by some unseen gun.

Having satisfied himself that everything was properly stowed away, Peter slipped through to the driver's seat. He flicked a sideways glance at Harry.

"Where to?" he asked.

Harry shrugged.

"I don't care," he said morosely.

Peter started the engine and headed off quietly in the general direction of the South Downs.

"I'm going to go again tomorrow," he said quietly.

Harry looked at him enquiringly.

107

"Again. It's the third time this week. Do you really think it'll do any good?"

"I don't know?" he replied.

"You haven't seen her, then?" Harry asked.

He shook his head.

"No. It's nothing like that. But I'm beginning to understand the movements of the rest of the family."

Harry lapsed into silence. However fed up he may have been with his lot, he knew that there was little purpose in trying to force his young friend into telling him what was in his mind. When he was ready he would speak, and that was the end of it.

"You're very sure of her, aren't you?" he said at last.

Peter smiled.

"Yes," he said. "Rationally I know I shouldn't be, but funnily enough she's the one thing I am sure about in all this. If we can only find each other, we won't be parted again. Julia and I feel the same way about each other as I think my grandparents must have done when they were both young."

Harry eyed him thoughtfully.

"Yes," he said at last, "I think you may be right."

* * * * * *

The rain was falling in great sheets, filling the overgrown graveyard with tiny rivulets as the water tried desperately to find its way back to the sea. Peter glanced upwards at the grey mass of the church's square stone tower and laid his bicycle carefully behind a large monument erected to the memory of some long dead local dignitary. Then, tightly clutching the shotgun which had once belonged to Hablinski's paid assassin under his raincoat, he walked quietly towards the door of the church.

The ancient door inside the porch creaked slowly open at his touch and he went inside. There were no lights on, and the heavy stained glass windows allowed little of the meagre daylight outside to penetrate. He glanced around to check that he was alone, and then walked purposefully towards the high seventeenth-century pulpit dominating the front end of the nave. Climbing up the stairs into his chosen hiding place, he crouched down low and began his silent vigil.

He had first spotted the Earl entirely by chance several weeks earlier as he had peddled through the village towards his regular vantage point just outside the main gate of the Southdown estate. It had been on a Thursday afternoon at about three o'clock, and just as he had passed the church he had become aware of a sleek black limousine pulling up outside the little wooden porch. Quickly dismounting, he had hidden from view and watched as the chauffeur had opened the rear door of the limousine. And then, to his amazement, he had seen the 15th Earl of Southdown emerge from the car.

It had been the first time that he had set eyes on the Earl since his brief sojourn at Southdown House the previous spring, but although only a relatively few months had elapsed the Earl's physical appearance had changed greatly. On the last occasion, although he had been preoccupied and aloof in his manner towards Peter, he had otherwise appeared perfectly healthy, a man in his prime. But now, as the chauffeur helped him clamber out of the rear seat of the car, he looked as if he had aged several decades. The lines on his face had deepened into a continual frown, and when he walked it was with a pronounced stoop, his downcast eyes appearing to keep a constant watch on a point about two paces in front of his feet.

He had exchanged a few quick words with his chauffeur and then, quite alone, walked up the path leading to the church and disappeared inside. About an hour later, again quite alone, he had re-emerged from the church and returned to his car. Moments later, they had swept off down the road in the direction of Southdown House.

It had been a strange performance. A quiet, sick-looking man going to a country church and remaining for exactly one hour before returning to his home, a home which was in any case equipped with a private chapel of palatial proportions which had served his family's religious requirements for many generations.

Peter had returned to the village the next day on nothing more than a hunch, a gut feeling that he had at last stumbled on something significant, something which might loosen the frustrating wall of ignorance which was preventing him from discovering Julia's whereabouts. So he had cowered behind the bushes in the churchyard and waited. And sure enough, at three o'clock precisely, exactly the same performance had been repeated.

The following day, Saturday, he had drawn a blank. And again on Sunday. But then, on the Monday, the Earl had reappeared, walking through the graveyard within yards of Peter's hiding place, and disappeared for what was quite clearly a regular visit.

Three sightings had been enough. The next day Peter had gone up to London to pay his grandmother's assassin a visit. He was temporarily housed in a disused commercial washing machine in the basement of a community centre on Leroy's estate. By now the man, who called himself Ronald Smith, had spent nearly three months hunched up in the old machine, regularly fed and watered by Leroy or one of his trusted associates. Although he was allowed out every other day for a brief exercise period, he had nevertheless developed a stooped and sallow appearance, a combination of his crouched position in the washing machine and the lack of daylight. But his physical condition was as nothing compared with the fear he endured day and night, because Leroy and his friends would regularly come and leer at him through the glass, laughing and joking that it would be terribly funny to put the machine onto a fast spin while he was still inside. He was therefore more than willing to talk freely about his former life as the gardener cum resident assassin at Southdown House when Peter promised to put in a good word with his jailors.

Ronald Smith's story confirmed something which Gertrude Farrington had hinted at during their conversations. It was Hablinski who was the real master of the Southdown fortune, carefully concealing his power behind the nominal control of the Earl and now his son. But it revealed more than that. There was tension in the relationship, a tension which disturbed Hablinski sufficiently to maintain the gardener-assassin as a permanent spy within the Southdown household, a spy who was paid handsomely by Hablinski to supply regular reports on the movements of his nominal masters.

Smith had also largely confirmed Peter's own fears about Julia's fate. It was common knowledge amongst the household staff that she was hated by her brother and her grandmother. They both regarded her as a sanctimonious intruder who was at best a nuisance. And although Smith still swore blind that he had no knowledge of what had recently become of her, he seemed more than certain that any of the three of them were capable of using her as a hostage if circumstances required.

But it had been when Peter brought up the subject of religion that he had received his biggest shock. For apparently, within Southdown House, it was a well-known fact that Rupert Troughton, the 15th Earl of Southdown, was and always had been a convinced atheist.

From outside the church there was the sound of a car drawing to a halt. Peter shrank down further into the pulpit. For a long time it was quiet, but then he could hear the sound of the wooden door creaking open and footsteps on the stone flagging. The footsteps came closer and closer until they were just below the pulpit, but then they stopped and there was silence.

Peter waited for a few moments and then, cautiously, peered round the side of the pulpit. Just below him, he could see the Earl, kneeling low in silent prayer. Peter pulled himself back into the safety of the pulpit and took several deep breaths, trying to prepare himself mentally for the challenge ahead. He lifted himself onto his knees, firmly clutching the shotgun in his right hand.

He was just about to stand up and confront the Earl when a sudden sound startled him. Somebody was unlocking a side door to the church. He shrank back, and moments later he could hear the sound of soft footsteps in the chancel.

"Good afternoon, your lordship." The voice was soothing, its sing-song tone rather high-pitched.

"Why vicar, how are you?"

The Earl's voice did not match his looks. It remained confident, authoritative, just as it had been six months before.

"I heard that you have become a regular visitor to our little community in the last few weeks. I thought I would come and tell you how pleased I am and ..."

His voice trailed off.

"Is there something troubling you, your lordship? Something you may wish to talk over?"

There was a pause.

"I have come to reflect privately with the Lord, that is all. But it was kind of you to offer."

"Well, if you change your mind, your lordship, you know where I am, at any time of the day or night."

The Earl muttered his thanks and the vicar's footsteps retreated softly into the distance. Moments later, Peter could hear the sound of the side door being closed and locked.

He waited until he was sure the vicar had gone. Then, after checking that the Earl was still in the same place, he rose to his feet, the shotgun in his hand.

The Earl did not hear him. He remained kneeling on the prayer cushion, his head sunk low in silent concentration.

For several moments Peter did nothing, watching the imposter who had stolen his title. He presented a strangely pathetic sight, a powerful man, one of the richest men in Europe, praying to a God in whom he had never before believed.

His hand tensed on the trigger.

"Are you praying for forgiveness?" he asked.

The Earl looked up. But there was no fear in his face, only a numb look of silent resignation.

"So you have come at last," he said quietly.

"Were you expecting me, then?"

"I didn't know when or where, but I thought it likely."

Not taking his eyes off the Earl for a second, Peter climbed slowly down the pulpit stairs until he was standing just in front of him.

"And you did not care?"

"I hoped you would come."

Peter thought he must have misheard.

"Why?" he asked.

"Because the Lord told me I should await you and seek your help. And who am I to disobey the words of the Lord."

Peter stared at him in disbelief.

"Where is Julia?" he asked.

The Earl raised himself slowly from his knees and sat down on the pew.

"I do not know. They have taken her away. I do not know where."

"Who has taken her? What are you talking about?"

The Earl sighed deeply.

"Those who I had believed were my own."

"James?"

"My son and my mother. They have conspired against me to take my dear daughter from me."

"But ..."

The Earl smiled thinly.

"You wonder how I could allow such a thing," he said. "How could a vastly wealthy Earl, a peer of the realm, allow such a thing to happen?"

Peter nodded.

"One day, perhaps, if you succeed in winning this terrible title and all that goes with it, you will find out that money such as I have possessed brings no pleasure with it. It will be like a shackle around your neck, no less than it has been for me. The Lord was right to praise poverty as a virtue."

Peter's mind was spinning. He had prepared himself mentally for one kind of conversation, yet now he found himself involved in a completely different and unexpected one.

"Why have they taken Julia?" he asked.

Again the Earl smiled.

"That, at least, you should know."

"I am right, then. They have taken her to ensure my good behaviour."

"Your good behaviour, but also mine. When you left our house, my mother's suspicions had already been aroused. She believed it possible you were the missing heir, the legitimate grandson of my father who had survived. She had planned to have you detained at the house the following morning, but before she could do so James had discovered you in the library with Julia and had you forcibly ejected.

"Shortly after you had gone they found a letter lying inside an old book on the desk in the library. It was a love letter, written by your grandfather to your grandmother. Yet it was obvious that there had been other papers hidden in the same book, papers which were no longer to be found. It suggested you had discovered whatever it was you were looking for.

"But Julia had been with you in the library. So my mother and James became convinced that she knew everything, that she had betrayed them and condoned your actions.

"While all this was going on Julia was locked in her room. I could hear her crying out, so I went to find out what was happening. It was while I was looking for the key that I met James and my mother. And it was then I saw a look in their eyes which I have never seen before, a kind of crazed contempt which I pray has passed me by as it has rolled down the generations from my mother to my son. And suddenly I knew that I was no longer master in my own house."

He paused, and his eyes ranged past Peter to the wooden cross on the altar.

"By the next morning Julia had gone. James told me that she had betrayed our family and had therefore been expelled from it. I protested, but my protests were in vain. I was not considered strong enough to protect the family's fortunes. He was taking over the direction of the estate and Julia's wellbeing was to be a guarantee of my co-operation ..."

"Did you not ask what had become of her?"

"I was told that she was safe."

"Nothing more?"

The Earl shook his head.

"And that was the last you saw of her?

"Yes."

For a moment there was silence. The Earl looked into his eyes.

"Do you really love my daughter? I think she must have believed that you did?"

Peter suddenly became aware that he was still pointing the shotgun at the man in front of him. He lowered it quietly to his side.

"Yes. I do love her. At first I used her, but then I fell in love with her. Despite our differences we are so ... alike."

"You are cousins. Why should you not be alike? I find nothing strange in that. And I see that you are a kind man. I pray that you may one day find sanctuary with my daughter."

113

It was a strange remark, but Peter let it pass.

"Tell me about Hablinski," he asked.

The Earl shrugged.

"It is Hablinski who is the real Earl. He controls everything. Now he even controls me."

"I thought you said it was your mother and your son."

"They are nothing more than tools in Hablinski's hands. When I spoke to Hablinski about Julia I could see immediately that he had been kept fully informed. For all I know it was his idea to use Julia as a weapon to force my silence."

Peter suddenly remembered his grandfather's fate.

"There are other ways to keep a man quiet," he said softly. "If Hablinski trusts your son so much, why does he not arrange for your own ... removal?"

Again the Earl smiled.

"I see you are perceptive as well as handsome."

"And the answer to my question?"

"Until recently I always trusted Axel. He was like a father to me after the sad accident which killed my own father. He spent much time with me as a child, teaching me the ways of the world, and although disquieting rumours sometimes reached my ears Axel was always able to allay my doubts and suspicions. But now, I have been forced to come to the conclusion that I have been the victim since childhood of a lifelong conspiracy to prevent me from seeing the truth. Only now, as I myself begin to approach old age, do the scales begin to fall from my eyes."

"You still haven't answered my question. If you are considered so dangerous, why are you still alive? Why have you not been killed as the man who was my grandfather and your father was killed?"

It was as if the Earl had been subjected to an electric shock.

"What are you saying?" he replied angrily. "Why do you say such a thing?"

"It was no accident. Your father was killed on the orders of your mother, or perhaps Hablinski. He was killed as you are now threatened with death, because he was planning to expose the façade of lies on which the whole rotten Southdown empire is based."

The Earl had begun to shake uncontrollably. He sank once again to his knees and began to mouth silently the words of The Lord's Prayer.

Peter grabbed hold of his grey hair and jerked his head violently upwards.

"Perhaps you have really been a dupe for all these years, but now you must face up to reality. Tell me why you are still alive. If you are such a threat, why are you not as dead as your father?"

Although he was still shaking, the Earl made a strenuous effort to pull himself together.

"I think Axel is frightened of James. He would rather keep me alive as a tool for his purposes."

"And James? James would seem to be the prime beneficiary of your demise."

The Earl looked horrified.

"He is my own son."

"As Julia is his own sister. That hardly seems an adequate explanation in your family."

The Earl shrugged.

"I don't know. I am still alive, as you can see. If what you say about them is true, then I must still serve some useful purpose, although I don't know what it is."

He looked up sadly at Peter.

"I have asked the Lord for guidance."

Peter nearly snarled at him again, but there was something about the Earl's tone which made him hesitate.

"Guidance?"

"My life has become loathsome to me, I have appealed to the Lord to allow me to bring it to a peaceful end so that I may join him in the heavenly pastures above, but he has steadfastly refused my appeals. It is the Lord's belief that I still have work to do in this world, and he has promised to send me guidance."

Peter stared at him for a moment.

"Perhaps I can offer the guidance you seek," he said calmly, careful to allow no cynicism to enter his voice.

The Earl looked at him thoughtfully. Again, he glanced briefly at the cross on the altar.

"I think perhaps you can. But what is it that you wish me to do?"

"Do you come here every day?"

"When I can, but only during the week when it is quiet. The Lord has told me to avoid the chapel in my home because it is unclean."

"And you always come at three o'clock?"

The Earl nodded.

"It is the Lord's wish."

"I believe the Lord wishes you to continue coming. Every day, at three o'clock. Sometimes I will meet you here. And I want you to tell me everything you know about your family and Axel Hablinski. And then, perhaps, I will be able to find your daughter. But outwardly you must always be pliant to their wishes, do exactly what you are told by your masters."

The Earl nodded.

"I will do as you ask," he said quietly.

Peter glanced silently at his watch.

"And now," he said softly, "it is high time you returned to Southdown House."

* * * * * *

It was only a small house, but it was quite big enough for the two of them. Peter watched Harry through the window as he set off for the local shops, a small wicker shopping basket in his hand. He breathed a sigh of relief that they had been spared the winter in the ice cream van, for in the chill autumn air Harry had started to develop a persistent cough. It could have developed into a serious problem, yet the warm central heating in their new home undoubtedly appeared to be having a beneficial effect on him.

Peter was now safely in receipt of a regular cash income from the Earl, passed silently across during the course of their regular meetings in the church. For the Earl it was a tiny sum, mere small change, but for Peter and Harry it was sufficient to guarantee them a comfortable life in a quiet suburb of Chichester. Peter had chosen the identity of a Mr Percy Jones, recovering quietly at home from the death of his young wife and parents in a car accident. It was a convenient story, explaining both his current lack of paid employment and the fact that he was living with Harry, who had adopted the role of a surviving grandfather. The story had proved useful both in discouraging the neighbours from becoming too interested in their affairs and in deterring various officials from pressing them too closely for proper papers.

Peter rose to his feet and went over to the small desk in the corner of the room. Pulling out a large file from one of the drawers, he once again started studying the growing mass of papers which lay within.

The file contained his own personal notes on the many conversations he had had over the weeks with the Earl of Southdown. The notes covered every conceivable subject, ranging from the organisational structure of the servants at Southdown House to the history of the family's various collections of antiquities. As a result Peter had been able to piece together a pretty good picture of the Earl's life, a picture which he hoped would help him in his quest.

The picture which was beginning to emerge was of a man who had hidden all his life behind a solid façade of aristocratic respectability.

Already as a child he had been encouraged to see himself as having a special mission in life, a responsibility to his forebears to maintain the good name and good fortune of the family estates. But he had also come to recognise, perhaps been encouraged to recognise, his own intellectual limitations. And in Axel Hablinski he had found a man he could trust absolutely: his sharp intellect, his acute business acumen and his low profile a perfect foil to the young Earl's own public role.

Hablinski had always been polite in the presence of the Earl, almost deferential, a man whose discretion could be trusted in all things. And slowly, almost imperceptibly, the Earl had become the puppet of his mentor, silently influenced and manipulated in all things.

From the beginning of his life the Dowager Countess Alexandra, the Earl's mother, had quietly concurred in her son's passive acquiesence in Hablinski's will. From as early as he could remember, she had encouraged the trust he placed in the émigré Pole, seeking to reinforce his growing authority at every turn.

Until very recently the Earl had known nothing of his father's first wife, Peter's grandmother, even less of the circumstances which had surrounded her tragic life. He had sincerely believed that he was the legitimate holder of the title, believing in his absolute right to hold and control the wealth and power it conferred with all the self-confidence of his class. So for decades he had reigned supreme, confident in his future and that of his noble line, a tribute to the durability of the British aristocratic tradition.

Yet slowly, in recent years, the edifice of self-perceived respectability had begun to crumble. At first the cracks had been small hair-line fractures which could easily be papered over and ignored. But gradually the rate of decay had started to accelerate, until the process could no longer be ignored. And finally, inevitably, he had ended up as Peter had seen him in the church, praying in silent desperation as he sought mercy and forgiveness from a God in whom he had never believed.

The Earl had first started to realise that something was wrong when his only son began to approach maturity. During James's childhood, he had always ascribed his violent temper and aggressive manner to youthful exuberance, a passing phase which would in time mellow into the relaxed manner of a mature young man. Yet as James had slowly passed from being a child to being a man his father had slowly been forced to accept that the traits which he had always disliked so much in him were becoming ever more pronounced, and

117

he had frequently found himself worrying about his son's mental health.

Then the rumours had begun. When he was out in public he had noticed that people of importance seemed to react strangely in his presence. They were never impolite, still less did they articulate whatever it was which was on their minds, yet he had sensed there was a fear, a widespread and growing fear, which was somehow connected with himself. When he had passed people they would whisper furtively to one another, flicking sly glances in his direction when they thought he was looking the other way. For a long time he had tried to convince himself it was a natural corollary of his vast wealth, a kind of twisted envy in the minds of those less fortunate. But then he had started to hear things, perhaps a half-articulated remark from one of his hunting friends, or an overheard comment during one of his infrequent visits to the House of Lords. It had been disquieting, unsettling, a cause of ongoing anxiety whenever he went out about his public duties.

The Earl's reaction to these difficult experiences had been to spend an ever greater amount of time at Southdown House. There, surrounded by all the splendour and trappings of power, he had been free to enjoy his wealth without worry, his concerns limited to the game in the forest and in the fields, finding friendship and solace with his faithful dog. When he travelled it was increasingly to places which were effectively extensions of his own private domain. If he wished to travel overseas, he would first of all arrange for Hablinski to buy a suitable area and make it secure from critical whisper and innuendo. Such it had been with his ever-growing private hunting estates in Zimbabwe, a vast tract of land in which everyone was obeisant for the simple reason that everybody was on the payroll.

The letters had been more difficult to ignore. As his commercial empire had outgrown its roots in real estate and stretched out into every conceivable corner of economic activity, disquieting letters had begun to arrive on his desk. They told absurd stories of double-dealing and duplicity, even of outright violence, by companies acting in his name. The letters were generally polite, appealing to him to reign in the activities of subordinates who had overstepped the mark of normal business conduct.

The Earl had been shocked by some of these cases. He had angrily summoned Hablinski to Southdown House and demanded an explanation of the disquieting events which had been drawn to his attention. But Hablinski had been as shocked as he had been, and had immediately rushed back to London to deal with the affair in question. It usually only took a few days to put things straight again, to soothe the ruffled feathers which had caused someone to write to him. And then, in due course, the Earl would receive a grateful letter or even a personal visit, in which the aggrieved party would thank him profusely for his kind intervention on their behalf.

But the letters, and sometimes telephone calls, had continued to flow in from all parts of the world, their frequency increasing as the years went by. It had become burdensome, an annoying distraction from the innocent rural pursuits he loved so much. So Hablinski had suggested running all his private correspondence and telephone calls through a central office which could ensure that effective and appropriate action was taken without the need to trouble the Earl.

And so the letters and the phone-calls had stopped. The Earl could continue to believe, as he sincerely wished to believe, that his business empire was a source of good in the world, bringing with it employment and innovation and economic prosperity wherever it went. And confident in that knowledge, he could set off with his dog and his gun for the hunting fields with a clear and easy conscience.

Lulled into this false sense of security, the hammer-blows of the truth, when they had finally come, had been all the more severe. After discovering his daughter's effective imprisonment within his own house, he had furiously confronted his mother and son in the drawing room, demanding to know by what right they had taken such action.

James had said nothing, lolling in a deep armchair and smirking silently to himself. It had been his mother, his own mother, who had finally confronted him with the awful truth. She had told him about the deceits and the killings which had guaranteed his false succession to the Earldom, she had told him of her own and Hablinski's origins in the Mafia world of inter-war America, she had told him how Hablinski and she had from the outset been determined to build a vast business empire through the application of Mafia methods to a whole range of legitimate economic activities.

The Earl had stood in silence, staring at the woman he had loved all his life with an almost slave-like devotion, and had suddenly realised that she hated him. She hated him because he was weak, because she had realised at an early age that he could not be entrusted with the truth, that she would have to protect and nurture him not just as a child but also as an adult, surrounding him with comforting stories of noble respectability which he could carry with him to the grave.

During the conversation he had seen her glance slyly at James, and he had instantly understood that she had found in her grandson a perfect replacement for the son who had proved such a disappointment. For James already knew everything, approved of everything, believed in everything, and James would succeed her as her true heir, carrying on a family tradition of greed and lust and envy.

The Earl had looked into their eyes and known that everything they said was true. His power was gone, his legitimacy was gone, the carefully-constructed self-delusion of respectability was gone. And all that was left to him was his daughter, a shining beacon whom he had long sensed possessed a moral fibre which he himself lacked. In a rage he had stormed out of the drawing room and down to the servants' quarters, demanding the key to Julia's room. But then he had discovered to his horror that the fear with which the Southdown fortune had been amassed stretched right into the heart of his own home, and there was not one member of his own domestic staff who would do his bidding.

He had become, almost as much as his daughter, a prisoner within his own home. He was allowed to retain the courtesies of his noble title, the outward respect his position demanded. But there was no longer any substance to his power, only the empty hulk of a broken man who could see no way forward except through Christ.

Peter looked up from the file. When he had found and controlled the Earl he had been so hopeful that he had made the breakthrough he needed. But for all his willingness to talk, for all his self-confessed desire to allow Peter to take possession of his daughter and his title, he had been a useless discovery. The Earl was as impotent as he was, and all they could do was sit beside each other in a vaulted nave and dream of happier times.

Closing the file, he carefully locked it away in the desk. Hablinski had the advantage of all ruthless men: he could play on the sensitivities of others less ruthless that himself in order to achieve his goals. So it was with the Earl and with Peter, both powerful men in their own way, yet both silenced through their love of a softly-spoken sixteen year old girl.

He walked across to the French doors and looked out into the small fenced garden beyond. It had been carefully tended by the previous tenants of the house, its trim lawn surrounded by neat flower-beds which somehow looked smart even in winter. It had clearly been their precious possession, and Hablinski knew well that nearly everyone had a precious possession, something which they didn't want to lose, something with which they could be threatened. It was why the violence was so rarely necessary. The mere threat was generally enough.

Peter turned away from the garden and sat down quietly on an old sofa. He would try a new angle, a thought experiment. Instead of concerning himself excessively with the problems and preoccupations of Peter Kirby, he would instead make a concerted effort to put himself into the shoes of Axel Hablinski.

* * * * * *

He could not yet see the house itself. It was set far back from an exclusive private road in Hampstead Garden Suburb, hidden from view by a high brick wall. But already, despite the anonymity of the external surroundings, Peter could sense Hablinski's presence within. The winter clouds hung dark and heavy overhead, and as he walked towards the solid iron gate set into the wall he could just feel the first drops of rain. The knot in his stomach began to tighten, and he felt an almost overwhelming desire to turn back, to return to the quiet if artificial domesticity of his semi-detached life in Chichester with Harry.

But the video camera set high above the wall had caught him in its view, for it was moving silently, tracking his progress as he approached the gate. There was a discreet little bell set into the wall, but before he had had a chance to touch it a man's voice addressed him from the tiny grill.

"May I be of assistance?"

Peter took a deep breath.

"I wish to speak with Axel Hablinski. Tell him my name is Peter Kirby."

"Will you wait, please," came the reply.

There was a long pause. And then, without a sound, the high iron gate began to swing slowly open.

Peter walked through and carefully examined the house beyond. It was a rambling brick building of early Victorian design, the strange assortment of neo-Gothic turrets projecting from every corner creating a rather chaotic impression.

He had been expecting to find armed guards to greet him, but there was no one to be seen. Behind him, the iron gate had swung neatly back into position, cutting off his last chance of escape to the outside world. Trying to control his nerves, he started walking along the cobblestone drive which led up to the house.

As he climbed the steps towards the entrance the door swung open to reveal a tall man dressed in the uniform of a butler.

"Please come in," the man said in a deferential voice.

Peter stepped into the hall. The gloomy appearance of the outside of the house was matched if not surpassed by the interior. All around him, heavy oak furniture complemented the early Flemish tapestries which adorned the walls, the dark colours merging and mingling to create a heavy and sombre appearance.

The butler took his coat and laid it on a chair beside the door. Then he turned to Peter with a slight bow.

"Would you be so kind as to allow me to search you, sir? It is Mr Hablinski's orders."

Peter nodded in silent acquiescence and spread his legs slightly apart. The butler's hands were quick and efficient, the trained hands of a professional, but the moment he had finished he stepped back politely and resumed his previous formal manner.

"Thank you, sir. And now, if you would be so kind as to follow me, I shall lead you to Mr Hablinski's study. He will see you there."

Together they walked down a low corridor to one side of the hall. The butler knocked respectfully on one of the doors.

"Come in," came a rather high-pitched voice from within.

The butler pushed the door open.

"Mr Peter Kirby!" he announced, before standing to one side for Peter to pass.

Peter walked apprehensively into the room. Before him, standing behind an enormous oak desk, stood a short elderly man with a stooped and unprepossessing appearance. He nodded to the butler, who quietly turned and left the room, pulling the door closed behind him.

It was only when he had gone that the man turned his gaze towards Peter.

"This is indeed an unexpected pleasure," he said slowly, and as the old man spoke Peter could feel himself being dissected by Hablinski's eyes, eyes that were cold and inquisitive and strangely lacking in the full range of human emotion.

"I wanted to speak to you privately," Peter said.

"So I see," Hablinski retorted. "Do please sit down so that we may do so."

They sat down opposite each other at the desk. Hablinski continued to observe him with taut attention.

"I fail to see why you have come," Hablinski said at last.

Peter shrugged.

"You think I'm mad, perhaps?"

Hablinski eyed him.

"No," he said slowly. "You do not have the look of one who is deranged. You have the look of one who is frustrated. A slightly desperate look, perhaps. But lurking beneath the desperation you are like a clever animal waiting for the chance to break free. I think you have come here to try and manipulate me.''

Peter reached into his pocket and pulled out a small manilla envelope. He placed it silently on the desk.

"I think you are looking for this.''

Hablinski reached forward and picked up the envelope. He pulled out the piece of paper within and quietly examined it for a moment.

"Your grandmother's marriage certificate,'' he said slowly.

He opened a drawer in his desk and carefully laid the certificate inside. Then his gaze returned to Peter's face.

"I must be excessively foolish, for I am still not sure of the exact purpose of your visit,'' he said.

"I want Julia freed,'' Peter began.

Hablinski's thin lips broke into a smile.

"Ah,'' he said. "The truth, I suspect, but only a small portion of the truth.''

Peter ignored his remark.

"Where is she?'' he asked.

"She is well. You do not seriously expect me to tell you any more than that.''

"Will you let me see her?''

Hablinski lent back thoughtfully in his chair.

"Do you think I have survived this long by being a fool, young man? Why do you come here and lie to me? Surely you realise that you have by your own actions placed yourself in a very weak bargaining position.''

Peter sat back in his chair and gazed Hablinski straight in the eye.

"Why is the 15th Earl of Southdown still alive?'' he asked.

It was as if he had punched Hablinski in the stomach. He sank back into his chair and stared at Peter.

"What are you talking about?'' he said at last.

"You know what I am talking about. He was useful to you in the past, but now he has become a nuisance. And yet he is still alive. There is a contradiction in that, isn't there?''

Hablinski was still staring at him.

"How do you know these things?'' he said.

"Let's just say I do know. Does it really matter how?''

At Peter's words a look of sudden anger flashed across Hablinski's face, pushing aside the urbane manner he had adopted since his arrival. But it was only for an instant. When he spoke, it was in the same controlled manner as before.

"I sense," he said, "that you already believe you know the answer to that question. Am I correct?"

Peter nodded silently.

Hablinski eyed him suspiciously.

"You are very perceptive," he said. "Very perceptive indeed."

"I have seen the young Viscount at work. He will be a difficult partner for you when he inherits the title. Perhaps even a dangerous partner. It must be causing you a lot of worry."

Hablinski's face remained expressionless.

"I think I begin to see the thrust of your argument," he murmured.

Peter shrugged.

"You might, of course, simply want to kill me," he said with a smile which pretended to a confidence he did not possess.

Hablinski pushed a little buzzer on his desk.

"Yes sir," came a metallic reply.

"We will need a sleeping draught," Hablinski muttered, before flicking a switch to close the connection.

He turned back to Peter.

"You must allow me to think upon your words," he said, "and then we will speak again. In the meantime, I do hope you will not mind taking a little nap while I arrange for you to be transferred to more appropriate surroundings."

The door opened and the butler reappeared, carrying with him a small silver tray on which was placed a red pill and a crystal glass full of water. He lowered the tray towards Peter.

"Your pill, sir," he said in a deferential tone.

Peter picked up the tablet and placed it in his mouth. And then, raising the glass to his lips, he took a large mouthful of water and swallowed hard.

* * * * * *

He became aware of the smell of white lilies long before he awoke. It floated lightly in the air, filling his nostrils with its youthful aroma, and it reminded him of Julia. For Julia had been wearing the perfume on the day they had made love, and ever since that day it had reminded him of her. He kept his eyes closed and dreamed of her as she had been then, her body and her mind laid bare beside him. It was a precious memory, a memory he did not wish to exchange for the real world.

A hand reached out and touched his forehead. He opened his eyes and thought he was still dreaming. For there, sitting beside him as he lay on the bed, was Julia.

"Are you all right?" she said tenderly, seeing that he was awake.

124

He was still not yet fully conscious. His limbs felt heavy and weary, and when he tried to raise himself he found he could not do so. He lay back and gazed at her in disbelief.

"Is it really you?" he said with an effort.

By way of answer she lowered her head and kissed his forehead.

"Thank God you've come," she said softly. "I've missed you dreadfully."

He looked at her gentle face and knew that he had been right to fall in love.

"Are you still mine?" he murmured.

"Yes," she whispered.

He drew her lips towards his and they kissed, quietly at first but then with increasing force. The hunger was mutual, the desire intense. As they kissed the life seemed to flow back into his limbs, and he drew her towards him on the bed, gently pulling the clothes from her body and caressing her as he had so often imagined caressing her during the long months of their separation. And as their bodies became intwined in eager embrace they thrilled at each other's touch, each content to enjoy a brief moment of peace and ecstasy in a world which had often seemed so cruel.

All energy finally spent, they lay together for a long time, gazing tenderly into each other's eyes. But then, like a cruel dream, memories began to seep back into Peter's mind, memories of a rambling house, memories of a courteous butler in a black uniform carrying a silver tray, memories of Hablinski's cold heartless smile as he had sat in his chair and watched while the sleeping draught had begun to do its work.

Peter raised himself up on one elbow and began to take in his surroundings. They were in a spacious and well-appointed bedroom. Outside, through a broad picture window, he could see a dense pine forest, and the trees were covered in thick white snow.

"Has it been snowing?" he asked.

She too raised herself up on her elbow and looked outside.

"There was fresh snow in the night. But there has been snow outside for several months."

Her remark shocked him. He stood up and walked to the window. It was locked, but he could see that they were on the first floor of a building, just beneath some large overhanging eaves which offered protection against the snow. But beyond the distinctly Alpine outlook there was no other clue as to their whereabouts, since the house appeared to be completely surrounded by pine forest.

"Where are we?" he asked.

She shrugged.

"The Alps, I think, or maybe the Black Forest. When they bring me groceries they've nearly always got German written on them."

He sat down in an armchair and examined her thoughtfully.

"Did they bring you straight here from Southdown House?" he asked.

At his words a cloud seemed to pass over Julia's face.

"No," she replied. "After you were taken away I was locked in my room. And then, the next morning, James came to me and told me that my family had decided to disown me. He said I was to be taken away and that I would never return. Shortly afterwards I was given an injection that sent me to sleep.

"When I awoke I found myself in a large unfamiliar house. It was somewhere deep in the countryside, far away from any other houses, and although I couldn't go outside I'm certain it was extremely well protected."

She shuddered.

"James's mental state is worse than even I had ever imagined," she continued. "The house where I was held was used by him and his perverted friends as a kind of secret playground where they could indulge their disgusting habits without fear of detection."

Again she shuddered.

"Did they hurt you?" Peter asked quietly.

She shook her head.

"No," she said. "They never once touched me, although I often thought they would. There were quite a lot of young people there of both sexes. Some were nearly as old as me, some much younger. Most of them were on drugs. But they were all there to be used."

Peter winced. He knew the kind of kids. They came from the back streets of central London, wastrels like he had been with no home and no family and no one to report their disappearance to the police.

"And James's victims were kept with you in the house?"

She nodded.

"I think I was the only person who cared what happened to them. Some of them were terrified, of course, but most of them seemed to accept passively what was going on."

Peter snorted.

"He really is mad. When he finally inherits full control of the Earldom nobody will be able to stop him."

His words were addressed to Julia but meant for somebody else's ears.

"I think it's already too late to stop him," Julia said angrily.

"How long were you there?" he asked.

"I don't know. But it was probably about six weeks. Then I was suddenly moved here."

"And this is different?"

She laughed dryly.

"This place is paradise. Here I'm just a prisoner, and a comfortable one at that. I can do pretty well what I like except leave."

"Have you seen James since you came here?"

She shook her head, and the relief on her face was obvious.

"Did you know that this house is under Hablinski's direct control?" Peter said. "It has nothing to do with James."

She looked at him sharply.

"What makes you think that?"

"It was Hablinski who sent me here. I'm sure James doesn't know anything about it."

She looked at him with surprise.

"Hablinski? What's all this got to do with him?"

Peter lay back and looked at the white plasterwork on the ceiling. He imagined Hablinski's sly face set into the plaster, looking down at them both as they lay naked on the bed. Then he looked back at Julia, and began to tell her a carefully edited version of the truth which he had been planning to tell for several weeks. Yet he had originally supposed it would be for Hablinski's ears alone, and now he had to adjust his story to allow for the fact that Julia was also listening.

The facts were the easiest to manipulate. He concealed all reference to his clandestine contacts with Gertrude Farrington and Julia's father, but other than that he recounted the story largely as it had occurred.

But if the facts were relatively easy to adjust, the crucial underlying value judgements were much more difficult to modulate, particularly now that Julia was listening as well as Hablinski. He suspected that Hablinski had been fully aware of that fact, which explained why he preferred to allow Julia to interrogate him rather than attempt to do so himself.

To Julia, Peter tried to paint by his words and tone a picture of an empire controlled and beginning to be corrupted by her sick brother James. Axel Hablinski, in contrast, was a respectable businessman who had spent a lifetime building up one of the world's most successful business empires in the name of the Earldom and who could now see the whole magnificent structure disintegrating around him as a result of James's growing hold on power. A power struggle was

127

therefore taking place within the empire between the evil James and the good honest businessman Hablinski.

In this carefully edited story, Peter portrayed himself as little more than a distraction in this developing conflict, an inconvenience which had temporarily forced James and Hablinski to agree a common policy to deal with an external threat. Julia's own fate since her incarceration had been a reflection of both the discord and the common ground between them, with the decision to use her as a hostage representing the common ground and the radically different treatment to which she had been subjected in her two prisons representing the discord.

Peter finished by explaining to Julia that he had come to Hablinski with the offer of a deal. Hablinski would secretly help Peter to usurp power from her father and brother and therefore remove the threat posed by James. With Peter and Julia safely established as the new Earl and Countess of Southdown, Hablinski would be left free to continue managing the fortune he had amassed in their name without undue interference.

But to Hablinski the sub-text of his story was entirely different. For Hablinski was aware that Peter knew the empire was far from the innocent business concern he had portrayed it to be. Peter was therefore providing him with a soothing and reassuring message, demonstrating how convincingly he could portray Hablinski, even to the one he loved, as an honest businessman running an honest business.

His story drew to a close. He looked anxiously at Julia, wondering how she would react.

"Do you think the old serpent's got the clout to do a deal?" she said.

Peter smiled at the thought of Hablinski listening to her words.

"I think so. Hablinski knows how the world works. With him on my side, I believe the Earldom's there for the asking."

* * * * * *

A week went by amidst the pine trees. And then another week. And as the days stretched by Julia and Peter gradually forgot about the wider world. They were not free to leave, but now that they had found one another again they had no particular desire to leave. Theirs was a special kind of happiness alone in their gilded cage, alone and undisturbed.

Every morning two casually-dressed men would call and collect their shopping list for the day. Later in the day they would return, laden high with groceries. After that, Julia and he would struggle with recipe books and kitchen equipment, turning the pile of groceries into a candle-lit supper. And then, when the evening meal was finished, they would retire to the spacious double bed and make love before drifting off to sleep.

But one day, after about three weeks, there was a sharp knock on the door. Expecting it to be the delivery men, Peter donned his dressing gown and went to meet them. But instead of the usual pair, it was Hablinski's London butler who stood before him.

"Good morning, sir," he said politely. "Mr Hablinski would be grateful if you could spare him a few minutes at half past ten."

And so, at ten-thirty sharp, he followed the butler to a smart office at the far end of the house.

When he arrived Hablinski was looking out through the window at a fine mountain view. A broad snowfield stretched away steeply towards a distant valley floor dotted with tiny high-roofed houses.

"Do you not find the view exhilarating, Mr Kirby?" he said without turning round. "It is a great pity you cannot see it from your side of the building."

Peter approached him silently and followed his gaze.

"Switzerland?" he asked.

Hablinski nodded.

"More beautiful than Hampstead, don't you agree?"

"Have I passed your test?" Peter asked.

Hablinski did not take his eyes off the view for an instant.

"Let us say you have aroused my curiosity."

He fell silent.

"Did you watch everything?" Peter asked.

Hablinski seemed affronted.

"I naturally possess the capability to watch, but you should know that I do not always choose to do so. I am not a filthy animal like James Troughton. What you do in bed is your affair."

There was a venom in his voice which conveyed true hatred.

"You agree about James, then?"

Hablinski turned and looked at him, and again the cold eyes were probing, as if trying hard to search out the truth from the lies.

"Oh yes," he said. "You are absolutely correct about James. He could easily spin completely out of control. When his father dies and he inherits absolute power over the Earldom he may destroy everything for which I have worked."

"For what exactly are you working? If I understood that I would know whether you and I can do business together."

Hablinski turned and glowered at him.

129

"You are really very young to speak like that to me," he said.

"Perhaps it's because I'm an Earl. It's in the blood."

Hablinski smiled thinly.

"You didn't come here without preparing yourself, did you, young man? So why don't you tell me what you believe me to be trying to achieve? Then we will see how perceptive you really are!"

Peter hesitated. He hadn't really thought about it much, supposing it to be self-evident.

"You are trying to build a business empire such as the world has never seen, an empire that will rival and surpass those of John Paul Getty and Howard Hughes and all the others. And you are single-minded in your determination to succeed."

Hablinski shrugged.

"That's a bit thin, isn't it? You haven't said why. What is the appeal of all this money I have amassed?"

"It's not the money. You already have more than enough of that. You want the power which the money buys."

Hablinski nodded.

"Exactly," he said. "But power is only useful if it is directed. It is always a means and never an end."

Peter stared at him uncertainly. Perhaps it was because he had been so poor and powerless, but he had always supposed that money and the power it conferred were ends in their own right, that they didn't need any further justification.

"So what are you working towards?" he asked.

Hablinski turned away from the window and lowered himself into a deep leather armchair.

"You are certainly better company than either James or his father," he sighed. "You at least have a brain. And you are humble enough to be capable of reflection."

He was silent for a while.

"I freely confess I am a ruthless man," he said at last. "But unlike James, I have never been and I will never be ruthless without purpose. The modern world contains some dangerous contradictions. It is technological, fast-changing, difficult to prevent from falling apart. In historical times, democracy and competition offered a way of controlling this chaos in a coherent fashion. But those times have long since passed."

He paused, and Peter watched as he gazed moodily at the valley below. But then he glanced at Peter's perplexed face and smiled a dry smile.

"You are perhaps surprised to see that the old serpent reflects upon such matters. You had supposed I spend my entire time planning brutal killings and the like?"

Peter met his gaze head on.

"Perhaps I underestimated you. But I still don't see why you take such a dim view of democracy and competition."

Hablinski laughed.

"I would have thought with your past you would understand that better than most," he said. "Democracy is a sham. Votes are bought and sold without shame. The media has always been manipulated, and as the media becomes more influential so those who own the media become more powerful. Did not your alcoholic friend Gertrude Farrington explain all this to you?"

Peter flinched.

"I see you are surprised I know," Hablinski observed. "But you must always remember that I know everything about you."

Peter remained silent.

"Miss Farrington is a good example of a free spirit." Hablinski continued. "But she too can be manipulated, as you see."

"How did you know about her?"

Hablinski grunted.

"She spoke to a newspaper editor who offered to run the story of your challenge for the Earldom in his paper. Miss Farrington believed he would cooperate with her because his newspaper was under threat from one of my subsidiaries. But instead the editor thought he could curry favour with me by telling me of her approach."

A thought occurred to Peter.

"If you knew about my meetings with Gertrude Farrington, why did you not kill me then?"

Hablinski laughed.

"More killings. You really must think I am possessed by a lust for blood, like some kind of obscene vampire?"

"You've killed before. It was you who ordered the death of my parents and my grandparents, wasn't it?"

Hablinski bowed his head in quiet acquiesence.

"I confess that I did originally intend to kill you. It was a panic reaction, an uncharacteristically impulsive move. But then, as I came to understand you better, I decided I should observe you quietly for a while, to see if you might possibly be able to serve my purposes. So you see, it is not just you who has quietly considered an understanding between us. I too was thinking along much the same lines."

Peter was still standing by the window. He turned away from

131

Hablinski and gazed across the snowfield, trying to grasp the full implications of the old man's words.

"Tell me why you think democracy and competition are dead?" he said, turning back to face him.

Hablinski thin smile returned.

"A democratic system seeks to provide some kind of check on the highly inegalitarian distribution of power that the market-place creates. Since not everyone is capable of making an equal contribution to society's economic requirements, some are able by their talents and abilities to earn far more than others. These inequalities build up over the generations through inherited wealth. Yet democracy hands out votes equally, and the equally-distributed political power should therefore act as a check on the unequally-distributed economic power, permitting a measure of redistribution from the rich to the poor.

"There may once have been a time when such a system of checks and balances would have been able to work, but that time is now fading fast. Technology is destroying the foundations of democracy. For a modern technologically-based economy requires fewer and fewer economically active people, a highly qualified and competent minority of the population who understand it. As time passes, everyone else is rendered economically redundant, effectively surplus to requirements.

"So how does democracy cope with this situation. Nominally, the political power remains equally distributed, but slowly those who possess the economic power, the well-paid and economically useful minority of society, seek to use their economic power to buy the votes they need to maintain political control. They manipulate the media, they cajole the voters with threats and sometimes offer them bribes. At first the voters are confused and uncertain, but then they swallow the lies and half-truths with increasing gratitude, grateful at least that someone is offering a blueprint for survival in an increasingly uncertain world. And as this happens, democracy becomes the sham of which I speak, an empty shell of a political system which offers little and costs dear.

"But if democracy fails there is another central concept in traditional thinking which offers a defence against tyranny, and that is the force of competition, the driving force of laissez-faire capitalism. But competition too is becoming a sham. A handful of giant corporations such as mine, the inevitable by-products of a modern technology which requires size to be effective, fight each other like crazy dinosaurs for control of economic resources. In order to sell at ever lower prices, they will rip and grab and tear at the very heart of the planet's survival system, not stopping until they, like the dinosaurs in their time, have become extinct.

"The result of all this is utter chaos. A chaos which is dangerous for rich and poor alike, a chaos which will lead to nothing but war and famine and disaster as the world's vital resources become scarcer and scarcer."

"And what is your vision?" Peter interrupted.

"My vision is of a world at peace with itself, a world organised by a single corporation, a corporation which will be able to control and utilise the world's economic resources for the good of all. I have made it my life's work to create that corporation. And soon, very soon, I will have succeeded."

He rose laboriously from his chair.

"Come," he said, "I will show you the scope of the empire you may yet inherit."

Peter followed him silently as he led the way through the corridors of the old Alpine house. Pushing open a door, he indicated to Peter that he should pass. As they entered, the room was bathed in a harsh metallic light. In the centre was a semi-circular console adorned with a discreet array of controls while on the far wall, beyond the console, there was a large blank screen.

"This is one of my offices," Hablinski murmured. "There are other identical ones in other parts of the world, so I can work wherever I happen to find myself."

Peter looked quietly around. Something about Hablinski's manner told him that very few other people were allowed access to this room.

"Sit down," Hablinski said drily, indicating a small chair carefully positioned to one side of the console.

Peter did so, watching Hablinski numbly as he sat at his desk by the console and started to fiddle with the controls. With his diminutive stature, he looked rather like a spider sitting at the centre of a web, waiting patiently for a passing fly to land.

The lights dimmed and a map of the world appeared on the screen before them. And as Hablinski spoke a succession of maps, pictures, diagrams and graphs appeared before them, illustrating and expanding upon the points he was making.

"Gamma Holdings started to emerge as a major player on the world stage shortly after the last war," Hablinski began. "It gradually branched out from its origins in property into other areas of economic activity. In 1952, for example, it acquired its first newspaper, a hitherto small-circulation British national daily which required a large infusion of cash in order to survive. With the massive funding it received, the paper gradually increased its circulation until it became a major player in the field, an important opinion-former in its own right ..."

Hablinski's clinical voice droned on for more than three hours. He described in detail how he had systematically established a stranglehold on first one sector of economic life and then another, always moving on towards a new target when the previous one had been attained. At first the focus of his attention had been on Britain, but then he had gradually expanded, first to America and Western Europe, then to the booming East Asian economies, the Third World and the crumbling relics left high and dry by the demise of the Soviet Empire. Yet there was no relish or pride in his voice as he spoke, merely a long recitation of facts and figures which described his holdings around the world. It amounted to a vast litany of power, a tight grip on the economic life of many nations, a grip which was growing slowly tighter and from which it would eventually be impossible to break free.

Eventually the screen faded and Hablinski turned to face Peter, his eyes once again probing.

"What do you think?" he said.

"I don't think you need James or me. Perhaps you needed an Earldom once as a cover story for your activities, but now you do not need it any longer."

Hablinski smiled.

"Do not be misled, young man. I have amassed a great deal of power and influence, but I still have not attained the critical mass for which I strive, the point at which my power will become unstoppable. That is still some way off. The Earldom was always a convenient cover story, a publicly recognised cloak of respectability behind which I could operate. And it will remain so for some time to come."

There was something in his eyes which told Peter he was lying. But there seemed little purpose in pressing the point.

"What exactly do you want from me, Mr Hablinski?" he said.

Hablinski frowned.

"I am an old man. I need a successor who will share my vision of the world. Someone who can bring the process I have started to fruition."

Peter hesitated.

"I'm not sure I like your methods. You dominate by fear, sometimes by violence. Your rise to power has hardly been fair."

Again Hablinski's lips cracked into a thin smile.

"You were happy enough to try and grab this empire and all the vast wealth that goes with it. That too was hardly fair. And do you not see that every system of ordering human affairs requires a measure of fear and coercion in order to function properly? Mine is no exception. But you must believe me when I tell you that I abhor violence: it is always an admission of failure, a recognition that fear itself was insufficient to deter transgression. It is rather like two countries who stand across a border from one another and argue about some pathetic territorial dispute. They should be terrified of war, with all the human suffering it brings in its wake. And if they are sufficiently afraid they will avoid conflict and tread the road of peace. It is only when they lose their fear of violence that war begins and violence ensues. Fear and violence are not bedfellows, they are in truth opposites.

"The fear I arouse in those who seek to oppose my will is indeed great. But the countless millions of ordinary people who work for my companies are not oppressed by fear. Instead they enjoy the fruits of the protective shield I have built around them. They live an ordered life within an ordered company, sheltered and protected from adversity by a rule I believe to be benevolent. That is – has always been – the other side of the coin."

Peter shrugged.

"So who are the people who continue to challenge your authority?"

"Politicians, bureaucrats, rivals in business, a motley assortment of do-gooders and hypocrites. There are still plenty who would take great relish in seeing my power crumble. So whoever succeeds me must share both my vision and my strength, and must be prepared to do whatever is necessary to subjugate those who stand in the way of progress ..."

Peter remained in silence, staring blankly at the console. He had been expecting Hablinski to be an evil power-crazed businessman, seeking nothing but power for power's sake. He had planned to trick that businessman, to persuade him that he, Peter, would be a safer and more compliant front man as Earl of Southdown than his cousin James. He had planned to bide his time and wait, and then, when he had amassed sufficient formal power in his own hands, to ambush Hablinski when he least expected it, to rip his empire away and restore it to the golden path of righteousness.

But now his carefully laid plans were slowly going astray. Instead of a power-crazed businessman, he had found a man consumed with a burning vision of a future without chaos, a future in which the affairs of the modern world would be ordered and controlled by a dominant corporation, a world power in its own right which could impose an era of peace and prosperity on the world as it entered the twenty-first century.

There was an ironic parallel between Hablinski's view of the world and the old perspective of an English noble house. For the aristocratic families of England had regarded the welfare of those who lived and worked on their great landed estates as a major concern in their lives. They had run their estates like benevolent dictators, a stable constellation rotating round a central star, a star sufficently remote from the ordinary concerns of ordinary people to be able to treat them with respect and dignity. And such was Hablinski's vision of the future, a world in which the power of the ruler was so vast that he no longer needed to oppress, leaving himself free to concern himself with nothing but the continued welfare of his myriad corporate employees.

But there was more. Because it appeared that Hablinski was offering him far more than the placid role of front man which was still being filled by Julia's father. Instead he was offering him the right of succession, the chance to take into his own two hands the vast power which Hablinski had built up.

He glanced nervously at the old man. His long speech had fatigued him, and as he sat slumped in his chair it became apparent to Peter that he might not have long to live.

"Why me?" he asked.

Hablinski slouched even lower in his chair.

"I am a builder, not a ruler. I think there is a difference."

Peter looked at him blankly.

"You were right to speak of violence," Hablinski murmured. "I have a great deal of blood on my hands. Perhaps I am like Winston Churchill, a good leader in time of war, less useful when peace returns. But since I have been observing you I have come to form the opinion that you have the right personality to succeed me. You are young, and therefore flexible in your thinking. You are strong, and therefore able to take difficult decisions. You are intelligent, and therefore able to take the right decisions. You are kind, and therefore able to take just decisions. But most of all, you believe in yourself, and that will give you the strength to lead where others follow."

* * * * * *

The sun was shining brightly when they awoke. Julia arose and pulled the curtains apart, looking unhappily out at the wintery world beyond. Only after a long time did she finally turn and look at Peter.

He was lying on his back, staring up at the ceiling with a vague numbed look on his face.

"I don't understand why you won't tell me what happened with Hablinski?" she complained again.

Peter frowned. Since his return from Hablinski's study the previous day he had said nothing to Julia of his conversation with the old man.

"Did you know he can see and hear everything that goes on in this room?" he said flatly.

She looked at him in horror, quickly grabbing a sheet from the bed and wrapping it around her naked form.

"How do you know that?" she said, glancing around the room to see where the secret cameras could be hidden.

"He told me."

"What a snake!" she hissed. "What an indescribably disgusting snake!"

Peter remained silent. He had only told her so that she would leave him alone, free to think quietly through the implications of Hablinski's words.

Julia suddenly unwrapped the sheet and threw it back on the bed.

"What the hell," she said. "If he can see everything, then he's seen it all already."

She stomped off angrily into the kitchen. He could hear her noisily pulling cups and saucers out of the cupboard.

After a while he rose to his feet and followed her through to the kitchen. Hurting Julia was the last thing he wanted to do, but in his current confusion he was uncertain of precisely what to say. Better in the circumstances to say nothing.

"I just need a bit of time to sort out my thoughts, Julia. Can you allow me that?"

She looked at his dishevelled and perplexed face and forced a smile.

"I suppose so. Time doesn't exactly seem to be at a premium around here."

She finished brewing the coffee and poured out two cups.

"Do you want some too, Uncle Axel?" she said, vaguely addressing the ceiling.

Peter grunted

"Do me a favour, Julia," he muttered.

"I was only being polite."

Peter picked up a piece of paper and a pencil.

"What about having lasagne tonight?" he said.

Julia shrugged.

"I don't care. Anything you like."

She was trying hard to conceal it, but there was something about the tone of her voice that told him the honeymoon was suddenly over.

"Are you all right, my love?" he asked.

She looked down sadly into her coffee.

"How much longer are we going to be kept prisoner here, Peter?" she asked. "Didn't Hablinski give you any idea?"

He looked at her sadly. For weeks he had known that their artificial idyll couldn't last, and now he knew it had come to an end.

"I don't know. He didn't say."

Julia poured out a bowl of muesli and started mechanically munching her way through it.

"I want to go outside, walk in the woods. Even if we have to have an armed guard with us." Her eyes turned up to the ceiling. "Can you hear me, Uncle Axel? I would very much like to go for a walk in the woods."

Peter remembered that she had been imprisoned far longer than he had been. She had seen summer turn to autumn, and autumn turn to winter. His arrival had broken the monotony and temporarily given her hope, but now the despair was creeping back, filling her whole soul with a frustrated bitterness which he knew could finally destroy them both.

There was a faint click.

"What was that?" Peter asked.

Julia looked at him morosely and shrugged.

"I didn't hear anything."

Peter glanced around.

"It sounded like the door being unlocked."

Julia didn't react. She remained as she had been before, slumped over her empty coffee cup as if trying to find some profound message lurking at the bottom.

Peter rose to his feet and walked out into the hall. He approached the external door of their flat, the one that was always locked, and cautiously tried the doorhandle. It turned. He pushed gently, and to his amazement the door swung wide open.

He had only been outside in the corridor once, the previous day with Hablinski's butler. But this time there was no one to be seen, only an empty corridor stretching away to the stairwell at the front of the house. He walked nervously out into corridor, fearful to go too far in case the door swung shut behind him, separating him from Julia. Yet still no one appeared to challenge him.

The stairwell leading to the ground floor was not far away. He crept quietly along the corridor and peered down. All was still, an ancient grandfather clock ticking patiently in the hall below. He turned, intending to return to the door of their flat, but as he did so he noticed an envelope lying on a small occasional table at the top of the stair-well. On the front of the envelope, neatly written in a bold hand, was his name.

Peter picked up the envelope and pulled out the contents. Again he looked nervously around to see if anyone was silently observing him. But there was still nobody to be seen. He looked back at the paper in his hand, wondering if he had mistaken it for a copy. But there was no mistake. The document in his hand was his grandmother's marriage certificate.

He shoved the certificate quickly into his pocket and hurried back to their flat. In the kitchen, Julia was carefully copying out a list of ingredients from a cookery book.

"Get dressed," he said urgently.

She looked at him sullenly.

"Why?"

"The door is open. I think we can go."

At first she didn't react. But then she rose quickly and went to examine the open door for herself.

"Why?" she said, her voice perplexed. "I don't understand."

But Peter was already in the bedroom, hurriedly pulling on some warm winter clothes.

She followed him through and started dressing, and as she did so Peter could see that her fingers were shaking.

"I'm frightened," she said. "I don't understand what's happening."

Peter was pulling on a pair of fur-lined snow boots he had found in the bottom of the wardrobe.

"Dress warmly," he said. "It'll be icy cold out there."

He left her dressing and walked quickly through to the kitchen. Grabbing some food, he pushed it all into a shopping bag and returned to the bedroom. Then, as an afterthought, he returned to the kitchen and fetched a sharp bread knife just in case.

Moments later, they were both out in the hall. Except for the ticking of the clock, the house lay in absolute silence as they crept along the hallway and down the stairs. The front door opened at their touch and they went outside. On the small road leading from the house, a sleek sports car was waiting for them, snow chains fitted and keys in the lock.

Peter pulled open the door and clambered into the driver's seat.

"Get in," he called to Julia, who was standing staring at the house in which she had been imprisoned for so long.

139

As soon as she was beside him he turned the key and the engine hummed into life. The snow lay deep on the road, but although there were signs that several cars had recently passed along it, it was impossible to tell if Hablinski had left the house or was still within. But of one thing Peter was quite certain. Somewhere, somehow, his clinical eye was observing their every move.

They drove for a long time in silence down the steep Alpine track as it plunged into the dark pine forest, snaking its way precariously down the mountainside. Julia was sitting rigidly beside him, her face full of a kind of strained nervous anxiety, glancing around from time to time to see if anyone was following them.

After they had been descending for about twenty minutes the trees cleared and the track turned into a more substantial road, winding backwards and forwards among opulent high-roofed Swiss houses dotted around on snow-covered open pasture. Far below, they could see the village which had been visible from Hablinski's room nestling in the valley floor.

"Look in the dashboard," Peter said suddenly.

Julia leant forward and pulled open the glove compartment. She gasped.

"How much?" Peter asked, unable to look as he steered the car around yet another treacherous bend.

Julia picked up the huge wad of Swiss francs and quickly flicked through them.

"Must be twenty or thirty thousand francs. How much is that?"

"About ten thousand quid. Hablinski's been generous."

"But why, Peter? Why's he doing this?"

Peter shrugged.

"I'm not sure," he said. Leaning into his trouser pocket, he pulled out the envelope containing the marriage certificate and passed it to Julia. She glanced at it for a moment.

"Does this mean he wants you to challenge my father for the title in the courts?"

Again Peter shrugged.

"That was my first reaction, too," he said hesitantly, "but now I really don't know."

* * * * * *

Night was falling fast. They had abandoned the car in the local town, bought new clothes and thrown their old ones away in case they concealed a bugging device, and then hitched forty or fifty miles with several different vehicles along little used mountain roads until they had reached a tiny hamlet nestling at the foot of a mountain pass. And at each stage in their journey Peter had checked and double checked to make sure that they were not being followed. Yet all the while he had been becoming increasingly certain that the precautions he was taking were completely unnecessary.

Peter had originally intended to cross the mountain pass before nightfall, but the car in which they had been travelling had dropped them off in the village and they had been unable to hitch another ride.

As they entered the tiny village square they could see only one place in which they could stay, a small inn with bright yellow light emanating from the windows set into its ancient oak framed walls. They pushed open the door and entered a room from which stags heads seemed to peer down at them from every wall.

There were only a few customers in the bar, a group of gnarled old men sitting round a table reserved for regulars and a middle aged couple sitting by the window. Nodding a silent greeting, Peter approached the bar.

A side door opened and an old woman appeared from the kitchen carrying two steaming bowls of soup. She flicked a suspicious glance at the newcomers before serving the soup to the middle aged couple. Then she returned to the bar and addressed them in an incomprehensible Germanic tongue.

"Do you speak English?" Peter asked.

The woman nodded.

"A little."

"We need a room for the night."

The old woman eyed Julia cautiously, clearly anxious about her age.

"One room?" she asked.

Peter nodded.

She frowned.

"Are you English?"

Peter nodded.

"I will need to see your passports."

"We don't have any with us."

"I need passports. I must register you for local tax. They are very strict in this canton and I will lose my licence if I am caught. If you have no papers I am afraid you cannot stay here."

Peter's face fell.

"Is there anywhere else?"

The old woman shook her head.

141

"Not in this village. But why do you not have papers? How did you get into Switzerland without papers?"

"They were stolen."

The woman looked palpably relieved.

"So you must have the special temporary papers issued by the police. They will do."

Peter was tiring of the conversation. He reached into his pocket and pulled out a five hundred franc note.

"It's late," he said, "and we need a room. Do you have one?"

The old woman was staring at the crisp new banknote in Peter's hand. Her mind made up, she quietly collected a key from behind the bar and led them up a narrow wooden staircase to a small bedroom. Then, without another word, she took the bank note and scuttled off down the stairs.

Peter watched her go and then pushed the bedroom door closed. A discreet sign on the door showed that they had paid more than four times the usual price of the room.

Exhausted, he threw himself down on the bed.

"If she's anything to go by, Hablinski was right," he said angrily.

Julia sat down wearily beside him and looked at his drawn features.

"What do you mean by that?"

"Democracy is a sham. If you've got the cash, you can buy your way out of anything. What the hell if some Swiss law says you need papers so long as you've got a five hundred franc note."

Julia frowned.

"Are you really surprised by that?" she asked.

Peter's face lightened.

"No, Julia. I understood that well enough when I used to sleep rough. But I never really stopped to think about it before."

Julia rose from the bed, removed her overcoat and washed her face in the sink. As she turned on the tap, it made a noisy gurgling sound which continued for some time after the tap was switched off. Finally she turned towards Peter.

"What's going on?" she asked.

Peter lifted himself from the bed and removed his overcoat and sweater. Then he joined Julia by the sink and splashed cold water on his face. Only when he had finished did he look up at her.

"How would you feel if someone had offered you the chance to rule the world, Julia?"

She stared at him in astonishment.

"What are you talking about?"

"It's Hablinski's offer. I think it's what he's putting on the table.

The car, the money, it was just his way of saying to me that I was free to choose without pressure, that I could bring you away with me and decide for myself."

Julia was staring at him blankly.

"What do mean rule the world? We're talking about an Earldom, aren't we?"

Suddenly, without really knowing why, he reached towards her perplexed face and pulled it towards his own, kissing her gently on the lips.

"Over the years Hablinski has built in the name of your father's Earldom a business empire of unimaginable size. He believes he has gathered together under his control enough money and power to exert effective control over even the most powerful of governments. And now he has grown old and wants to bequeath his empire to someone who will govern it wisely."

Julia suddenly burst out laughing.

"And he's chosen you?"

The expression on her face made him stop short.

"Yes," he said.

"What's so special about you?"

He stepped back from her.

"I thought you loved me. I thought you wanted to share your life with me."

Again she laughed.

"I do want to share my life with you. You're a pretty good sort of bloke for an erstwhile tramp. But you're not God, you know."

Her words echoed around inside his head and again he stepped backwards. And suddenly, for the first time in a long time, certainly for the first time since his grandmother had walked into his bedroom at Harry's and told him he was the Earl of Southdown, he felt utterly and totally foolish.

Julia turned to the mirror over the sink and straightened her hair.

"Come on," she said. "Follow me. This isn't London and if we don't go down soon the cook will go home. And then for all your magnificent powers we'll have to go to bed hungry."

Without a word, Peter followed her down to the dining room. The regular drinkers had all gone, and they sat alone as the old woman scuttled grumpily backwards and forwards to the kitchen fetching their food.

"O.K., Julia," he said when they were alone. "What do you think I should do? I didn't ask for all the things in my life to happen to me. I didn't ask to be abandoned before I can remember so that I could be

passed around an endless series of institutions until I was old enough
to be chucked out. I didn't ask to sleep rough on the streets of London
because nobody cared what happened to me. And I certainly haven't
asked to be told by a fantastically rich old man that I can inherit a
fortune which will give me the power to challenge governments. But I
have been offered, and now I have to decide what to do. So should I
accept, or should I send him this damned marriage certificate in the
post and walk away?"

Julia looked at him cynically.

"Don't act the innocent, Peter. You knew perfectly well when you
began your quest that the Earldom of Southdown would make you an
enormously rich and powerful man. It didn't stop you moving heaven
and earth to grab it. You just seem to have inherited even more than
you bargained for, that's all."

Peter slumped back forlornly in his chair. He knew she was right,
that when his grandmother had told him about the fortune which
could be his he had acted with undue haste, that he had never really
stopped to contemplate the reasons behind trying to lay claim to such
a vast fortune. He had of course constructed all sorts of reasons which
could justify his actions: revenge for the injustices inflicted on his
family; a desire to escape from his hum-drum life as an ill-educated
member of some kind of urban underclass; a need for a feeling of
self-worth and importance. But now he saw that they had all been
nothing but excuses, crude attempts to allay his own inner doubts
about what exactly he was attempting to do.

"Why did you read those history books?" she asked suddenly.

Her words cut across his thoughts.

"I don't know ... I was interested, I suppose."

She smiled.

"You've always wanted the power to control, haven't you? The
power to move events on a grand scale. The power to make history
rather than merely participate in it."

He thought for a moment.

"I've known what it's like to be powerless," he offered.

She looked at him wryly.

"If you take such power for yourself then others will be as powerless as you were once. Doesn't that worry you?"

Peter remembered the fast set of London life, the opinion-formers
and power-brokers of a supposedly sophisticated democracy he had
seen around him every day, looking down on him and his cardboard
boxes with that strange mixture of pity and hate. If he had had
sufficient money and clothes to be allowed to converse with them,

they would have talked about pluralism and democracy and a caring compassionate society. You could see it in their faces. They were proud of the way they used their power, but they didn't use it wisely.

He looked at Julia.

"Despite appearances, I don't think Hablinski's all bad," he said. "I think he wants to clean up his act before he dies, to leave a memorial which is more than that of a corrupt Mafia boss. And the power exists, it's a simple fact. If I don't take it, all that will happen is that it will fall into somebody else's hands. Maybe even somebody like your brother."

Julia looked at him sadly.

"You're a good man, Peter. I recognised that from the outset. But they say that power corrupts and absolute power corrupts absolutely. I've seen it happen in my brother James. I don't want it to happen to you, that's all."

Peter remained silent for a long time. Then he looked up at her.

"I'll promise you something, Julia. Right here and now. If you ever tell me to abandon the Earldom, to smash Hablinski's empire into a thousand tiny fragments and walk away into suburban obscurity, then I'll do it."

She looked at him long and hard. And then she leaned across the table and kissed him gently on the forehead.

"One day," she said softly, "I might just hold you to that promise."

FIVE YEARS LATER

Peter Kirby Fitzpatrick Troughton, the 16th Earl of Southdown, lifted his eyes from the thick gold-encrusted file lying on the desk before him and gazed out across the broad expanse of water beyond the glass. The late afternoon sun was glinting off the ornamental lake, causing the thin ripples pushed up by the breeze to shimmer with that delicate clarity peculiar to a late English summer.

Rising to his feet, he started to pace up and down, moodily gazing down at the smooth white marble beneath his feet. He was able to walk for some considerable distance in each direction before he reached the turn, because the personal office through which he was pacing, the inner sanctum he had made his own private preserve, was the white gallery at Southdown House. It was the same room in which his wife, the Countess Julia, had lain on the floor as a child and dreamed of a future which had now arrived, gazing above her at the vast choir of angels flying down from on high. Peter had added a large inlaid walnut desk to the collection of Queen Anne chairs which had dotted the room for many years, yet other than that he had changed little in the white gallery or indeed in the rest of Southdown House, preferring to leave the domestic arrangements to Julia's father.

He stopped pacing and stood beside one of the long windows overlooking the formal gardens. In the distance he could just see the thin aquiline figure of his father-in-law, his faithful dog as ever by his side. He was setting off for his late afternoon walk in the woods beyond the gardens, a routine repeated every day at exactly this hour. Always a man of regular habits, he had become even more so since his loss of the Earldom. Yet he appeared to be content in his new-found role as estate manager, rarely leaving the confines of Southdown House. It was as if he had finally permitted himself to withdraw completely from the real world, happy enough to allow others to assume responsibilities which he had always found burdensome.

When it had finally come the formal transfer of the Earldom to Peter had been swift and painless. The marriage certificate had been filed, the incumbent Earl had freely acknowledged the legitimacy of the claimant, and the House of Lords had been left with little alternative but to grant him the title.

To this day it made Peter smile to remember the day when Hablinski had broken the news to James Troughton that he had switched sides. At his request the young Viscount had come to Hablinski's Hampstead house and settled himself into one of the large leather armchairs with all his customary smug self-confidence. Hablinski had then entered the room alone while Peter watched the encounter through a hidden camera.

At first Hablinski had said nothing, waiting patiently while the young man presented a series of wholly absurd ideas for new business initiatives. And then, quite without warning, Hablinski had told him that he had reached the conclusion that the young man known as Peter Kirby would have to be recognised as the rightful Earl.

James had stopped in mid-sentence, his mouth wide open. But then he had risen to his feet and started moving menacingly towards Hablinski. The butler, who had quietly entered the room during the course of the exchange, had stepped smartly forward and caught firmly hold of his arm. Once restrained, James's anger rose to new heights. He spat and cursed, foam running down his cheeks like a rabid animal. But all the time the butler held him firmly in his grasp, waiting patiently for the storm to subside.

Eventually the tempest finally abated. James had slumped silently back in the armchair and listened while Hablinski had coldly dictated the arrangements for the transfer of power. James's grandmother, the Dowager Countess Alexandra, was to be allowed to leave England and live out the rest of her life in quiet obscurity. But Hablinski had different plans for James. He had always considered him a menace to society, an evil perverted creature whose bizarre sexual activities had gone unchecked for far too long. And if the old Earl had been too spineless to exert any effective discipline over him then Hablinski was not. So James was to be quietly certified by two doctors and removed to a private psychiatric clinic owned by Gamma Holdings where he could live out the rest of his natural life without harming others.

And so one chapter had closed and another begun. The true line had been restored, the injustices of the past put right. And Peter Kirby had at last entered into his inheritance as the new Earl of Southdown.

Peter turned and looked at the portrait of his grandfather hanging over the fireplace. He stood tall and upright, his proud face surveying an unseen view, and now more than ever before Peter could see the strength of likeness in the portrait. He paused, wondering what his grandfather would have made of the extraordinary wave of events which had brought his grandson, the sole direct descendent of a clandestine romance with a servant girl, to such an extraordinary pinnacle of power.

For Peter now understood that Hablinski had not been exaggerating when he had described the vast extent of his fortune and the power which was its necessary corollary. In nearly every country around the globe, shielded behind a complex network of subsidiary holding companies, the long arm of Gamma reached into every corner of economic activity, dominating and controlling even where it did not formally own. And as the new young Earl had travelled and studied under Hablinski's careful guidance, he had come to see that the old man's declared goal of global domination was a far from idle dream.

But it was more than the sheer size of the empire he had inherited which had come as a surprise. For he had also discovered that the crude Mafia-style brutality with which Hablinski had built his empire in the early post-war decades had almost completely ceased. Gamma Holdings had become such a powerful player on the economic scene that raw violence was hardly ever required. If a rival company posed a commercial threat, it could be purchased; if national politicians or the grandees of some upstart international institution sought to control, they could be bought off. Where previously the gun had been required, the chequebook now sufficed. It seemed it had all collapsed into a money game, and Gamma Holdings had the money.

For five long years Peter had struggled to understand the intricacies of the business empire over which he would one day assume full control. It had been a hard task for a young man with painfully little formal education: sometimes he had despaired of being able to match Hablinski's instinctive grasp of the endless power game in which he was involved. But in recent months he had begun to sense in himself a new confidence, a growing ability to take decisions involving the lives of millions of people, moving the pieces around on the giant chess board with a new decisiveness and authority.

Yet despite his new-found confidence he knew that he was still the trainee, still waiting in the wings until the master died. For he understood full well that Hablinski was not the sort of man to retire into quiet meditation in the evening of his life. The manipulation of power was his whole being, and he would continue to sit inside one of his many identical private offices, pulling the levers of power until he drew his last breath.

His thoughts were interrupted by the sound of an approaching car. Peter smiled wryly, not needing to look out of the window to see who the unexpected visitor could be. For filling the previously tranquil summer air, growing ever louder as the car approached, was the heavy rhythmic thumping of overloud reggae.

A few minutes later the door to the white gallery swung wide open and Leroy strode into the room, clutching under his arm an enormous bundle of papers. Peter started walking the considerable distance towards him.

"Your office is too big, man," Leroy said, displaying his still perfect set of gleaming teeth.

Peter grinned.

"I know," he said. "But I like it. It's got a good view."

Leroy stared out of the window.

"Mine's better," he replied with a malicious grin.

Peter remembered the weeks he had spent sharing Leroy's bedroom at the top of the tower block. The view had indeed been fine, an aerial view of the affluent heart of London from a downtown slum.

"To what do I owe the pleasure?" Peter asked.

Leroy looked at him askance.

"'To what do I owe the pleasure?'" he mimicked. "You're starting to talk like a toff, man. You ought to watch it. It's me, Leroy, remember."

Peter looked at him and frowned.

"Of course I remember. How could I ever forget?"

They were silent for a while, but then Leroy shoved the papers in his hand at Peter.

"What's all this rubbish I find in my office, man?" he said.

Peter took the papers and glanced through them. They related to an urban renovation programme instituted some years before by Gamma Holdings.

He shrugged.

"How should I know? It's your programme. I just pay for it."

"There's a twenty per cent capital programme budget cut. That's too much, man!"

Peter frowned.

"It's got to be reined back, Leroy. You think money grows on trees."

Leroy grunted. Then he paced over to one of the Queen Anne chairs and sat down.

"Don't think there's no gratitude out there on the streets. Gamma's programme for attacking urban poverty is recognised even by some of the most determined grumblers as being the first serious attack on the problem for years. But you're still only papering over the cracks. There's plenty of work which still needs to be done."

Peter stood by the window and looked at Leroy's anxious face. He had aged and mellowed considerably since that bleak night on the dark walkway when they had first met. Responsibility and hope had numbed the grim humour of the ghetto, forcing Leroy to face up to difficult questions which he had never before addressed. But if his humour had faded, the sense of almost revolutionary zeal which had always been apparent had found new vigour.

The urban renovation programme had been Leroy's brainchild, a way of harnassing a small part of Gamma's vast wealth to the needs and interests of the urban poor for whom he had always cared. He had sold the idea to Peter, and Peter had sold the idea to Hablinski. And then the money had begun to flow, pouring economic wealth and expertise into some of the grimmest areas in Britain and around the world, bringing hope to people who had started to lose all faith. It had not been without a price for Gamma, since the investments freely undertaken were amongst the least profitable in the company's portfolio. But it had also brought a considerable gain in terms of political influence, surrounding Gamma with a new aura of political respectability which did much to ameliorate the sense of fear which had hitherto been its only trademark.

"How much do you need?" Peter asked quietly.

Leroy looked at him with a surprised expression.

"Another billion a year over each of the next five years will help, channelled mainly towards infrastructure and the construction industry. People want real jobs to do, not just welfare handouts."

Peter walked over from the window and sat down opposite Leroy.

"Do you really think I've become a toff?" he asked.

Leroy looked at him thoughtfully for a moment and then shook his head.

"No," he said. "Not yet."

Peter leant back in his chair.

"You don't approve of me living here, do you? I should perhaps have taken a flat in your tower block, somewhere where I could see the problems with my own two eyes. Instead I'm living here in this over-large palace as if I was the Sun King."

Leroy fidgeted uncomfortably in his seat.

"Why're you asking me all this, man? You don't really want to know, do you?"

Peter shook his head sadly.

"I'm not sure I do, but you can tell me anyway if you like."

Leroy stopped fidgeting and met Peter's gaze.

"You scare me a bit, man, that's all."

"I scare you. Why?"

"I don't know. It's probably not you, because you never scared me when you was poor. It's probably all this money you've got."

"I'm trying to use it wisely."

Leroy smiled gently.

"I know you are. Really I do. But what if you stopped using it wisely? What if you woke up one morning and changed your mind. Because you can do what the hell you like with it all, can't you? You've become like some kind of god."

He could see the anxiety in Leroy's face as he realised what he had just said. He had come to ask for more money for his pet project, not to utter words which would cause offence to the rich benefactor on whose munificence the success of the whole programme depended.

Peter was still sitting opposite him. He rose silently to his feet and walked towards his desk. Only when he was behind the desk did he turn to face his friend.

"You must excuse me, Leroy," he said stiffly, looking down at the papers on the desk. "I've got a lot of work to do."

Leroy rose to his feet with a glum expression.

"I didn't mean to offend you, man," he said sadly, turning and walking quietly away. He had already opened the door and was about to leave when he heard Peter call his name. He turned.

"Thanks for coming, Leroy," Peter said quietly, looking sadly at his departing friend. "I'll see what I can do about the money."

Moments later he was once again alone. He sat down quietly at his desk and flicked a switch to activate a small computer screen. Moments later the order had been given, the order which would sanction the contracts required to reverse the planned clawback in capital allowances which had prompted Leroy's unexpected visit. And as his fingers touched the buttons he knew that it was only his debt of gratitude to a man who had saved his life which had prompted him to do it.

He had hoped that the giving of the order would reassure him, helping him to justify the possession of power through its generous application to alleviate social ills. But instead of making him feel better it only seemed to make him feel worse. He stared at his fingers in a kind of numbed surprise, wondering how it had come to be that they could wield so much power as they played over the tiny computer screen, stimulating electronic impulses which would trigger thousands of people in every walk of life to dance to his tune and his tune alone.

Angry with himself at the mood of melancholy sweeping over him, he closed down the computer terminal and walked silently towards the window. Looking down, he could see Julia talking quietly to Leroy beside his car. Leroy smiled at her, kissed her on the cheek, and then stepped deftly into the car and roared off down the drive. Grateful that he had gone, Peter waited until the music could no longer be heard and then left the white gallery, walking through the silent house towards the front door.

He found Julia outside in the garden, carefully tending some roses which had recently become her pride and joy. She looked up reproachfully as he approached.

"What did you say to Leroy?" she asked.

Peter shrugged.

"Nothing. Why?"

"He seemed unusually subdued. Not at all his usual self. I asked him to stay to dinner but he wouldn't."

Peter snorted.

"He wanted more money. I've just given it to him. I don't see that's anything for him to feel subdued about."

Julia said nothing. Instead, she turned deliberately away and continued to pluck the deadheads from the rose bushes.

Peter caught her arm. He felt unusually lonely, which was why he had sought out her company.

"Sorry, my love," he said softly. "I didn't mean to sound so short."

She stopped fiddling with the roses and turned to face him.

"Did he say something which upset you?"

Peter nodded.

"Do you think I'm acting like a god?"

She started to laugh.

"Is that what Leroy said?"

"Yes. He said I scared him, that I'm acting like a god."

"I'm sure he didn't mean it badly. Leroy is very fond of you."

Peter looked at her smiling face.

"You haven't answered the question," he said firmly.

She grew serious.

"I imagine people with power have always looked like gods to those who don't," she said. "There's nothing new in that."

He shrugged.

"Does it worry you?" he asked.

She looked at him.

"It's different for me. Easier, perhaps. I've grown up with money so I'm used to bossing people around. Unlike me, you had nothing. I suppose it makes it harder for you to give the orders."

"Is it a problem?"

"A problem but also an advantage. Because you were once so powerless you try to use your new-found power wisely. Anyone including Leroy can see that."

Peter shrugged again.

"I try," he said. "But it doesn't alter the fact that the power is mine for the asking. I gave Leroy the money he wanted because it was my whim to do so. It doesn't seem an entirely satisfactory basis for taking decisions."

Julia was about to say something, but before she had a chance to speak one of the maids appeared at the front door of the house.

"There's a telephone call for your lordship from Mr Hablinski's office," she called. "They say it's important."

With a silent glance at Julia, whose liking for the old serpent was still no greater than it had been before, Peter turned and walked towards the house. Taking the hall phone from the maid, he listened silently for several minutes. By the time he handed the phone back to the maid, Julia had joined him from the garden. She could see the grim expression on his face.

"What's happened?" she said.

"Hablinski's had a heart attack. His doctors don't think he's going to last more than twenty-four hours. They haven't told him anything but he seems to have worked it out for himself."

"And he wants to see you?"

"Not just me. He has specifically asked to see us both."

* * * * * *

The limousine swept through the broad iron gates into the grounds of Hablinski's Hampstead home. Although the sun was sinking lower in the sky it was still shining brightly, but it did little to overcome the air of gloom and despondancy which hung over the grim Victorian structure of the old man's private abode.

As the car pulled to a halt, Peter stepped swiftly out and climbed the steps to the house. But then he paused and turned, waiting for Julia to join him. She was slowly climbing the steps, anxiety at the coming encounter clearly written on her face. During the years in which she had been married to Peter, she had seen Hablinski as little as possible. It had been an arrangement which had seemed to suit them both, because Hablinski appeared to feel as uncomfortable in Julia's presence as she was in his. Yet now, strangely, Hablinski had specifically requested that she be present by his bedside.

The door opened and Hablinski's butler appeared. After his rise to the Earldom, Peter had realised that 'butler' was something of a misnomer for Dmitri Petrovski. For in truth he was the closest thing Hablinski possessed to a confidant, a kind of intimate personal advisor who seemed to understand almost instinctively his master's wishes. Indeed, it had been Petrovski who had undertaken much of the more mundane aspects of Peter's initiation into the complex workings of Gamma Holdings, teaching him to recognise and replicate the reactions of his master in a whole variety of difficult business dilemmas.

Petrovski's face was grim and drawn.

"Thank you for coming so swiftly, my lord," he began.

Despite having been his teacher for many years, Petrovski always referred to Peter as 'my lord'. Yet there was no trace of sarcasm in his voice, only a deep respect which Peter had been forced to conclude was a reflection of his master's wishes.

"How is he?" Peter asked.

153

Petrovski frowned.

"Weak. The doctors say he will not last the night."

Peter nodded.

"I don't need to ask why he isn't in hospital, I suppose."

Petrovski tried to smile.

"You know the master. He does not like to be away from the levers of power for an instant, even when he knows he is dying."

Peter looked into Petrovski's expressionless face.

"Are you sure he knows?"

Petrovski nodded slowly.

"I am sure that he knows. That is why he asked to see you both."

For a second he flicked a thoughtful glance at Julia, a glance which suggested that he knew why she too had been summoned to Hablinski's bedside. It was a look heavy with meaning.

Moments later Petrovski had led them up the stairs and steered them into Hablinski's bedroom.

The room was not large, completely dominated by a heavy oak four-poster draped with dark red damask curtains. The old man was lying in the centre of the bed, his naturally slender form looking even more sallow than usual as he lay between the bedclothes. His eyes were closed, making it appear as if he had already sunk into a coma.

Julia hung back by the door and Peter approached the bed alone. Sitting down on the ornate quilt, he touched Hablinski's cold hand.

"Axel," he called gently.

The old man's eyes slowly opened and he looked blankly at Peter.

"Where is she?" he asked. "I thought I left instructions for you both to come."

Peter flicked a glance at Julia to tell her that she should approach. Reluctantly she did so, perching herself uncomfortably at the far end of the bed.

Hablinski smiled weakly at her.

"That you for coming to see the old serpent before he dies," he said.

She smiled faintly but said nothing, trying hard to avoid his gaze. His face twisted into an odd kind of grimace.

"Do you hate me so very much?" he began, and his voice seemed to croak under the strain of speech.

She shook her head.

"No, Uncle. I don't hate you."

Again he smiled.

"You lie to appease a dying man. That is typical of your kindness and I am proud of you for that. It shows that you are better than I can ever be. My only mistake was to fail to recognise your qualities far earlier."

This time Julia could not help herself. She looked up at him with a confused expression, uncertain why he had addressed her in that way.

Hablinski laughed.

"I am a man of surprises, Julia. Of that at least you should be aware."

She nodded.

"And with what do you wish to surprise me today, Uncle?"

Hablinski turned to Peter.

"Young man," he said, "would you be so kind as to lift me a little higher. I have become a little weak."

Peter leant forward and lifted Hablinski back onto the pillows. As he did so, he noticed how light he had become, as if his body was physically ebbing away with every passing minute.

From his vantage point propped up on the pillows, he fixed Julia with a penetrating stare from which she did not dare look away.

"What do you remember about your mother?" he asked.

She shrugged. Peter knew it was a subject she preferred to avoid.

"I don't remember much about her. I was only five years old when she died."

"But do you remember anything?"

A perplexed and anguished look came over Julia's face.

"I remember her smell. The smell of roses. Her face I only know from photographs. But why are you asking me, Uncle?"

Hablinski turned to Peter.

"Why is she not yet pregnant?" he demanded curtly.

Peter looked at him with open amazement.

"She's only twenty-one, Axel. Give us a chance."

Hablinski checked himself.

"I'm sorry. Sometimes I forget your extreme youth. But I hope you are planning to have children. It is important to me that you should have children."

Julia looked at him with surprise.

"You're a strange person to say that, Uncle. You never had any children."

Hablinski eyes drifted back to her. He seemed to be growing more tired, visibly fading under the stress of their conversation.

"Didn't I?" he whispered, not taking his eyes off her for a second.

Julia was sitting rigidly at the end of the bed, staring at the old man lying before her. She swallowed hard, making an extreme effort to control herself.

"What are you saying, Uncle? I don't understand you."

With an effort Hablinski lifted his arm and indicated a small vase of roses beside the bed.

"You were right to remember the roses. Your mother always wore a rose scent."

The look of horror was growing ever more pronounced on Julia's face. She said nothing, not daring to speak the words.

"Yes, Julia. That is why I have called you to be beside me when I die. The man you call your father is not really your father at all. He was just the front man, in this as in all else. He was only ever a front man."

She looked at him numbly.

"You?" she mouthed.

He nodded slowly.

"Your mother was a fine woman. She was young, vivacious, intelligent and ambitious, a woman who could have become something in her own right if she had so wished. Instead she agreed to help me complete the inheritance for which I have strived."

Julia was still sitting speechless at the end of the bed, staring at the man she had always loathed but who now claimed to be her father. He looked at her sadly.

"It was one of the biggest mistakes I made in my life to think that James was a more worthy successor than you," he muttered.

Peter looked sharply at him.

"So that's why you let him live. I always wondered why you spared him."

Hablinski nodded.

"James is sick. He may be my only son but he is sick. And despite the filthy things his sickness has caused him to do I could not bring myself to order his death."

Peter glanced at Julia. The numbness appeared to be passing, but he could already see that it was gradually being replaced by a seething anger. But for the moment she said nothing.

"And is that why you made me Earl?" Peter asked quietly.

Hablinski flicked an irritated glance towards him, and suddenly Peter realised how utterly unimportant he was in the old man's calculations. He had just happened to appear in the right place at the right time, a suitable and necessary stud to ensure Hablinski's genes transcended his own inevitable mortality.

Hablinski must have read his thoughts.

"You have played your part with a commendable zeal," he said. "When you first appeared out of nowhere I believed you could rip away everything for which I had worked so hard. I was determined to stop you, to wipe you out before you could pose a real threat. But then you fell in love with my daughter and I began to see that I might be able to write you a different part to play. As you correctly surmised, my son's violent excesses were becoming so extreme that even I, his own father, could not escape the inevitable conclusion that he was stark raving mad. So I began to look at Julia more carefully, wondering whether you might between you hold the secret to my succession ..."

Julia suddenly rose to her feet.

"You filthy bastard," she cried. "You knew what James was doing to those children in that house where he kept them, didn't you? You could have stopped it if you'd wanted to. But you just let him carry on. You didn't give a damn."

Hablinski sank back onto the pillows under the strength of her verbal onslaught. It was clear that her words had wounded him, pinpointing a deep sense of guilt and shame that lurked within him with a savage accuracy.

"It was not so easy as you suppose," he said. "James had vast power in his own right, just as your husband now does. Until I was sure of you, sure you would not throw everything I had built away, I could not dare to challenge him openly."

Julia looked at Hablinski with a look of profound contempt.

"You didn't need either of us. Your whole corrupt empire was not worth one of those children you allowed your son and his friends to molest."

Hablinski smiled at her.

"That was always the side of you that frightened me, Julia. It is your mother's side, a soft and sentimental side. It was the side I always saw when you were a child. But now that you are growing older I see another side, my side, and I know that you will be capable of bearing me heirs who are worthy of my life's work."

The arrogance and confidence with which he delivered these words temporarily reduced his daughter to silence. She stood up and walked away from the bed, standing with her back to them beside the window.

Peter looked at Hablinski. The exertion had tired him, and he had sagged back onto the pillows.

"Why did you tell her? Was it really necessary that she should know?"

Hablinski looked at him.

"I judged it so. I thought it might assist you."

"Me? Why should it assist me?"

"I judge she is the weak link, not you. She is the one who might throw it all away. I wanted her to understand that she carries my blood within her veins, that as my daughter she shares my guilt as well as my inheritance. It will make her think again about herself, gird herself up for the challenge that will soon be upon you both."

There was something about Hablinski's words which made Peter stop in his tracks. Hablinski smiled slyly.

"There will be a challenge," he repeated slowly.

Peter glanced at Julia. She was standing looking out of the window, apparently not listening to their conversation.

"Why should there be a challenge? Why now?"

"Because I am dying. You understand that I am dying, of course."

Peter looked at him for a few seconds.

"Yes," he replied. "I know you are dying."

Hablinski seemed to relax, pleased that Peter was not going to make some pathetic attempt to protect his sensibilities by denying the truth. Then he closed his eyes briefly, as if trying to summon up the strength to explain his fears.

"You are aware of my theory of the danger zone."

Peter nodded.

"Yes," he replied. "It is a period of time when Gamma Holdings has become sufficiently powerful to seriously threaten major governmental institutions without being powerful enough to overcome all challenges. During this interval of time, it is possible that a concerted international attempt will be made to break the company's power before it is too late. I am also aware of your belief that we are now in the danger zone and that it will last for a further ten years or so, after which Gamma will have become sufficiently influential to destroy all further challenges."

Hablinski nodded.

"I believe that my death, once it becomes public knowledge, will precipitate the challenge."

Peter sighed.

"And who do you think will be the one to coordinate this challenge?"

Hablinski smiled.

"You are really no fool," he said. "You have learnt your lessons well. You ask me immediately who is the focus of opposition, who it is who must be broken on the wheel."

"And the answer?"

"I believe it will be Ronald McKenna, the new President of the United States ..."

Peter looked at him askance.

"McKenna? But I thought his election was largely funded by Gamma?" Peter interjected.

Hablinski grunted.

"So it was. But I have received information that McKenna is very resentful of our patronage during the election. He strains at the leash and craves to break free. If he sees a chance, I believe he will release the dogs."

Again Peter glanced at Julia. She was still standing by the window with her back averted, but now he could tell that she was listening carefully to every word that Hablinski uttered.

"And your advice?" Peter asked.

Hablinski shrugged.

"At first you must try to head him off. Dance and weave and dodge. Without conceding an inch, try to appear reasonable and conciliatory. But then, if he persists, you will be left with no choice but to act decisively. Vice-President Smith is far more pliant, a fool who craves nothing but the outer trappings of office."

Suddenly Julia turned to face them both. The anger on her face had if anything grown even more intense.

"Why don't you stop speaking in riddles, Hablinski?" she shouted. "You just mean kill him, don't you? You mean reach for your chequebook and pay someone to kill the President of the United States, just as you have paid to kill so many others in the past."

Hablinski sunken eyes swung away from Peter to meet his daughter's angry face. They seemed to smile, as if relishing the fire he had aroused in her.

"Before it was so easy for you, little Countess," he whispered. "You could blame the old serpent for everything that was distasteful or unpleasant and retain for yourself an aura of sanctimonious superiority. But now, I fear, you must learn to think for yourself."

Julia moved forward, trying to think of some appropriate riposte, but before she could speak Hablinski's whole body seemed to contort into spasm and his face was filled with an intense burning pain. And then, before either of them could say or do anything, he fell back limply on the bed.

* * * * * *

It had begun under the guise of an anti-trust action in the US Federal Courts. But although the argument was technical, the language couched in the strange rambling dialect of the legal profession, there could be no longer be any doubt that Hablinski's prophecy was beginning to unfold. Ronald McKenna, the very candidate Gamma Holdings had so recently bought and bribed and financed into the Presidency, was trying to break free of his paymasters.

At first little had happened. Gamma's lawyers, including many of the best paid in the land, had done exactly as Hablinski had recommended they do. They had weaved and dodged and squirmed, introducing one technical obstacle after another to prevent the courts from moving against the core of Gamma's crucial American power-base. For months they had succeeded, but the President had persisted, the courts had somehow seemed to sense his determination, and now the tactics of filibuster and delay were finally beginning to crumble into dust.

Peter flicked a switch on his desk in the tiny windowless office he had made his own since shortly after Hablinski's death. The room sank into darkness, leaving only a few tiny lights on the console before him glimmering in the gloom. The office was an exact replica of the one in which Hablinski had once worked, newly installed at Peter's instructions in the basement of Southdown House. It was linked to all the other identical offices in other Gamma offices around the world with the most secure computer technology money could buy.

Peter relished the sense of almost total blackness which now engulfed him. He allowed it to seep through his body, soothing and softening the pain of the decisions he had recently found himself obliged to take. They had been hard decisions, and although he was sometimes filled with a kind of nervous exhilaration at the power he now possessed, there was often a sense of bitter resentment at having been thrust so young into such an awesome position. Today was one such occasion, a day when only darkness brought relief.

A soft knock at the door reminded him that for the owner of Gamma Holdings such relief could never be more than temporary. He flicked a switch again and the room was filled with soft fluorescent light. Swivelling his chair round, he faced the door.

"Come in, Petrovski," he called, for he had recognised the respectful knock of Hablinski's erstwhile butler.

Petrovski entered the room and silently closed the door behind him. Officially he had assumed new duties as the butler at Southdown House, but unofficially he had continued in his role as intimate confidant to the ruler of the empire, seemingly content to serve his new young master with all the slavish devotion he had lavished on his predecessor.

"Well, Petrovski?" Peter asked, making an effort to suppress the vague irritation he always felt at the butler's excessively reserved and deferential manner.

"I hope I am not disturbing you, sir, but some news has reached me which I thought should be brought to your attention without delay."

Peter indicated a chair but Petrovski remained standing.

"And what is this news?"

"Our sources in the White House indicate that the President is considering raising the company's role in global economic affairs at the Security Council of the United Nations."

Peter looked at him sharply. He had been expecting the move, but its timing had come as a shock.

"When?"

"Soon. Possibly within the month. The President is apparently keen to resolve his dispute with Gamma by the time of the next Congressional elections. He does not wish to be seen as a man who tried but failed."

Peter's face sank. It was exactly the development he had feared, a development which could transform a series of rather poorly co-ordinated national attempts to bring Gamma to heel into a powerful single attack under the auspices of the ever more potent organs of the United Nations.

"Are our sources sure of this?" he asked.

Petrovski nodded.

"I fear so, sir. The President has already ordered papers to be prepared for submission to the Secretary General."

Peter looked at Petrovski's expressionless face. He was standing by the door, awaiting a single word, a word that would unleash the vast flow of cash required to 'act decisively' against President Ronald McKenna.

"You agree with my analysis that McKenna is the lynch-pin, of course?" Peter asked.

Petrovski's body seemed to relax by an infinitesimal degree at Peter's question and he stepped deferentially towards the console.

"May I, sir?" he asked, indicating the controls.

Peter nodded. Petrovski leaned over his shoulder and his fingers lightly touched a number of buttons. On the large wall screen beyond the console, a complex flow chart appeared.

"I took the liberty of preparing this some while ago. It lists the changes which I would expect to ensue from McKenna's ... removal."

Peter examined the chart. His own analysis was almost exactly the same in every respect. The first and most obvious consequence of McKenna's demise would be the automatic succession of Vice-President Smith, a weak and ineffective man who had been selected largely for his inability to offend any significant section of the American electorate. With Smith in the White House instead of McKenna, there seemed little doubt that the sting would rapidly fade from any further action against Gamma by the US authorities. And with the United States removed from the scene of battle, the other national challenges which had emerged in the wake of McKenna's powerful stand could be dealt with one by one through a variety of veiled threats and tempting promises. National leaders, fearful perhaps that they might soon meet the same fate as the American President, would be unlikely to try and invoke the intervention of the United Nations. Even if they did, the weakened posture of the United States would make it unlikely that effective action would emerge from the Security Council. The Secretary General of the United Nations, although himself no friend of Gamma Holdings, would be left powerless to act.

All this was summarised on Petrovski's flow chart. He had now retreated a respectful distance from the console and was waiting patiently for his master's response.

"Gamma's survival would seem to point to McKenna's removal, then," Peter muttered.

Petrovski nodded but said nothing. He knew Hablinski would not have hesitated in ordering the decisive strike, would perhaps have rejoiced at being able to consolidate his political stranglehold with so little loss of blood. But he was still uncertain how his new master would react.

Peter remained silent for a while, staring with unseeing eyes at the flow-chart on the wall. He wished Petrovski would go away, that he could once again plunge the room into darkness, but he just stood there silently.

"Can it be done?" he whispered.

Again Petrovski seemed to relax. He sensed his master was moving inexorably towards the right decision, forced along the narrow path by the ruthless logic of his own power. Again he took a small step forward.

"A straightforward assassination should not prove overly difficult, in view of our heavy penetration of the President's bodyguard. But there are several essential elements in any attempt which present particular difficulties. On the one hand, it must not be possible to trace the President's demise directly to any agents of Gamma Holdings. On the other hand, and apparently contradicting the first requirement, there must be absolutely no doubt in the mind of anyone of importance that Gamma was indeed responsible. So the question is not whether the President can be removed, but rather whether he can be removed in such a way as to fulfil the two requirements I have just specified ..."

He hesitated.

"And your proposal for meeting these two requirements?" Peter asked.

Petrovski lowered his eyes.

"I believe, sir, that you should invite the President to a private meeting, a meeting which should be held here at Southdown House. At this meeting you should try to resolve the differences between you."

Peter stared at him in amazement.

"A meeting! You must be crazy! McKenna would never agree to a meeting."

Petrovski's face remained passive.

"With respect, sir," he said, "it is my view that he would. Our sources within the White House, sources which are highly reliable, have indicated that McKenna is confident of his ability to outwit you. He believes you are not only young and inexperienced, but also lack the essential ruthlessness of Mr Hablinski in these matters. It is for this reason that he has chosen to act at the present time. The President would therefore be likely to view a private request for a personal meeting as a sign of weakness, an opportunity for you to try and negotiate a face-saving compromise. From the President's point of view, a negotiated agreement which critically weakens Gamma's position would be far better than all the uncertainties and imponderables of a protracted conflict which he knows he could yet lose. I therefore think he will agree to your request for a meeting."

Peter's head was spinning. As so often before the logic of Hablinski's methods, so accurately mirrored from beyond the grave in Petrovski's softly spoken words, seemed to have him tightly in their grasp. It was almost as if Hablinski were still alive.

"And the assassination?" he asked.

"It is essential to transmit to other world leaders the vital message that despite the change of management the vital interests of the company are not to be tampered with. It therefore follows that the President should meet with his unfortunate accident right in the middle of his visit."

Peter cast his eyes back uneasily at the flow chart taunting him on the wall. Yet he was already well aware of the logic of the argument, for there could be no escaping the fact that unless McKenna was removed speedily from the scene of battle the whole of the empire would crumble rapidly into dust. But despite the logic, despite the smooth rationality with which it presented itself to anyone who cared to look, he still felt unready to accept the inevitable conclusion.

"Leave me now," he said quietly, without looking round.

He waited silently until Petrovski had gone and then punched several more keys on the console. The flow-chart disappeared and was replaced by a series of graphs and diagrams, each summarizing Gamma operations in different sectors of the globe. He wanted to remind himself of what he already knew, that Gamma's activities were on the whole benign for the communities whose lives depended on them. The tighter the stranglehold, whether it was on a sector of an economy or a whole country, the better it appeared to be for those affected. For under Hablinski's and now his own tutelage Gamma had developed into a role model of high capitalism, an organism which cared not only for its own employees but also for the wider society in which it operated.

Gamma didn't just produce goods and services to satisfy a crude materialistic demand. It also concerned itself directly and indirectly with a whole variety of other tasks. It ensured political stability, because political stability was as essential requirement for successful business activity. It campaigned for and funded an efficiently-organised health service, because a healthy work-force was required for effective production. It built old people's homes and play centres for young children, because these were a crucial element in a society which was strong, stable and self-confident in the image of the company which dominated it. In the modern world, public relations had become a way of life, so Gamma offered the whole package, a secure life from cradle to grave. A closed system, perhaps, but a system in which it was possible for people to lead lives of fulfilment and personal satisfaction.

Peter's thoughts turned to Leroy, his erstwhile ally on the streets. His reconciliation with Gamma was typical of the reactions of so many who came into contact with the company's munificence. For while they might resent the extreme concentration of power in so few hands, they also valued the benign utilitarian manner in which that power was being exercised in order to create a society which was stable, happy and secure.

There was no doubt that Ronald McKenna had the power to undo all that. For McKenna didn't wish to break Gamma's power so that he in turn could do good in the world. It was far more straightforward than that. For all the rhetoric, he simply wished to grab a larger slice of power for himself, transferring a small portion of Peter's influence into his own grubby hands. And for the poor and disadvantaged in his country and elsewhere, there was little doubt that Ronald McKenna would be a far less benevolent ruler than Peter Kirby Troughton would ever be.

Suddenly he became aware of a small hand on his shoulder. He looked up and saw that Julia had quietly entered the room.

"You're in here again," she said softly, in the faintly disapproving tone with which she often spoke to him these days.

"Yes," he said. "I have to think."

"Why have you stopped working in the White Gallery, Peter?" she asked.

He flicked a glance at the console.

"I need this lot. You wouldn't really want all this junk up there, would you?"

She walked around to the far side of the console, leaning down on her elbows and fixing him with a penetrating stare.

"That's not the reason and you know it."

He looked at her sadly. He so badly wanted to tell her the truth, to tell her that he preferred to avoid the White Gallery precisely because it made him reflect. But she had been acting so strangely since Hablinski's death, becoming ever more withdrawn with every day that passed. It was as if she didn't wish to know about the vital decisions he was having to take about the company's future.

He stood up and leant over the console, kissing her gently on the cheek.

"I got more than I bargained for, didn't I?" he said with a wry smile.

She pushed him away.

"You've got too much, Peter. I'm not sure you can handle it. Sometimes I think the company controls you, that despite his death Hablinski is still in charge, controlling and manipulating you from beyond the grave."

Peter looked away.

"I'm trying to do something constructive with it. Use it responsibly. Look at that damned urban renewal programme I finance. When do you ever see young people on the streets of London these days? And who exactly do you think is responsible for providing them with jobs and decent housing? It's no good trying to liken me in every respect to your father."

She winced. The jibe was deliberate and she knew it. Whenever he wanted to hurt her, he always referred to Hablinski as her father, a

165

pointed reminder of her hereditary connection with the ruthless methods he had employed in building up the company, a veiled suggestion that somewhere beneath the soft exterior she was nothing more than a chip off the old block.

She looked at him strangely.

"What are you going to do about McKenna?" she asked.

The question caught him completely off guard. Of late she had asked him so little about the business, so little about anything beyond the trivial, that he had almost forgotten he had once supposed she could read his mind.

"What do you mean?" he asked.

There was a fire burning in her eyes which reminded him of her father.

"You know perfectly well what I mean. He hasn't just gone away, has he? In fact he's the main reason you sit down here in this stinking little hole every day. So now I'm asking what the result of all your deliberations has been. To put it bluntly, I'm asking you if you're going to follow my father's advice and order the assassination of President Ronald McKenna?"

Peter glanced at her. There was that sanctimonious sneer in her voice which he had always found difficult to tolerate, a holier than thou attitude which completely ignored the realities of the world in which they were both living. Her voice reminded him of pacifists who refused to take up arms against even the most ugly of enemies for fear they would jeopardise their own moral purity.

He thought of the billions of dollars the company had been pouring into social welfare projects around the globe at his personal behest, as Gamma Holdings began to turn its vast might on the myriad evils which beset the world's poor. For unlike Julia, he had personal experience of what it was like to be poor, powerless to help either himself or others. And now that he had the power, he was determined to use it wisely, to shelter and protect with effective measures backed up by hard cash those who were too weak to help themselves.

Again he thought of Ronald McKenna, a greedy self-serving politician who had never been poor and who cared nothing for the plight of those who were. There was not an ounce of benevolence in Ronald McKenna, and for all Julia's moral purity, McKenna would bring nothing but misery to the very people Peter wished to help if he succeeded in his struggle to break Gamma's power.

Peter looked into his wife's eyes. She was still waiting for an answer to her question. He dearly wished he could share her purity, preserve for himself the private cloak of respectability which came when others took the decisions. Yet he could not do so, for one of them at least would have to inhabit the real world in which the hard issues had to be faced.

But one of them was enough. McKenna was probably the last real obstacle, the last serious challenge which could not be bought off with cash alone. There was no need for her to know the truth, no need for her to suffer the agonies and dilemmas of a soldier in the front line.

He met her gaze full on.

"No, my love, I'm not going to assassinate Ronald McKenna. In fact I've decided to invite him to meet with me at Southdown House. We'll sit down together and try to reach a negotiated solution."

She nodded silently . And then, without a word, she walked quietly from the room and closed the door.

* * * * * *

It was the calm before the storm. The vast army of presidential security guards who had arrived at Southdown House several days before had long since finished their preparations and had melted unobtrusively into the background, uneasily sharing the servants' hall with Peter's own domestic and security staff. Southdown House itself had become a kind a neutral zone, checked and double checked by both sides to ensure that neither of the principle parties to the forthcoming summit would be under any physical risk during their two day encounter.

Peter paced apprehensively up and down the full length of the White Gallery, listening attentively for the sound of the President's approaching cavalcade sweeping along the drive towards the imposing classical portico below. He knew they had already left Windsor Castle, speeding their way towards West Sussex amidst a plethora of screeching police sirens and low flying helicopters. Soon, very soon perhaps, they would arrive, and Peter would descend with his wife to greet the President at the white curving steps which swept up from the drive to the main door.

Out of the corner of his eye he could see Julia. She was sitting bolt upright in one of the Queen Anne chairs, staring out of a tall window towards the ornamental lake. Still she carried the same sullen look she had carried for weeks, the tense and distant expression which suggested her mind was lost in some private thoughts in which he was not being invited to participate.

He forced himself to look away from her, to concentrate on the difficult opening meeting with the President which lay ahead. From an official perspective the visit to Southdown House was a strictly private affair. The President had already concluded a two day state visit to the United Kingdom. He had had talks with the Prime Minister and attended a formal banquet with the Queen at Windsor Castle. But in reality the state visit was merely a cover story, a series of photo opportunities behind which the President could accept an unexpected invitation to negotiate with the world's most powerful businessman.

Petrovski's sources within the White House had already confirmed the glee with which the McKenna had received Peter's invitation to direct talks at Southdown House. The proposal for a face-to-face meeting had come as a surprise to both the President and his staff, but they had interpreted it in exactly the way Petrovski had predicted, seeing in it a desire by the new young Earl to find a face-saving formula by which he could capitulate. And so, without undue hesitation, the President had agreed to the meeting and temporarily suspended his plans to raise the status of Gamma Holdings at the Security Council.

Yet despite the President's acceptance of his invitation to talks, Peter knew that the end game in which he was now involved would be far from straightforward. For he knew that McKenna would arrive in his limousine as a conquering hero, expecting instant concessions to prove that he had not been duped, and if he did not get those concessions there was a good chance he would simply walk out, return to Washington and summon an emergency meeting of the Security Council of the United Nations. And then, as Petrovski and he both clearly understood, all of their carefully laid plans would go astray.

A gentle hum slowly became audible. Peter stopped pacing up and down and looked out of the window. In the distance, beyond the formal flower beds which surrounded the House, he could see a long line of black limousines sweeping into view from behind the cover of the distant rhododendron bushes.

Julia rose to her feet, her flowing green dress reaching nearly to the floor.

"We'd better go down," she said quietly.

Peter took her by the hand, leading her through the corridors and down the grand staircase to the main hall. In the shadows, hidden away in little nooks and crannies, they were continually aware of the President's security team, advance emissaries of an occupying army preparing the ground for the arrival of a victorious enemy general.

Moments later they were outside and waiting at the end of the red carpet which stretched out from the House. There were seven sleek identical limousines in the approaching cavalcade, their windows covered in darkened glass so that it was impossible to see who was sitting within. If terrorists had attempted a strike at the President while he was travelling, they would have had to take out all of the cars in order to be sure they had achieved their objective.

The first three cars drove past the end of the red carpet and pulled to a halt, allowing a team of black-suited security men to tumble out and surround the fourth car, the Presidential car. Only when they were all in position did one of them open the door to allow the President to emerge.

Ronald McKenna stepped out with difficulty from the limousine. He was an overweight man in late middle age, his puffy face red and bloated. Yet there was a sharp and canny intelligence in his face as his eyes rapidly scanned his younger adversary.

"Welcome to Southdown House," Peter said, stretching out his hand and trying to sound more authoritative than he felt. For McKenna had somehow succeeded, as few people succeeded these days, in making him aware of his extreme youth for a man with so much power.

The President took the outstretched hand and shook it thoughtfully.

"It was kind of you to invite me, your lordship," he said in his soft Alabama drool. "I'm sure our discussions will be most productive."

He turned to Julia and bowed slightly.

"Countess," he said respectfully, shaking her by the hand.

Julia smiled graciously but said nothing. The President's arrival had clearly done nothing to dispel the mood of silent reflection with which she had awaited his arrival.

Peter led McKenna into the House. Before and behind them the President's team of security guards swept and scanned, maintaining an ever constant vigil. In view of the extensive advance preparations which had already been made, there seemed something excessive about their exaggerated movements, as if the President was doing everything in his power to remind his young adversary that he was visiting Southdown House to receive a private yet unconditional offer of surrender.

As soon as they were inside the House Peter turned to face the President.

"I expect you will wish to freshen up before we talk. My man Petrovski here will show you to your suite."

Petrovski stepped forward from the shadows and bowed politely.

The President glanced at Petrovski with a strangely knowing look and then returned his gaze to Peter.

169

"I freshened up at Windsor, your lordship," he drooled. "If it's all the same to you I'd rather get straight down to business."

The words were polite enough but the underlying tone was not. McKenna sensed total victory and was eager to relish the moment of capitulation.

"We will go to the library, then," Peter said. "Are you happy for us to meet alone?"

McKenna smiled.

"Alone or in company. It's all the same to me."

Peter led the way silently towards the library. Moments later they were sitting alone in two deep leather armchairs, each waiting for the other to speak first.

McKenna seemed to become impatient.

"Well then, your lordship, tell me why you have asked me to meet with you?"

Peter tried to smile.

"I think you know that. For some reason best known to yourself you have been trying to attack the business interests of my companies in the United States for several months. I felt it opportune that we should talk."

The President's face grew sour.

"Your companies are too damned powerful. Somebody needs to put a check on them and that's what I'm doing."

"You were happy enough to take the campaign contributions when you were seeking election."

McKenna's face became even more sour.

"We're not getting very far, are we, your lordship? Who was I to refuse financial support when it was freely offered? But now that I have the duties of the Presidency on my shoulders I have wider responsibilities to consider. But I've not come to England to discuss my campaign contributions. I'm here to see if we can reach an ... an accommodation."

Peter rose slowly to his feet and walked to the engraved walnut drinks cabinet.

"Before we proceed, may I offer you a drink?" he asked.

The President looked slightly surprised. But then he smiled and nodded his head.

"Why thank you," he said. "Mine's a Scotch."

Peter smiled quietly to himself and poured out two drinks. Alcohol was the President's private weakness, the reason why his bloated face was so red and blotchy, and in time it would be his undoing. Yet there had always been a danger he would refuse, that he would control his secret craving for just long enough to complete his talks at Southdown House.

Peter handed the drink to the President.

"What kind of accommodation would you suggest?" he asked.

The President sipped the drink gratefully and visibly relaxed. He thought he had Peter on the run, about to stop the shadow boxing and begin with the serious concessions.

"Firstly, Gamma Holdings must divest itself of all its operations in publishing and the media," he began. "Second, it must reduce its market share in all sectors of the economy to below fifteen percent. Third, it must openly submit its internal records over the past forty years to a full congressional inquiry to determine whether it was involved in criminal activities whilst under the day-to-day management of Mr Axel Hablinski. These do not seem to me to be unreasonable demands."

Peter sipped his drink.

"They will cripple the company, that is all."

The President shrugged.

"I agree that they will undermine the company's political power. It will have to compete in the market place like every other business. But sadly I must insist on immediate and unconditional acceptance of each of these points. If you feel unable to concede then there seems little reason to continue with our current discussions and I will feel obliged to return immediately to the United States ..."

Peter flinched. There was a harshness about the President's manner which made it clear he was not bluffing. There was only one thing to do.

"I seem to have little alternative," Peter said thoughtfully. "Provided that we can agree the practical arrangements to ensure there is no undue loss of face, I am prepared to agree to your terms."

McKenna relaxed. It had been the reaction the President had hoped for, the reaction of a weak ineffectual young man when confronted by the steely resolve of an experienced and tough politician.

"Maybe we can do business after all," he said with a dry smile. "And in the meantime, why don't we have another drink."

* * * * * *

It was already ten o'clock in the evening by the time the formal dinner had finished. Peter slipped away to his small windowless office, the one room in the house to which the Presidential security team had been denied access. It was a condition they had been happy to accept only because it was so far removed from the state rooms where the President was to be entertained for the duration of his stay.

At the touch of a button the room was filled with soft light. Peter walked slowly to a deep armchair in the corner of the room and sank down gratefully into it. In his mind's eye he could still see the President's arrogant face as he had sat in the library and openly demanded the total destruction of Peter's inheritance. For the President and Peter had both understood that the three conditions laid down would not just weaken Gamma Holdings but destroy it. With control of the media removed and a congressional inquiry into Gamma's history underway, the whole sordid history of the company's foundations would be revealed for all to see. A wave of deep revulsion would sweep across America and the world, bringing in its wake further calls to bring the guilty to justice. And in the ensuing witchhunt any residual power left in the hands of a rump Gamma Holdings would quickly crumble to nothing, leaving only a cold memory in its wake.

Peter sighed heavily. He knew full well, better than most perhaps, the evil which had surrounded the construction of the empire over which he now ruled. Had not his own parents and grandparents been the victims of that evil? And his own childhood, the children's homes and the cardboard boxes on the streets of London, had not they too been a reflection of the evil of Hablinski's methodology?

But his vision was different. He had come to believe that even out of evil could come good. And now that it was he rather than Axel Hablinski who was the ruler of the empire, there was little doubt that the strategic direction of the company was changing radically, directed under his personal guidance towards putting right some of the many things that were wrong with the world in which he found himself.

Again Peter's mind turned to Leroy. Leroy's own growing empire, spawned in Peter's image and with his money, had already done so much to ease the conditions of those living in Britain's inner cities. Other similar organisations constructed along similar lines were doing the same in other countries. Yet the likes of Ronald McKenna would never allow the urban renewal programmes to continue, for while a vastly rich benevolent dictator such as Peter might choose to fund such projects out of a sense of social conscience, there seemed little likelihood that the ordinary working taxpayer, prosperous yet not prosperous enough, would be prepared to take up the burden. And so, as his empire crumbled, a great many other people's hopes and dreams would crumble too.

Peter's thoughts made him shrink back into the armchair, for in reality he had deliberately conjured them up because he was still not sure, still not certain of his right to take the actions he was proposing to take. Yet all the time Hablinski's logic was bearing down on him hard, forcing him along a hard and difficult road. And to reflect too long would merely undermine his conviction that he was doing the right thing, that the utilitarian principle – the greatest happiness of the greatest number – was sufficient alone to justify and excuse his actions.

Not wishing to be alone any longer, fearful that he would lose his nerve at the eleventh hour, he rose to his feet and walked slowly towards the console, pressing the little button which would summon Petrovski to his presence.

No sooner had he pressed it than the door swung silently open and Petrovski entered. Despite himself, Peter looked down at Petrovski's hand, the hand in which he was carrying the tiny vial containing the drug with which Peter would kill his adversary.

Petrovski followed his eyes. He stepped forward and placed the vial gently on the console. Then he stepped back again and waited for Peter to speak.

Peter looked up at Petrovski's expressionless face.

"What are you thinking?" he asked.

Petrovski looked at him in surprise.

"What do you mean, sir?" he said slowly.

"I mean what are you thinking, Petrovski. You're a clever man but you never seem to reflect on what you are doing. You never seem to have any ... feelings."

"I try to serve you well, sir, just as in the past I attempted to serve Mr Hablinski well."

Peter shrank back from him. There was a coldness about Petrovski that reminded him so much of Hablinski, as if the servant had become a pale reflection of his erstwhile master.

"Hablinski wouldn't have hesitated about this, would he?" Peter asked.

Petrovski nodded slowly.

"No, sir, he would not."

"Do you think the worse of me because I do?"

Petrovski looked offended.

"It is not my place to make such judgements," he replied.

Peter gave up trying to understand the man. He went over and picked up the vial.

"Are your people absolutely certain this stuff isn't detectable?" he asked.

Petrovski visibly relaxed.

"The President is a secret alcoholic. This is not known to the general public but is well understood by his doctors. He has been repeatedly advised to reduce the quantity of alcohol he consumes but has rejected all advice. As a result, his body faces the continual threat of heart attack through alcohol excess. This drug merely precipitates a condition from which he is in any case likely to die soon. It will not show up at any post-mortem examination.''

Peter picked up the vial and pushed it into his pocket. He had to admit there was a certain cleverness to Petrovski's method of dealing with the President. The library was routinely searched before each of their meetings. So Peter would simply enter with the vial in his pocket, pour the President a drink and quietly add the poison. Minutes later, the President would suffer a massive coronary from which he would not recover. The crime, if such it were, would be undetectable. Yet the suspicion would linger for evermore in the minds of the world's leaders that McKenna had met his death because he had started to tangle with Gamma Holdings. The aura of suppressed fear which had once surrounded and protected Hablinski would transfer neatly to Peter. His empire would be left alone, free to grow ever stronger. They would finally have passed through the danger zone of which Hablinski had so often spoken, emerging into a new era of unchallenged and unchallengeable power.

He turned to Petrovski.

"Go now," he said quietly.

Petrovski vanished. For several minutes Peter remained alone, fingering the little bottle in his pocket, but then he too left the room. Wearily, he walked along the silent corridors of the House towards his bedroom. Having decided upon the course of action he was to take, he now wished the night would pass quickly. When day came he would be able to finish the business. And only then would he feel better, able at last to find the inner peace which had been evading him ever since Hablinski's death.

He pushed open the door of the bedroom and went inside. It was already late, and he had been expecting to find Julia asleep in the massive four-poster bed they had made their own. So it was with some surprise that he saw her sitting by the dressing table, her back to him, slowly combing her hair.

She made no effort to turn as he entered, but remained exactly where she was, pulling the comb quietly through her hair.

He took off his jacket and laid it on the bed. Then, aware that she had still not turned, he approached her and laid his hand on her shoulder.

"Are you all right?" he asked.

She stopped combing her hair and laid the comb on the table. And then, with a flash of anger and a suddenness of movement which caught him completely unawares, she walked across the bedroom to his jacket and pulled out the vial from his pocket.

Peter watched her speechless as she lifted the poison before his face.

"Fancy a drink?" she said sarcastically, and the bitterness in her voice ran deep and hard.

He struggled to find some words but none came. Without speaking, she marched into the adjoining bathroom. He could hear the sound of the toilet flushing. And then she returned, the empty vial clutched tight in her hand.

There was an anger in her that ran so deep it was terrifying.

"How?" Peter asked.

Julia's eyes flared.

"As you take such pleasure in constantly reminding me, perhaps I am after all my father's daughter. I too can lie and cheat with considerable accomplishment if I so choose."

His mouth fell open.

"You bugged me."

She smiled.

"Of course. And I'm jolly pleased I did. I might yet be able to pull you back from the brink."

"You've been watching me for weeks," he repeated.

She nodded bitterly.

"And it's not been a pretty sight, I can tell you."

He could feel his legs giving way beneath him. He sank down weakly onto the bed. Again it was as it had been on the day he had first met her, the day five years before in a school classroom. And he knew now as he had known then that her strength was a thousand times greater than his would ever be."

Peter looked at the empty vial.

"I had too," he said weakly. "It was the only way."

Julia glowered at him.

"I thought you had so much power," she retorted. "You managed to live penniless on the streets without crime, yet now you have so much you feel you are somehow justified in murdering people. Can't you see it's simply wrong?"

"He's just one man. And he's going to die soon anyway."

"Don't you see he's just the first? Soon they'll be another. And then another and another. You'll look at more flow charts and you'll kill again and again and again. Because you have to, don't you? It's the logic of a man like my father. Gamma was built on violence and it can only be maintained by violence, because somebody somewhere will always want to be free."

Her words shocked him. He had genuinely believed that McKenna would be the last, that his death was the last piece of unfinished business hanging over from the Hablinski era. He had believed that would be the end of it.

Julia could see that her words had shocked him. Her face suddenly softened.

"I feel so sorry for you, Peter," she said. "I know you're a decent man. You've been poor yourself and you loathe poverty. And then, by a strange quirk of fate, you find yourself in a position to help others whose lives are as wretched as yours once was. You accept the challenge. But in the process you've forgotten something central about human beings. You've forgotten that the desire to be free is as strong as the desire to eat. And that's why what you're doing is so wrong."

He looked at her.

"And you think someone like that drunken creep McKenna is right?" he asked.

She shook her head.

"Don't you see it's not as simple as that?" she said. "For all I know McKenna needs to be taken down a peg or too as well. But that's not your job, Peter. There are other people in the world besides you and they've got responsibilities too. It's not all up to you."

"But they don't have the power and I do."

"Well then," she snapped back. "Give it to them."

He turned away.

"Don't think I don't want to sometimes," he said. "Do you really think I like it that my words carry so much clout, that a whim of mine can affect a million lives? But I do it because I know that the power Hablinski built up is not really divisible, and that if I allow the empire to be fragmented everything I have tried to achieve will simply crumble into dust."

"In other words you think you're indispensible?" she asked quietly.

He turned to face her.

"No ... No, I don't think that."

"What would happen if you died? You're not immortal, you know."

He sank down on the bed and buried his head in his hands. Before he had returned to the bedroom he had tried so hard to convince himself that he had known what to do. But now Julia's words were stirring up once more all the deep feelings of self-doubt which had filled his every waking moment for many years.

"I don't know," he said forlornly.

She took his head and pulled it roughly upwards, forcing him to look her in the face.

"I'll tell you what will happen," she said harshly. "Somebody else will take over."

Something about the tone of her voice stopped him in his tracks. A sense of urgency which suggested that what she was about to say was more than idle speculation.

"What do you think of Dmitri Petrovski?" she asked pointedly.

Peter shrugged.

"You know what I think of him. I don't like him much, but he's a useful man to have around."

"And what do you suppose Petrovski thinks of you?"

"I ... I don't know. I suppose he thinks I'm a pretty poor boss compared with your father."

She looked at him in despair.

"You still don't realise, do you, Peter?"

"Realise what?"

"That Petrovski will turn on you. Perhaps not now, perhaps not for months or even years. But eventually Petrovski will claim what he believes to be his due. And when he does, you will find yourself cast aside as ruthlessly as Ronald McKenna."

He looked at her sharply.

"What makes you think Petrovski would be disloyal?" he said.

"He was loyal to my father, or rather he feared my father. But now I am certain he is biding his time, waiting for the right moment to claim what he considers to be his own ..."

"But it's not his!" Peter interjected.

"His. Yours. What's the difference? Power belongs to those who wield it."

"You don't need to worry," she continued. "I don't think he'll act yet. The company's still in that danger zone my father kept talking about. Still vulnerable to a concerted attack. It suits Petrovski to allow you to front for him and take the risks. But eventually, when he's ready, he'll strike you down, cancel the absurd fiction of this Earldom, and finally be able to feel the thrill of ruling the empire in his own name."

Peter remembered Petrovski's expressionless face when they had spoken earlier. He had taken it for a simple lack of emotion, but it could perhaps have been a mask.

177

A thought suddenly occurred to him and he pushed it forcefully aside, fearful that Julia would again read his mind. But it was already too late.

"Yes," she said simply. "You could kill him too."

He looked at her numbly. And as he looked at her he began to understand that she was right, that Petrovski would not be the last any more than McKenna would be the last. There would be other McKennas, other Petrovskis, a lifetime of challenges to be fought off with violence and brutality.

"However good your intentions may be, Peter, the sheer concentration of power in your hands is bound to attract the attention of others. They may be outside the organisation, like McKenna, or they may be insiders, like Petrovski. But there will always be someone. And even if your own rule proves to be broadly benign, one day somebody else will be sitting at your desk and pulling the levers of power."

Julia sat down beside him on the bed and laid her hand gently on his shoulder.

"Let it go," she said quietly. "Its foundations are rotten. And whatever you strive to achieve will go sour in the end. All that will happen is that you'll try and fail."

He nodded slowly. She sensed his capitulation.

"Tomorrow you must agree to McKenna's demands," she said quietly. "Then we can plan the next step."

Despite himself, he could feel a wave of relief flowing through his body at her words. It was as if a terrible burden had suddenly been lifted from his shoulders.

She knelt down before him. The anger had completely vanished, and as she gazed up into his eyes he remembered how much he loved her.

"Do you know how long it is since we've made love?" she whispered.

Peter looked at her sadly. He'd tried several times in recent months, more because he felt he ought to than because he really felt like it, but on each occasion it had come to nought. And more recently he had given up trying.

"I'll tell you," she said in reply to her own question. "You haven't made love to me since the night you inherited my father's empire."

Peter allowed her to push him gently back on the bed and then in turn pulled her on top of him.

"Has it ever occurred to you," he said with a wry smile, "that it's not easy for gods to make love?"

It was strange how you could feel an emptiness in your pocket, but as Peter entered the library the following morning he could actually feel the absence of the poisoned vial.

The President was already there, clutching a sheaf of papers in his hand. As soon as the door was closed, before they had even sat down, he handed the papers to Peter.

"You wanted some more details of my proposals for resolving our differences, your lordship," he said with a scarcely concealed look of self-satisfaction.

Peter took the bundle of papers and sat down at the desk. The President ambled over towards the drinks cabinet.

"Do you mind if I help myself?" he said absent-mindedly.

Peter nodded quietly and started to read through the document. But he had only read about two sides before he looked up at McKenna, who was sitting in one of the leather armchairs quietly sipping his Scotch with a slight smirk on his face.

"This isn't what I agreed to," Peter declared angrily.

The President smiled.

"Well," he began. "There's been a slight change of plan. We now feel it would be best to transfer the US assets of Gamma Holdings into the hands of an official receiver appointed by the Federal authorities pending the outcome of the congressional inquiry. The receiver will supervise the disposal of Gamma's surplus assets, holding the proceeds of such sales as collateral against any claims which might emerge during the course of the inquiry."

The anger passed and Peter smiled wryly. Hablinski would have told him this would happen. As Hablinski's student he had himself known that this would happen. But the speed of the impending collapse nevertheless came as a surprise. He looked thoughtfully at the President's Scotch and once again became aware of the emptiness of his pocket.

"It amounts to total expropriation," he said slowly, wondering if he could rescue anything from the wreckage.

McKenna smiled maliciously, relishing his moment of triumph.

"It amounts to a settling of the account," he said slowly. "You will be left with Gamma's extensive holdings in other countries, and of course any profits from the U.S. operations will be passed by the official receiver into your personal account. Provided you co-operate fully with our investigation into Gamma, you will easily remain one of richest men in the world."

Peter nodded. In this at least he was certain that the President was as good as his word. He represented the prosperous classes of the most prosperous country in the world. Reducing the Earl of Southdown to penury was not the name of the game.

He quickly read the document through to the end. On the final page was a place for each of them to affix their signatures in the presence of witnesses.

"You agree, then?" McKenna asked.

Peter nodded.

"I agree. I do not see that I have much alternative but to agree."

McKenna's body seemed to relax. He had clearly been expecting Peter to put up a slightly harder struggle than he had done, and now he was relieved that he could return to Washington with such a complete victory. He rose and poured himself another large Scotch.

"Want one?" he asked.

Peter shook his head.

The President looked at him thoughtfully.

"Hablinski was a tough act to follow, eh?"

Peter nodded.

"He wasn't all bad. He was a successful businessman, the ultimate embodiment of the American dream."

McKenna shrugged.

"Do you know what his father was? He was a bootlegger during prohibition, a Polish bootlegger who was clever enough to adopt Mafia methods. That's where Axel Hablinski learnt his tricks."

"And do you think the other corporations of high capitalism have always been so pure in their methods. Yet you don't seek to expropriate their assets."

Again McKenna shrugged.

"A question of degree, your lordship. Hablinski knew no limits. He didn't accept the idea of a self-denying ordinance."

Peter quietly poured himself a mineral water.

"What about the social investment programmes I've begun?" he asked. "Will your official receiver continue with them?"

The President scowled.

"That's up to him. There was an lot of crude vote-buying in those programmes you began. A lot of feather-bedding of people who need a fire-cracker under their backsides to get them working a bit harder."

Peter sighed. Of course it was possible to misconstrue his actions. He should really have known better than to ask. And McKenna was not the sort of man who could easily understand the true reasons he had spent his money on the poor. But it was all rather academic now. He had to accept that by letting McKenna live he had made his last real decision. Now it was for others to look after themselves.

McKenna walked to the desk and sat down, picking up the document and thumbing casually through it.

"Since you agree to sign, I suggest we call in the pack. I have a television team on stand-by to record the official signing."

McKenna began to rise to his feet, but then, without warning, a strangely anguished look came over his face and he slumped forward over the desk. For a second Peter stared blankly at his limp body, but then he rushed for the door and pulled it open with a cry.

The corridor outside was packed with people of every description. As he pulled the door open they all poured into the library, crowding anxiously round the desk where the American lay. After a few minutes an elderly man elbowed his way through to the President and started to examine him. The crowd in the room fell silent.

For several moments the doctor said nothing. But then he straightened himself up and turned to address the crowd. His words, when they came, were little more than a whisper.

"I regret to say that the President is dead."

There was a shocked silence which lasted several seconds. And then one of the President's security men, who had positioned himself next to the door, quietly pushed it closed.

"I would suggest," he said, "that we all remain in this room until the Vice-President has been informed."

The crowd were still silent. In the far corner, two dark-suited men had opened a small black briefcase and were trying to raise Vice-President Smith.

It was at this time that Peter first became aware of Petrovski's presence in the room. He had slipped in quietly with the rest of the pack, and now he elbowed his way towards the security man by the door.

"The Earl of Southdown will need to pass," he said in a commanding voice. "In the circumstances it is imperative that he inform the Prime Minister personally of the President's tragic demise during the course of his visit here."

Petrovski's words cut through the silence like a knife. But the eyes in the room did not fall upon Petrovski, they fell upon him. Peter scanned the room, looking back at the faces which were looking at him, and suddenly he saw how infallible Hablinski's simple method had been. For on each of the faces arrayed before him there was a single emotion, and that emotion was fear.

181

Events had been moving fast, and it was nearly nine o'clock in the evening by the time the maelstrom abated. His first action on leaving the room had been to place a call to the Prime Minister to inform the British authorities of the President's death. Then he had telephoned the Home Office and personally invited Scotland Yard to come down to the House and begin a full inquiry into the circumstances of the President's death.

Half an hour later Southdown House had been been placed under a virtual state of siege, its outer perimeter protected by a contingent of the British army in order to prevent the prying eyes of the world's press from gaining access. The President's body, after careful examination by British and American detectives in the library, was then removed to begin its long journey back to a forensic examination in the United States. Only then had the tides of officialdom gradually started to ebb away, taking with them their vast baggage train of equipment and supplies.

As the sun began to set peace finally returned to Southdown House. Peter went out into the garden and walked alone in the formal gardens for quite some time. The look of fear he had seen on the faces in the library had had a strange effect on him, as the dawning realisation began to seep in that the President's death through natural causes had achieved his earlier objective without any need for violence on his behalf.

Several phone-calls during the day had confirmed everything which had appeared on Petrovski's neat flow chart. Vice-President Smith had expressed regret that the President had met his death while on a private visit to Southdown House in such an obsequious manner that it had made Peter wince. The British Prime Minister, himself gradually plucking up the courage to initiate action against Gamma Holdings' assets in the UK, had also adopted a conciliatory and respectful tone. And messages were continuing to flow in from government leaders, media chiefs and other influential figures around the world expressing sadness at the tragic news from Southdown House.

Peter sat beside the lake and quietly watched an overweight goldfish swimming in the gathering gloom. Its red and blotchy appearance reminded him of McKenna shortly before his collapse, an overconfident President who had dared to challenge Gamma Holdings but did not dare to challenge his own fatal addiction to alcohol. And as he watched the fish he wondered whether it had been a sign, a signal from some higher being that Julia had been wrong to make him concede, that a stronger man would not have listened to her weak womanly words.

He glanced up at the House and suddenly realised he had not seen her since the President's death. With a sickening sensation in the pit of his stomach, he realised that she might have falsely assumed that he had broken his promise and secretly asked Petrovski for a further supply of the poison she had poured away.

Rising to his feet, he walked quickly through the gardens and into the House. Seeing one of her maids, he called after her sharply.

"Mary!"

She turned.

"Do you know where I can find the Countess?"

The maid looked at him askance.

"Why, your lordship, didn't you know? She left early this afternoon. She said she didn't know when she'd be back."

Peter stared at the young servant.

"Left! Where did she go?"

The maid shrugged.

"I don't know, sir. She took one of the cars and drove herself. It was while all those comings and goings were happening this afternoon."

A sense of panic was seeping through Peter's body. From the manner of her going he was sure that she had left him. She had assumed he was guilty of the President's murder, taken his rejection of her advice as a rejection of his love for her, and simply decided to walk out. Taking the steps three at a time, he leapt up the stairs to their bedroom. And sure enough, there on the pillow of their bed was an envelope with his name printed neatly on the front.

He opened the envelope and pulled out the note.

"My dear Peter," it began. "It is clear to me that despite our conversation last night you have chosen my father's path. It is a path I do not wish to tread. I have therefore decided to leave you now so that I can build my own life in my own image. I had hoped – no, I had believed – that you were worthy of my love. The distress I feel on discovering that your greed and love of power has pushed aside your love for me cannot easily be put into words. But perhaps I am too hard on you. Perhaps you are merely the living embodiment of the old saying that power corrupts and absolute power corrupts absolutely. You do not need to fear I will speak out, because I will not. And despite your foolishness and my hurt, I wish you well. Julia."

Peter read the note several times and then laid it carefully down on the bedside table. It was growing dark outside and a wind had started to pick up, causing a strange anguished howl to emanate from the chimney. He lay down on the bed and buried his head in the pillow, trying to avoid the sound of the wind. And then, silently and alone, he started to sob.

For a long time he lay alone on the bed. In his mind's eye, he remembered the extraordinary way in which their relationship had developed. He remembered her as she had once seemed to him, arrogant and aloof, the victim of a lonely childhood of aristocratic privilege. And then he remembered her as she had been during the solitary weeks they had spent together in her father's gilded cage in Switzerland. During that time she had been so strong, a beacon guiding him through the night. Only later, after he had succeeded in winning Hablinski's backing and gained the Earldom, only then had the problems started to emerge. For although she had loved him greatly she had always been uneasy with the new role he had adopted as understudy to Hablinski. It was almost if she had preferred him as he had once been, a penniless yet innocent child of the streets. The vast wealth he had inherited had failed to impress. Instead, by slow degrees, it had served to corrupt a relationship that had once been so pure. And now, with her final letter of reproach, she had finally bowed to the inevitable. She had given him up as lost.

He rose to his feet. It had been a mistake, a terrible mistake. For the previous night he had accepted her demands. McKenna's death, for all that other people might secretly hold him responsible, was nothing to do with him. And now, this very night, before her rejection of him became too ingrained, he would go and search her out.

But where? That was the question. She had left no clue, no indication of her whereabouts. She could have gone anywhere.

Unable to remain in the bed they had once shared, he rose to his feet and started wandering aimlessly through the House. But wherever he went, her ghost seemed to follow him. For in every room, in every corridor, there was the faint afterglow of her presence. So eventually, after he had walked completely around the House several times, he found himself back in the bedroom again, alone, afraid and uncertain.

Time flowed by. Evening became night. He changed for bed and tried to sleep, but no sleep came. Only thoughts of Julia, the Julia who had once seemed so unreachable and was now unreachable again. And now that she had left, the whole vast empire over which he ruled seemed like an empty shell, the altruistic dreams as much as the wealth and power a cruel trap into which he had allowed himself to fall. For without Julia it was worth nothing, and he knew he would willingly give it all up for the touch of her arm.

It was three o'clock in the morning before he finally gave up trying to sleep. The sense of loneliness was becoming overpowering, a stifling anxiety which he feared he would soon no longer be able to control. If he had had parents he may have turned to them for help in his hour of need, but he had no parents. There was only one person who could help him through his hour of crisis, only one person who could counsel and advise him on what he should do next. And that person was Harry.

He had neither seen nor heard much of Harry during the years in which he had ruled the Southdown domain. Like Julia herself, Harry had seemed to prefer him as a young man out of luck. Once, shortly after his accession to the Earldom, he had made the mistake of offering Harry money, a generous pension with which he could live out his days in comfort. And on that day he had learned that Harry was not a man who liked to be patronized, that despite his apparent obsession with making money he was not in fact obsessed by it, but rather by the desire to stand on his own two feet, to be independent and free. After that Harry had returned to his crumbling cafe in Hackney and carried on with his life much as before. From time to time Peter had visited him there, but the conversations had become increasingly strained and Harry had steadfastly refused all invitations to stay at Southdown House. So eventually, as the years had passed, they had stopped seeing each other at all. Yet now, suddenly, Peter wanted to see the old man again.

Dawn was just beginning to break by the time he pulled his car up in the street outside the cafe. He had chosen the least prestigious car in the garage, a white Range Rover, yet still it looked incongruous amidst the elderly crocks of central Hackney. He clambered out of the car and looked fondly at the cafe. Even the building seemed to lend him comfort, reminding him that he too had once been a simple man with simple concerns, a man like any other.

All was quiet. Knowing that Harry would ignore the doorbell at that time in the morning, taking it to be a prank by kids on the street, Peter picked up a stone lying on the pavement and threw it up at Harry's window. For several minutes nothing happened, so he threw another stone. Eventually Harry's bony face appeared at the window.

Shortly afterwards Peter was sitting on his sofa in Harry's dingy living room, looking uncomfortably at the old man as he quietly prepared a cup of tea by the stove. Eventually Harry turned.

"Well then, Peter, why the unexpected visit?"

Peter looked down at his feet.

"Julia's left me," he blurted out.

Harry looked at him as if the news had not altogether come as a shock.

"Why?" he asked.

"Because she thinks I killed McKenna."

"Well. You did, didn't you?"

Peter looked at him sharply.

"Why do you say that?"

"Everyone knows McKenna was after your blood. Then he visits your house to negotiate with you and suddenly drops down dead in the library. It's rather convenient. What do you expect me to think?"

Peter sank his head low.

"I admit I was planning to kill him, but then I changed my mind. Julia changed my mind. And then the creep just goes and keels over in my library. So now everyone thinks it was me, which it admittedly could have been but wasn't."

Harry observed him quietly for a moment.

"Look at me and say that, Peter," he said.

Peter raised his eyes and met Harry's gaze.

"I didn't do it, Harry. McKenna died of natural causes, probably caused by his surprise at the ease with which he'd just walked all over me."

Harry nodded uncommitally. He rose to his feet and to Peter's amazement started pouring out three cups of tea.

Then he handed two to Peter.

Peter looked at him with a perplexed expression.

"Why are you giving me two?" he asked.

Harry winked.

"One for you, one for her. She turned up here yesterday afternoon in a pretty distressed state. She didn't want to go in a hotel and didn't have anywhere else to go. So I put her up in your old room."

It took several seconds for the words to sink in, but then he jumped up and suddenly embraced the old man.

"Thanks Harry," he exclaimed, grabbing the two cups of tea and starting for the door.

"Peter!"

Harry's exclamation brought him to a halt and he turned.

"I believe you," he said, "but I think you'll find she's a tougher nut to crack."

Peter nodded. And then, carefully carrying the two cups of tea, he started down the stairs towards his old bedroom.

When he reached the door he didn't knock. He gently pushed it open and slipped inside, laying the cups down on the small bedside table. Julia was fast asleep, and although she stirred she did not awake. Peter sat down quietly at the end of the bed and watched her sleeping face. It was calm and tranquil, as if the decision to finally leave him had lifted a burden from her shoulders, a burden which had been oppressing her for a long time. The expression disturbed him, and he laid his arm gently on her shoulder.

She opened her eyes. For a second or two she said nothing, clearly disorientated, but then her memory of the previous day's events must have flooded back to her and she sat bolt upright.

"What are you doing here?" she asked angrily.

"I came to see Harry. I didn't know you were here."

"Harry's upstairs. Leave me alone."

Peter could see the hurt in her face.

"I didn't kill him, Julia."

Her words caused her to pause, but then she laughed cynically.

"Do you think I'm stupid? Of course you killed him."

"I didn't. I'd just agreed to everything he asked, and then he dropped down dead."

Julia smiled hautily.

"Very convenient."

"Perhaps it is. But it's also true. I swear it."

Julia rose to her feet and pulled her dressing gown on. Then she sat down in the hard wooden chair and examined him closely.

"Maybe it doesn't matter whether you killed him or not, anyway."

Her words surprised him and he looked at her sadly.

"How can you say that?" he said. "I thought we loved each other."

"We did. Perhaps we still do, I don't know. But you've become obsessed by the power you've grabbed. You've started thinking of yourself like some kind of superman, the arbiter of good and evil in the world. You've become so insufferably arrogant."

Peter looked at her unhappy face.

"When I first met you I used to think you were arrogant," he said.

"When you first met me I was afraid. I was afraid of the money with which I'd grown up and of the effect it could have on the people around me and the way they dealt with each other. I had to protect myself from it and that's why I carried that shell around with me. And now I'm becoming afraid of you. It's as if the money has taken control, turned you into someone you're not. That's what sickened me so much about McKenna. It was the fact that you could even contemplate murdering him in order to cling on to what you thought was yours. It showed me that the long slow process of corruption was almost complete, that despite your persistent attempts to buy off your conscience you really had sold your soul to the devil."

Peter hung his head low. There was no purpose in presenting her with a carefully-constructed justification of his actions as the Earl of Southdown. It wasn't what she wanted to hear.

"I love you, Julia. I'll do whatever you want in order to win you back."

He could see that his words were beginning to have some effect. She lifted the cup of tea to her lips and took a sip.

"There is a way," she said slowly. "I've thought about it often over the years, ever since I was a child in fact, and now I'm finally sure it's right. But I really don't know if you've got the courage to do it."

FIFTY YEARS LATER

The sun glinted off the ornamental lake as the tourists slowly assembled for the beginning of the last afternoon tour. Their tour guide, a pretty young student who was earning some extra money during the summer holidays, stepped up neatly onto a stone step beside the lake and waited patiently for silence. Only when she was sure she had everyone's attention did she begin.

"Welcome to Southdown House," she said rather grandly, surveying the motley assortment of what she guessed to be Australian tourists with a slightly disparaging air, as if a lesson in architectural history would probably be far over their heads.

"The house was built in the early years of the eighteenth century by the Troughton family, one of England's richest noble houses ..."

She droned on for several minutes in that rather mechanical voice which inevitably results from repeating the same speech over and over again. After a while the tourists started shuffling their feet and looking rather bored, as if they wished she would hurry up and begin the tour of the house. The girl sensed their impatience but was not alarmed by it. If past experience was anything to go by, they would soon be listening with keen attention to the story she was about to unfold.

"But the most interesting period in the history of Southdown House was undoubtedly the time when it was occupied by the 16th and last Earl, a young and handsome man who emerged from obscurity and claimed the title for his own in circumstances which remain to this day more than a little obscure ..."

Despite herself, the girl hesitated. For there, standing at the back of the crowd, was an elderly man whose face she found disturbingly familiar. She tried to place him, yet try as she might she could not work out where she had seen him before. But there was no time to reflect too long, for just as she had predicted, the crowd had fallen silent at the note of intrigue she had introduced into her account and were waiting eagerly for her to continue.

"It transpired that the 16th Earl was the grandchild of the 14th Earl's clandestine marriage to a servant girl in the late 1930s. But when this secret marriage was subsequently discovered by the 14th Earl's parents he was forced to conceal his first marriage and marry again. The Earldom and the estate then passed to his descendants by this second illegal marriage and did not return to their rightful owner until claimed over fifty year later."

The young girl looked at the man more closely, annoyed by her inability to place him. He was rather shabbily dressed in an old sports jacket, although something about his manner told her it was from preference rather than lack of money. But it was not so much his clothing which struck her as odd as his expression, a quiet detached expression which suggested that he, unlike the other members of the party, found her whole exposition monumentally boring.

"When the new young Earl claimed his inheritance towards the end of the last century, Southdown House was at the pinnacle of its power. The Earldom, always rich, had become the largest repository of privately owned wealth in the world. The new young Earl, a man who had spent his childhood in abject poverty, was therefore thrust overnight into a position of almost unimaginable wealth and power."

She was sure that the elderly man in the shabby jacket had stopped listening altogether. He was peering into the lake, absent-mindedly tracking the progress of a large pink goldfish as it swam steadily by. But then, as if he had sensed her hesitation, he looked up and smiled gently, as if to reassure her that he was indeed attending. She looked away, deliberately focussing her eyes on the other members of the party, and forced herself to continue.

"But even more extraordinary than the story of how the 16th Earl came into his inheritance were the events which followed. After only five years as Earl, while still in his mid-twenties, the 16th Earl suddenly renounced his title and with it all the vast wealth the Earldom had amassed over the years. Within a year the businesses and real estate had all been sold off and the proceeds channelled into a vast array of charitable foundations around the world. Eventually only the house and grounds were left, and then they too were handed over to the National Trust. And after that, without leaving a trace, the erstwhile Earl and his pretty young Countess simply vanished from the face of the earth. They have never been heard of or seen again."

The group of tourists around her stood in numbed silence, as all tourists did when she reached that particular part of her narrative. It presented her with something of a technical problem, since by delivering the most interesting part of her story so early in their visit it was hard to keep up momentum, so that when they were inside and examining the interior of the house she found it difficult to keep their minds from wandering.

She stepped down from the stone step and led the party into the house itself, starting off in the state rooms on the ground floor. Out of the corner of her eye she could not prevent herself from tracking the movement of the man in the shabby jacket. He was lingering at the back of the party, his pace slow and hesitant, and in his eye there was the distracted look of one whose mind was far away. Constantly aware of his presence, she tried to concentrate on her talk, repeat the words of an exposition she had given a hundred times before, but sometimes they would elude her and she would stumble, completely forgetting a date or a name in the strange state of agitation which had come over her.

Presently they entered the library. It was a fine old library, its ancient leather-bound volumes representing one of the most valuable collections of old books in the country. Pulling up some old library steps, she climbed up several feet above her audience and waited for silence.

"This is the library," she began rather obviously, and then completely lost the thread of what she was saying. She looked for the man in the shabby coat, temporarily unable to see him among the sea of faces, but then she noticed he had moved slightly to one side of the crowd and gently lowered himself into an ancient leather armchair, totally ignoring a discreet little sign which asked members of the public not to do so. He was leaning forward slightly, gazing down thoughtfully at a spot on the carpet in the centre of the room.

She cleared her throat, fearful that an act of such flagrant indiscipline would encourage the other Australian tourists to themselves begin flaunting the rules.

"Excuse me, sir," she began.

All heads turned to examine the disobedient old man.

He looked at her with a bemused expression.

"I'm sorry, sir, but that chair is very old. I wonder if you would mind ..."

With a muffled apology, the old man rose to his feet and stood obediently beside the other tourists. She collected her wits and continued with her exposition. It did not take long, because she had already decided to cut out quite a lot of the detail in order to complete the tour a little earlier than scheduled. For the old man, with his attentive yet detached expression, was for some quite inexplicable reason beginning to disturb her, and she felt she wanted to be rid of him as soon as possible.

It was however with some considerable degree of alarm that she realised several rooms later that she had got rid of him even sooner than expected. Since the incident in the library she had been studiously ignoring him, concentrating instead on a dumpy middle-aged woman with a wholly unsurprising face, fearful that if she did not pull herself together and give a competent talk one of the visitors would complain to the crusty old custodian who supervised the House. But now that the talk was nearing an end she could not resist one last glance at her strange visitor, and cast her eyes around to see what he was up to.

But he was gone. Somewhere between the library and their present location, he had managed to give her the slip.

She felt her heart miss a beat. All the tour guides were warned about this sort of thing when they got the job. Financial stringency in recent years had meant that Southdown House had inadequate staff to supervise every room, so instead of allowing the public to wander freely around, they had to be accompanied by the tour guide at all times. The tour guide was to enter a room first and leave it last, thereby ensuring that visitors were supervised throughout their tour.

She caught the eye of the dumpy middle-aged woman.

"Have you by any chance seen that old man, the one who sat in the leather armchair in the library?"

The dumpy woman looked surprised.

"No, dearie. Sorry."

Other people had overheard her question and shook their heads. The question was repeated, passed around the group, but nobody could remember seeing him since the incident with the leather armchair.

The tour guide looked uncertainly around. For now she had little alternative but to assume the old man was some kind of thief. Southdown House was filled with countless numbers of priceless

191

treasures. They could not easily be picked up during the course of a tour, but a person left alone in a room might well be able to steal something of value.

She muttered a few final words of thanks to the tourists and hustled them as quickly as she could out into the courtyard at the back of the house. Locking the door, she started carefully retracing her steps towards the library. She was determined to at least try and track down the impostor herself before confessing her error to the custodian, a humourless old woman who might well give her the sack without further ado.

Quietly she unlocked the library door, half expecting to find the room ransacked and the windows smashed, its best treasures stripped away by an experienced if elderly cat-burglar. But instead, to her surprise, she suddenly caught sight of the old man. He was tottering on the very top of the library stairs, clutching in his hand an eighteenth century copy of the Parliamentary Gazette.

He had not heard her enter so she remained silent, watching him as he pulled several handwritten sheets from his pocket and laid them into the book. Then he carefully replaced it on the shelf and turned to climb down the stairs.

He was half way down when he caught sight of her standing by the door. For several moments he studied her reproachful face, and then, ever so slowly, a broad smile spread slowly across his wrinkled face.

He climbed gingerly down the rest of the stairs.

"I have a strange feeling of déjà vu," he murmured as he reached the floor.

His inexplicable words silenced her before she had spoken. She stared at him in bewilderment.

"Are you a student?" he asked.

She nodded silently.

"A history student?"

Again she nodded.

"I should think you are a good one. And you should become a teacher of history one day. From the way you spoke I think you will make a good teacher."

Before the girl had found him somehow menacing, a hindrance to the mechanical rhythm of her talk, but now she suddenly became aware of the extraordinary tranquility in his face, a tranquility which made her realise that this was no ordinary man.

He had lifted up the heavy library steps and had begun to carry them across the room to their usual resting place. But after a few paces he stopped and lowered them wearily to the ground.

She stepped forward and took them from him, carrying them to where they were supposed to be.

When she turned again his face had grown serious.

"You even look like her," he said so quietly that she was not sure she had heard him properly.

"Like who?" the girl asked.

The old man smiled again, his soft eyes meeting hers.

"Like a girl I once fell in love with."

The student frowned.

"What were you doing in here?" she asked.

He carefully lowered himself into the leather armchair he had sat in before.

"Guess!" he said with an impish smile.

She looked up anxiously at the copy of the Parliamentary Gazette.

"You were putting some papers in that book."

He smiled.

"Caught in the act by a pretty young girl for the second time in my life," he murmured. "I really ought to be more careful."

She remembered the first words he had spoken.

"What did you mean before by 'déjà vu'?"

He said nothing. Instead, he rose to his feet and started walking towards one of the bookshelves behind the desk.

"I expect you're wondering how I gave you the slip?" he asked.

She nodded.

He carefully reached his hand behind one of the books and pulled gently. The shelves came away from the wall, revealing a narrow servants' passage behind.

She looked at him in amazement.

"While you were waiting for all the tourists to file out I quietly slipped in here," he explained.

She followed him and peered into the passage. Then she turned.

"Who are you?" she asked.

He walked slowly to the desk and sat down.

"I thought maybe you'd already guessed. I thought already outside by the lake that you'd rumbled me."

Deep down inside she could feel a growing sense of excitement, a thrill which made her shiver to the core of her being. And then, suddenly, she knew where she had seen him before.

"You ... ?" she mouthed.

He nodded.

"I'm afraid so."

"The 16th Earl?"

Again he nodded.

She looked at him in abject amazement. And then she started to laugh.

"Sorry about telling you to get out of your armchair," she said.

Peter looked at her as she laughed and wondered by what strange twist of fate he had come across such a girl at such a time. For she really did bear a remarkable similarity to his wife as a young woman.

He smiled at her gently.

"I haven't set foot inside this house for nearly half a century," he said.

She looked up at the old copy of the Parliamentary Gazette.

He followed her eyes and smiled.

"Once before I allowed a young girl to look inside that book," he said. "And now, if you wish, I will allow you to look. But before you do so, please promise me that you will not reveal what you find until after you are sure that my wife and I are dead and gone. We do not wish the tranquility of our last years shattered by a swarm of impatient reporters."

She looked at him hesitantly, just as Julia had done so many years before.

"What is it?" she asked.

"Give me my promise, young lady, and then go and look for yourself."

Again she hesitated, but only for an instant.

"I promise," she said with a smile, and then fetched the library stairs from the far side of the room.

Peter waited in silence while she climbed up the stairs and retrieved the papers he had left. Then she climbed carefully back down again and lowered herself into a deep armchair where she began to read.

Nearly an hour passed before she looked up again.

"I still don't really understand why you chose to disappear like that?" she asked.

Peter smiled.

"When I was a very young man I had nothing at all," he said. "At that time I suppose I was rather immature, and I thought that all I needed to make me happy was a generous portion of money. And then, as you know, I suddenly found a portion which was more than generous. It was like a dream come true, and only later did I discover it was a false dream. For the money gradually changed me, gave me delusions of grandeur, made me feel that I was far more important than the tiny speck of cosmic dust which I have subsequently discovered myself to be."

He hesitated. The girl looked up at him.

"Why did you vanish, though? You could have given most of your money away and still stayed here. I don't see why your abdication was so utterly complete."

Peter smiled.

"I was sorely tempted," he said. "And perhaps, if an American President had not collapsed and died in this very room, I would have done just that. But his death precipitated a crisis with a girl who turned out to be my conscience, and a complete denial of all that had gone before was a condition imposed by her. At the time I doubted her when she assured me it would be for the best. I feared that because she had always been vastly rich she did not understand how hard it would be to make our own way in the world. Only much later did I really begin to understand why she had made me do it, and only later still that I came to accept she was right."

The girl looked at him thoughtfully.

"It must have been hard to give up all this?" she murmured.

Peter gazed thoughtfully around the room for a while, his mind drifting back over the decades to the days when it had been his own.

"You'd think so, wouldn't you?" he mused. "But you'd be wrong. Southdown House and the fortune which went with it were a poisoned chalice when they fell into my hands. I was very young, scarcely any older than you are, and I felt it was my responsibility to try and use my wealth constructively for the general welfare. A late twentieth century variation of the old notion of noblesse oblige, you might say ..."

He hesitated for a moment, and then began to chortle.

"But I think," he continued, "that there is something about the human condition which makes people crave independence. Perhaps, you might say, they have an irrepressible desire to be free, a desire which transcends all other motivations. And so my power was inevitably going to be resented by others, whatever good deeds I may have succeeded in accomplishing."

She looked at him.

"And Australia?" she asked. "Australia must have been hard. You say in this that you took no money at all with you into your new life."

Again he smiled.

"We took no money, but we took ourselves, and somewhat to my surprise that turned out to be enough."

As he spoke the library drifted slowly away from his consciousness. For his time as a wealthy Earl had really only been a tiny part of his life, swamped and dominated by the rich and varied life he had subsequently led on the other side of the world. For despite his deepest fears Australia had been an easy land in which to make a fresh start, an open and welcoming society used to accepting the rejects and misfits of another continent.

At the time, the best part of a lifetime ago, he had been amazed at the transformation which had come over Julia in their new life. He had always sensed that she had loathed the position into which she had been born, that she had loathed the wealth and privilege which had relentlessly washed over her from her earliest years almost as much as he had loathed and feared the poverty of his youth. Her inherited wealth had been like a millstone around her neck, stifling and suppressing her own sense of self-worth, but once she had been cast free she had seemed to find a new vigour. In Australia she had worked and studied, studied and worked, until eventually she had risen by her own efforts to become a history teacher and then the headmistress of a secondary school catering largely to the needs of Australia's disadvantaged poor. Now she had become a highly respected figure, something of an authority on urban social policy.

For Peter too the change of lifestyle had brought fresh opportunities. At the time of his abdication he had secretly feared it would be a return to the status quo ante, that he would become once again the fearful and insecure young man he had been when he had worked in Harry's Cafe. But his fears had been proved unfounded, because it transpired that he had won something far more valuable than money when he won the Earldom. He had won himself. And with the new-found self-confidence that comes when a person recognises that he is the true master of his own destiny, he had begun the long hard climb to fulfil a dream he had secretly cherished since the days of his adolescence in a south coast children's home. He had become an academic historian. And although the Chair was only a small and insignificant one, the University at which the tenure was held perpetually short of funds and threatened with closure, he too had found his career a long and profoundly satisfying one.

Once again his thoughts turned to Julia, the wife who had shaped and moulded his life through so many difficult crises. To this day he was not certain why she had been so determined not to have any childen of her own. Perhaps she had been reluctant to perpetuate her father's genes. Perhaps she had been fearful lest a future son discover the truth and accuse her of abandoning his birthright. Or perhaps, as she always claimed, she had simply been too busy.

He had tried hard to persuade her to return with him for one last visit to her childhood home, but she had preferred to remain behind.

For her the memories were too painful, the conflicts and dilemmas of her past life too dangerous to reawaken. And so he had come alone, determined to honour the search for historical truth to which he had devoted his professional life, and leave behind for posterity the strange story of the 16th Earl of Southdown.

He suddenly became aware that the young girl in the library, the girl who resembled so uncannily Julia as a young girl, had risen to her feet.

"We have to go," she said softly. "The security staff will be round soon to check everything's in order."

Peter looked at the sheaf of papers in her hand. She followed his eye, and then a thought seemed suddenly to occur to her. She held up the papers.

"These are a bit brief, aren't they? You've got so much to say, it deserves a whole book."

There was a glint in her eye which revealed what she was thinking.

"And you want to write it?" he asked.

An impish grin consumed her whole face. It would be a thesis to remember, the historical equivalent of a journalistic scoop.

He thought for a moment.

"Even if I agree, you couldn't publish it until after Julia and I are both dead. You do understand that?"

She nodded, the growing sense of excitement written all over her face.

Peter walked over to the window and looked out at the gardens beyond. If the truth be told he had written the story so briefly because he found it painful to recount, because with the benefit of hindsight and maturity he found many of the actions of his youth foolish and naive. But from a strictly historical point of view the girl was right. His story deserved a fuller treatment.

His mind made up, he turned to face her.

"All right," he said, "but there's one further condition."

She looked at him expectantly.

"When you finally publish the book I would like you to give it a particular title. It's just an old man's whim, I suppose. But I would like the title of your biography to reflect my feelings about what I attempted to do during my brief time as the Earl of Southdown."

"I don't mind," she said. "What is that title?"

He smiled, and the whole long memory of his life seemed to stretch away behind him.

"If you would, simply call it 'Castles in the Air'."